The Play's the Thing

The Cricket Club
Book 2

MARGAUX THORNE

ARE YOU SIGNED UP FOR DRAGONBLADE'S BLOG?

You'll get the latest news and information on exclusive giveaways, exclusive excerpts, coming releases, sales, free books, cover reveals and more.

Check out our complete list of authors, too!

No spam, no junk. That's a promise!

Sign Up Here

www.dragonbladepublishing.com

Dearest Reader;

Thank you for your support of a small press. At Dragonblade Publishing, we strive to bring you the highest quality Historical Romance from some of the best authors in the business. Without your support, there is no 'us', so we sincerely hope you adore these stories and find some new favorite authors along the way.

Happy Reading!

CEO, Dragonblade Publishing

Chapter One

London, England 1848

Miss Anna Smythe slammed the newspaper down on her lap. "I'm going to be sick!" she exclaimed irritably, fiddling with the corners of the rag paper, thinning out the wrinkles made by her incensed grip.

Across the carriage, Sir John Smythe's head popped up from his latest book on fly fishing, and he frowned at his eldest daughter. "I told you not to read. You always get sick when you read in the carriage. The bumps have never agreed with you, my dear."

"It's not the bumps on the road, Father," his other daughter said. Miss Beatrice lifted a lovely, arched brow at Anna. "It's the bumps in the article that are making her stomach roll. *Yet again.*" The girl swiped the newspaper out of her older sister's lap. She took her time, straightening and folding the pages until they rested harmlessly and small in her own hands. "That article was written months ago. Why do you keep torturing yourself?"

Anna averted her gaze, staring out the window of the carriage where the lush open fields were beginning to become swallowed up by the well-worn signs of a village. Charming little houses and perfunctory, squat gardens swam into view, informing her that their ride was almost over. It wasn't a long journey—an hour was hardly anything to complain about—but perhaps she *should* have chosen better reading material.

Nevertheless, she wasn't about to admit that to her nosy little sister. "I'm not torturing myself," she huffed, avoiding yet another arched brow from Beatrice. "We're staying at the man's house; I just thought it would be important to memorize every word so when I confront him, I will be ready."

Her father finally dropped his book to his seat, revealing his entire confounded face. Though now firmly entrenched in his middle years, Sir John seemed to be one of the lucky few who aged like a fine wine. Tall and barrel-chested, he had refused to give over to the softness of an easy living, and his hair—at one time, as fiery as a summer sun—had mellowed into a respectable and less shocking auburn with only the faintest hints of gray bordering his temples.

Even the wrinkles on his distinguished face were barely noticeable … when he wasn't scowling at his middle child so harshly. "Confront him? You absolutely will not be confronting anybody. For the next month, we will be guests in Lord Newton's home. You will not"—he leaned over his seat, firmly catching Anna's eye—"I repeat, you will *not* start any confrontations, especially on something as ridiculous as cricket."

Anna's mouth dropped as heavy as a brick to the floor. "Cricket is not ridiculous! And I'm not going to confront him in a malicious manner… I'm merely going to ask why he wrote such a rude and outlandishly untrue and foul article. That's all."

"It was hardly rude," Beatrice contended.

"Nor was it untrue," Sir John added.

Anna tossed her hands up in the air, settling back into her seat smugly. "Thank you. Both of you agree that it was foul. I know it was! And I want—nay, need—to ask the *viscount* how he had the gall to write it."

Beatrice and her father shared a knowing look before pursing their lips. Anna was used to this encounter. Many a conversation between the trio had ended with it, and Anna was always on the receiving end. Beatrice was just as similar in looks to their father as she was in temperament, but, luckily for her, she never had to go through the red-carrot stage of her hair and instead skipped straight to the lovely auburn portion. Though everything about Beatrice was lovely, from her slender form to her long limbs. She had only just turned sixteen and men were already lining up to fill her dance card. Anna should have been excited for her sister. She tried to be. However, with age came wisdom, and even though Anna was only three years older than Beatrice, it seemed like she had a lifetime of worldly knowledge under her belt. And most of it wasn't optimistic about a young woman's future.

"For heaven's sake, the article wasn't foul," Beatrice replied, throwing the newspaper back onto Anna's thighs. "He even said your cricket match against the matrons was a success. He acknowledged the talent of the players and the large crowd of people that had come out to see you play. How can you find fault in that?"

"Because …" Anna started, lengthening out the word like she was beginning a speech in the House of Parliament, "the tone of his article was one of shock, as if the *viscount* hadn't expected it to be such a success."

"It was not," Beatrice argued. "You're reading into it."

"Hardly," Anna countered. "And also, do I have to remind you of that little part at the end? The one where the *viscount* said that women's cricket was a fad and that it wouldn't catch on? The problem, according to this wise man, was the women's game was slower and we couldn't hit the ball as far as men. He said it would hinder us from gaining more supporters in the future. Can you believe him? The nerve! He thinks women are weak!"

"He does not!" Her father cocked his head. "And why do you keep saying it like that?"

"Saying what?"

"Viscount," he answered. "You keep saying it oddly. *Viscount.* With a demeaning emphasis on the word. Why?"

"W-well," Anna blustered, gripping the paper, "he's new to the job, isn't he? He's only been the viscount for a couple of years. He didn't even know he was the old viscount's cousin until someone informed him. He was working for that newspaper in London when he found out. I heard all about it."

Indeed, she had. The captain of her cricket club, Miss Myfanwy Wright, was the old, deceased viscount's daughter. After the funeral, she'd had to move out of her family home when the new viscount moved in, though it turned out all right in the end. Myfanwy was now blissfully engaged to her guardian, Mr. Samuel Everett. But that fortuitous turn of events was beside the point!

"What does that matter?" Sir John asked.

Anna shrugged her shoulders. "It just does."

"Why?"

"I just don't think he should be putting on airs. How many viscounts do you know that work? It's odd." She punched her fingers into the maligned newspaper. "He's an odd man with odd ideas."

"I've heard he's given up that writing business," her father replied. "And how exactly is he putting on airs?"

Anna tugged at the hair at the nape of her neck, twirling a tendril around and around her finger. She caught herself staring at the long curls framing her sister's oval face. Her hair had once been that full and glorious, the tips grazing her lower back. It had been taken from her three years ago, chopped off when she'd been too delirious with fever to stop the doctors and their large, commanding scissors. Not a day went by that she didn't think about it. Still … she could never decide if she truly missed it or not. Perhaps she just missed what it represented.

"Anna?" her father repeated sternly. "Did you hear me?"

Anna's hand dropped from her hair. She cleared her throat. "Don't play with me, Father. You know exactly what I mean. How preposterous it is, making us come stay with him for such a long period of time. You asked his mother to marry you and she said yes. There's no reason to prolong this courtship. It's not like you're children, and yet this *viscount* is making you grovel. It's ridiculous. That, dear Father, is putting on airs. You should be offended. You're a baronet, not some second-rate chimney sweep."

Finally, her words seemed to strike a chord. Sir John jostled uncomfortably in his seat, and Anna knew it had nothing to do with the plush pillows at his back or the length of time in the carriage. "On the contrary. I'm not offended in the least. Lord Newton seems like a fine young man with a good head on his shoulders. In her letter, Mrs. Wright informed me that he wasn't against the match. He didn't say she *couldn't* marry me. He only wanted her to wait to make her decision after we've spent more time together. It is a sound and reasonable request. Especially since ... especially since ..." He let his words fall. With a quick flicker, Sir John dashed the curtain out of the way to glance outside the window. If Anna didn't know any better, she would think her father's nerves were getting the better of him.

Helpful as ever, Beatrice picked up the sentence. "Especially since you haven't actually seen Mrs. Wright in thirty years."

Sir John's Adam's apple jumped, and he gave his daughter a tight smile. "Precisely."

"It's so romantic," Beatrice went on, her voice heavy with the kind of dreaminess that only a sixteen-year-old can muster. "It's like a fairy tale. How can Lord Newton not recognize it too? You and Mrs. Wright were childhood loves and grew up together. You wanted to marry her, but your father wouldn't let you, and when you broke the news to her, she ran off and married another. Now, all these years later, after your dear spouses have departed, you reached out to her again, asking for her hand. You don't know what she looks like, who she's become, and yet you still want her. She could be all wizened and prune-y by now."

"She's younger than I am," Sir John piped in wryly.

"She could have a wooden leg."

"She's not a pirate—"

"She could have a glass eye, missing teeth, a hunchback, a disease where she smells like old, dirty feet all the time—"

"Beatrice, good Lord," Anna interrupted. "Are you trying to scare him to death? Look at our father. He's gone positively green."

Beatrice's large eyes went wide, and she hugged her father's side. "I'm only teasing you, Father. I'm sure she's none of those things. The point I'm trying to make is that it doesn't matter what she looks like now. You'd still love her. That's what makes this whole thing so wonderful. Mrs. Wright is so fortunate to have you."

Anna didn't think it possible, but her father appeared even more uncomfortable. "I am the fortunate one," he said gruffly. "I was angry—furious—at your grandfather for many years, but I had to forgive him in the end. I married your mother, and she gave me the loveliest children a man could ask for." After a pause, the wrinkles returned to his face, as if the picture he created could only satisfy his nerves for a short time.

An unsettled, cagey feeling sank into Anna's bones. She hated to see her father so uncertain, almost lost. "I know that we already talked about this ... however, I want to ask you one more time," Sir John said, peering at his daughters through heavy lids, imploring them for their truths. "You are fine with my marrying again ... with adding to our family? Please know that I would never do this if I thought it would hurt you in any way. I loved your mother the best I could, but she's been gone now for over five years. I tried to do right by you; I tried to be the best parent I could be—both mother and father."

Anna couldn't take it anymore. The idea that her father believed he hadn't been everything to them—to her in particular— was more than she could bear. She leaned across her seat, knocking the newspaper onto the floor of the carriage, grabbed her father's hands, and locked them between her own. "We couldn't have asked for a better father," she said, holding his gaze. A silent conversation flowed between them even as she continued to speak. "You have done more, given more to me, than I could have ever asked for." Anna could feel Beatrice watching them, feel the curiosity rising from her like the heat off a sidewalk, but she didn't want to stop. "You gave me a second chance at happiness. Now it's your turn to do the same."

The anxiety in Sir John's face melted, leaving a smile that brought an ache of homesickness to Anna's stomach. Her father always seemed to be a content man, but smiles like that had been few and far between in recent years. Slowly, he untwisted a hand from Anna's grasp and palmed her cheek, squeezing her face just enough to let her know that he valued everything she had just told him … and understood so much more.

"Thank you, my dear," he said softly before turning to his youngest daughter. "Thank you both. I love you more than words can ever say." He chuckled, reclining more into his cushions, as if a weight had been ripped from his shoulders. No longer a worrying father, he was back to being a confident would-be bridegroom. He peered out the window again, musing in a quiet plaintive voice, "We're almost there. What will they think of us?"

It was a rhetorical question, but Beatrice answered anyway. "We're not so rough around the edges," she said, laughing and sharing a look with her sister. "We may surprise the viscount. He may even grow to like us when everything is said and done."

I doubt it. If the viscount made a list of all his friends, Anna was positive that her name wouldn't be on it at the end of the month. Not that she cared! Her only goal was to make the shortsighted man see that there was room in the world for women's cricket. If that meant she had to be a little heavy-handed, even confrontational, then so be it. Naturally, she wouldn't do the *confronting* when her father was around. What the man didn't see couldn't hurt him.

"And just wait until he meets David," Beatrice continued. "No one has ever met David and not taken to him immediately. Besides me, he's the most likable one of all of us."

Anna let that little comment slide, along with the tongue that Beatrice stuck out at her in silly fun. "When is David coming?" she asked instead.

"Not for a few weeks, but please don't get your hopes up, Beatrice. His ship might be delayed," her father answered, his tone immediately thickening with pride. "It's been so long. God, I missed that boy. I can't thank the Lord enough that he's coming home to us safe and sound. I'm never letting him leave again."

Sir John would get no arguments from his daughters there. David, the eldest of the Smythe children, had surprised them all three years ago when he decided to take a position as a clerk in the East India Company alongside his best friend, Mr. Phillip Williams. Sir John had bribed his only son and heir with everything under the moon to stay home, but to no avail. The Smythe children might have been attractive and well mannered, but they were also exceedingly obstinate and opinionated. A fire ran in their blood that Sir John had never been able to contain. Even threatening to cut David off financially did nothing to curb the boy's zeal for adventure. So, to India he'd gone, taking Sir John's potential line with him.

"Is … um… Is he bringing anyone with him?" Anna asked, lowering her head. She couldn't look at her father while she asked the question. It was too much. She was embarrassed enough when the words left her lips so haltingly.

"I don't know, my dear," Sir John said gently. "You mustn't worry about it."

"I'm not worried," Anna replied quickly. Her finger was back to twirling a short curl. "I just … You know … I don't want to overburden the viscount with so many people. I don't want to be rude."

"Oh, so now you're worried about being rude." Beatrice chuckled. "It's too late anyway. We're here!"

Sir John patted the young girl's hand excitedly. "So we are!"

The next few minutes were interminable. The carriage took its time as it bumped and shook its way down the long drive to the large home, eventually coming to a stop. Sir John inflated his lungs with a steadying breath before exiting the vehicle. Then, with single-minded purpose, he helped his daughters out of the carriage one by one as if they were as delicate as china.

The day was bright, and it took Anna a couple of seconds to acclimate to the scene presented to her. A line of servants flowed down the steps of the country house, as commanding and awe-inspiring as an army readying for battle. A diminutive woman stood out front at the base of the steps, absurdly dwarfed by the gigantic Georgian-styled house behind her. Anna had attended a garden party at Newton Place months before, but she was still taken aback by the splendor and ceremony laid out for them. She felt like royalty being received this grandly. A statement was being made, although Anna couldn't be certain what it was saying or who was saying it.

The tiny woman bobbed gracefully as Sir John came to meet her. He was hesitant at first, and his legs appeared to be trudging through mud, slow and cautious. Anna remained behind her father, so she couldn't see his expression, but the lady's said it all. Like the rest of her, the older woman's face was tiny, her features plain and unassuming, and yet the moment she gazed upon Sir John, light flooded out from her like a broken dam. Extreme, unrelenting pleasure poured from every inch of her pale skin. If someone would have told Anna that the woman was a star, she would have believed them. Was that what love did? Turn the impossible into the possible? Anna tried to remember but quickly slammed the door on those memories. Now wasn't the time, and this certainly wasn't the place.

Sir John jerked forward, outstretching his arms as if to take the woman into an embrace. However, years of gentility halted his progress, and he cleared his throat. "My dear Mrs. Wright," he said gruffly, his voice stuffed with the feelings he crammed inside. "I cannot tell you how glad I am to be here. Finally."

Mrs. Wright also seemed to remember herself and where she was. Her ebullient smile relented into shyness, and she dipped her head in a way that reminded Anna of Beatrice. Childlike. Overcome. She was a handsome woman, though Anna wouldn't call her beautiful. Her hair was pulled back drastically and formed into a bun at the nape of her neck, which only accentuated the sharpness of her straight nose. Her chin was just as long and pointy. But there was something in her cheeks that was soft and pleasing. Age might have withered some of the plumpness, though it was easy for Anna to imagine the round, fleshy cheeks that once graced her face. How creamy they must have felt. How welcoming for a kiss.

As Sir John introduced his daughters to his old love, Anna didn't miss the hesitant way the older woman addressed them, or her growing apprehension. Mrs. Wright was nervous to meet the girls. It hadn't dawned on Anna that it would be so. She'd been too caught up in her own drama, and no doubt her continued silence was only making the hostess feel even more inadequate.

"You have a lovely home," Anna finally said, her voice a little higher than she would have preferred.

Mrs. Wright nodded warmly. "Thank you. It's my son's." She glanced over her shoulder almost like she was unsure if the large structure would disappear at any moment. "To be honest, we're still getting used to it."

"I can imagine," Anna returned easily. However, now that the elusive son had been brought up, it seemed as if he was all anybody could think about. Just like a man, Anna thought dismissively. He wasn't even here, and yet he commanded all the attention. How could they all prostrate themselves at his feet and slide into his good graces if the viscount couldn't be bothered to greet them? Was he rude or just ignorant? Did it matter?

Anna couldn't stop herself from pressing further. "Will we be meeting your son while we are here?" she asked. Wasn't that the point, after all? For them all to be one happy family?

"Yes, of course!" Mrs. Wright replied, visibly shaking as if the question had startled her. "He's here now. He's only ..." Her brow pinched. "He's working ... writing."

Anna stole a look at her father and sister and pursed her lips in displeasure. Sir John ignored her, but she knew she'd got her point across. *Given up that writing business, indeed.* "Still writing?" she drawled. "For the newspaper?"

The older woman's pleasant veneer cracked slightly. "I'm not sure, to be honest," she said. "My son likes to keep to himself. Are you familiar with his work?"

Anna's laugh was as light as a summer breeze. "You could say that, Mrs. Wright. I most certainly am."

Chapter Two

THE COTTAGE WAS shaking. Strike that. No, someone was just attempting to break down his door.

"Jacob Wright. Open this door this instant!" his mother called from the outside. For someone who could be mistaken for an elf, his mother definitely had a pair of lungs on her. Jacob hung his head, dropping his pen on his half-finished paper. With a sigh, he trudged to the door.

He swung it open easily, hoping that the conciliatory action was enough to curb some of his mother's ire. It wasn't.

Her glower could have blinded Polyphemus's one eye in seconds flat.

"I lost track of time," Jacob said quickly as his mother charged into the snug cottage. Her face was red, and wisps of her dark hair clung to the sheen of sweat on her cheeks. Jacob couldn't be sure if it was anger or the walk that had done it to her. The hermit's cottage was a decent twenty-minute jaunt away from the house, which was precisely why he liked it so much.

She rounded on him, her skirts splayed out like daisy petals ready to be plucked. Despite her current appearance, his mother had taken pains to look exceptional today. Her dress was new and made from an expensive dark green silk that made her look like an exotic jewel. Irritation pinched him. The last thing his mother needed to do was *try* for Sir John Smythe. That man deserved nothing from her.

"Don't tell me you lost track of time," she said. The hairs on the back of Jacob's neck stood at attention. They never failed to do that when her voice sharpened to that steely edge with him. It didn't matter that he was coming on thirty and was at least three heads taller than her. A mother's displeasure never stopped hitting its mark.

Rose Wright's fingers rested on her temple as if she were trying to hold back a headache. "You told me you would come. You told me we would greet them together."

"Mother, I'm sorry. As I said, I lost track of time. I didn't do it on purpose."

The wary look she gave him meant that he would surely have to work on lying a little better. "Well, it certainly didn't help that you were here," she replied with a weak-willed sigh. "This cottage has one window, and it's so dirty one cannot even tell if it's daylight. Remind me to clean it next time I come out."

Jacob snatched her hands in his and dragged her to the chair behind his desk. It was the only place to sit in the cottage beside the bed. Sparse was how Jacob liked it. Sparse meant his mind could do all the work it needed without interruption. Over the past couple of years, his life had been one big interruption after another. And by the worry on his mother's face, it wasn't going to stop anytime soon.

"Oh no you don't," Jacob said adamantly, placing his mother in the seat. He leaned over her, settling his hands on the arms of the chair. "Your cleaning days are over. What's the point of having a son for a viscount if you're going to keep trailing behind him with a bucket of soap and water in your hands?"

That elicited a pathetic chuckle from her, and he relaxed back to standing. "Honestly, Jacob," she said, rolling her eyes, "I don't mind cleaning every now and again. It gives me something to do. Besides, I do it better than the servants anyway."

"Then hire better servants," he returned dryly.

Her laughter grew thicker, more authentic. It warmed Jacob's heart. His mother had laughed so little when he was growing up that being the cause of it still made him feel seven feet tall. "Oh, Jacob, stop changing the subject. You know why I traipsed all the way out here."

"You needed exercise?"

Her mouth tightened. "You've been rude."

Jacob dug his hands into his pockets carelessly. "I'm always rude. Besides, I'm a viscount now, which means it's socially acceptable to be as rude as my heart desires."

Rose's lips twitched, fighting a smile. "Yes, but we're not talking about your heart. We're talking about mine." She paused, allowing the realization to spread across Jacob like an ink stain. "I asked that you not be rude today. I asked you to be pleasant and welcoming to the baronet's family."

Jacob turned away, stalking to the dirty window in the cottage that his mother deemed so unworthy. At one time, the pair of them would have been quite happy with that window and the space in that cottage. Not anymore. Not since he'd received the news that the old viscount died and, by some strange piece of luck, Jacob was his heir. Now, things that were once good enough for them were not anymore. But who made those rules? Who was the judge of such things? Sir John *fucking* Smythe?

Jacob couldn't hide the bitterness in his voice. "And I told you to wait until my investigator got back to me with the information I requested. It's been thirty years, Mother. Thirty years! And you go ahead and accept a proposal from a man you barely know. I don't understand it!"

"Jacob, we've discussed this—"

"I know what we've discussed," he spat. Why did he suddenly feel like a five-year-old? Why couldn't he disagree with his mother without acting like a spoiled child? Maybe because she'd given her life to making sure he always had a full belly and an education. And now, the fact that he was withholding his happiness for her marriage made him seem ungrateful and rotten.

Why couldn't she understand that all he was doing was looking out for her best interests? Why did she hold Sir John *fucking* Smythe in such high esteem? That lazy baronet wasn't fit to lick his mother's boots. And Jacob couldn't wait to tell him that.

He heard the chair creak as his mother stood, her steps calm and measured as she walked up behind him. Rose rested her hand on his broad shoulder. "Jacob, my son, you have to trust me. I know you think you've taken care of me for a long time, but I was taking care of myself long before that. I know what I'm doing. It might not seem like that. To you, it might seem … I don't know … willful? Fanciful? But I know Sir John Smythe. I can't force you to call off your investigator, but I still wish you would. There's nothing there that will change my decision. I will be his wife, as I always should have been."

Jacob's throat burned. So many harsh words threatened to burst out, and they crackled and popped against one another, creating a fire that seemed impossible to stifle. He wanted to rail at this woman who had been everything to him for most of his life. This woman who had never tired, never stopped, never felt sorry for herself. When her husband had died and she had a small child to take care of, she didn't hole herself up in her room, relying on the charity of strangers and family. She got to work, renting out rooms in their modest home, taking in her two sisters when they needed their own charity, and even resorted to sewing and mending to make ends meet.

Jacob had been raised by women. Good women. Strong women. So strong that even after losing his father when he was ten, he never lamented the casualty of that commanding presence. His mother and his aunts had ably taken over.

So, to see his mother falter now—to see her finally hiccup and trip down this road of insanity for this man, this man that had used her and abused her so dangerously in her youth—was beyond the pale. Jacob couldn't wrap his head around it. But his vision was clear. He could see his mother's path if she ended up in this overgrown man-child's hands. And he couldn't allow it. Jacob had always believed that his mother would move heaven and earth to give him what he needed—not what he wanted. And now it was his turn to repay the favor.

There would be no wedding between the Smythe and Wright families. He would see to that.

As his mother's callused hand increased its pressure, Jacob spun to face her. Two years of gentile living had done much to soften his mother's visage, though the strains of her past were still present. Try as they might, with all the new clothes and servants and soft pillows, no one would ever mistake Rose Wright as a true mother of a viscount. The lines that bracketed her mouth were too deep; her gray eyes held too many storms of experience. Adding another problem for her to battle seemed unconscionable to Jacob.

So, he would have Sir John *fucking* Smythe do the dirty work for him. Jacob could be gracious. He could play the dutiful son. He loved his mother, after all. That was why he'd invited the baronet and his family to his home for a month. Thirty days was a sufficiently long time. Even master manipulators couldn't bury their crimes and lies for that long. Being forced under the same roof would provide all the pressure Jacob needed.

Sir John would show himself; Jacob was sure of it. And then his mother would finally see that memories—even good ones— deserved to live and die in one place … the past.

Chapter Three

EVEN IF HE hadn't written such a rude and outlandishly untrue and foul article, Anna would have disliked the man. In fact, everything about the viscount was unlikeable, including the way he ate his food in such a perfunctory, hurried fashion, as if the taste was something to be tolerated and not enjoyed. She disliked the way he sat, all tall and grand, as if his spine would bend for no one. She disliked the way he spoke, with such monosyllabic, bland answers that others, presumably, should be grateful for. But Anna intensely disliked the way he looked at her. Jacob Wright—she refused to call him Lord Newton in her head—had a terrible way of casting his gray eye upon her, as if he were a sponge soaking up everything, as if all her fibers and sinew and atoms and muscle were on display, there for his taking, there for his probing. Like, if he concentrated enough, he would be able to identify where her bone ended, and her spirit began.

Yes, Anna hated the way he looked at her, but especially how that searing intensity made her feel. Hot and fiery inside. Desirous to act.

It had thrown her, how jarring it was, how invasive. Anna had barely had a moment to contain herself during their introductions before the families were whisked around the dining room table and she was left to sense his gaze as it wandered back to her again and again. Like she was the Rosetta Stone, Jacob was searching for answers, trying to decipher her code.

Anna hadn't expected the viscount to be so mindful … or attractive. He certainly didn't look like a newspaperman, whatever that meant. Jacob was tall and lean, with midnight-black hair and a long, confident chin. His nose was straight and noble, his forehead high. It confounded (and annoyed) Anna, but he was the picture-perfect version of a viscount, down to his arrogant behavior. She'd predicted that he would continue his dismissiveness at dinner and be as boorish as he'd been when he left his mother to fend for herself that morning with the guests.

But Jacob *wasn't* dismissive, sitting at the head of his lovely oak table, surrounded by his fine crystal goblets and sumptuous food. Curt, maybe. Terse, most definitely. Rude, undeniably. But not aloof. From the angle of his pointy, pronounced jaw, the way his head cocked this way and that, the way his sharp eyebrows twitched after someone spoke, Jacob Wright was all too aware. All too perceptive.

And Anna didn't like being on his receiving end of such scrutiny. She had a distinct feeling in the pit of her stomach that nothing good could come of it. And yet she was drawn to him. Drawn to the way her skin prickled whenever his attention fell on her; the way her temperature rose as his silence hung in the air, almost lying on top of her like a blanket of snow. Uncomfortable, but also so very satisfying.

Anna didn't know what had come over her. She couldn't explain it. Those types of intimate, alarming sensations hadn't hounded her in years. She'd made sure of that.

Thank goodness for his aunts. Iris and Violet Sherman were two people that one had to experience to believe. Quick to laugh, poking constant fun at one another and their older sister, Rose, they salvaged the awkwardness of the night with a steady stream of lively chatter. Thanks to Jacob, Anna found it difficult to follow their giggles and inside jokes; however, the sound of their voices—high and mellifluous—kept her in a relative state of ease.

The sisters had no qualms amusing the newcomers with their life stories, informing the guests that neither of them had ever married. At a young age, they'd begun a life of service for a neighboring gentry family but had moved on to working in the kitchen of Rose's home, feeding the needy boarders. They stated all of this in such a matter-of-fact tone that Anna was too caught off guard to be embarrassed by the topic. The Sherman sisters discussed money and hardship as naturally as if it were the weather, something to be dealt with on an everyday basis, but nothing to cry over. To the sisters, every situation in life could be handled with either despair or hope, and it was obvious to all what they chose.

"Of course, all that is over now," Violet finished, wiping a dab of horseradish cream off the side of her mouth with her napkin. The oldest of the girls, she was a portly woman, tall and robust with an ample chest that appeared to settle on the edge of the table whenever she leaned over. "Our working days are behind us, or so our nephew keeps telling us."

"Do you have any brothers?" Beatrice asked. Not as adept at hiding her emotions as Anna, her adoration and curiosity for the sisters were written all over her face. Anna wasn't sure if that was a good thing or not. Unfortunately, she would have to wait and see.

Iris laughed before taking a rather *long* drink from her goblet. The footman came to her shoulder, filling the glass with wine without being asked. "It's always just been us," she said cheerfully, two spots of red warming her high cheekbones. Like Violet, Iris was a big woman—big bones, big voice, big personality. With their dark blonde hair and matching plain features, Anna would have mistaken the sisters for twins if they hadn't pointed out the ten-month age gap between them. Although, on closer inspection, Violet's chin was long like Rose's, making her face not as round as Iris's.

All the girls were named after flowers, and yet Anna couldn't find anything dainty or delicate about them other than Rose's tiny size. They were plain and riddled with thorns; however, that was what made them so charming.

"Our father, bless his soul, never cared about that, though," Iris went on. "He treated us well and never stood in our way when we wanted to learn anything," She motioned her goblet toward Jacob. "He was a good, decent man, the very best … just like Jacob. But like our poor nephew, he was destined to be surrounded by women."

Anna spied Jacob and caught the corner of his mouth inching up, surprising her with a distinct dimple in his cheek. He shook his head, not so much annoyed at the attention as amused by it. Even he wasn't immune to his aunts' cheerful antics.

"He won't be alone for long," Beatrice piped in. "Our brother is coming home soon. How fortuitous that he will be back before the wedding—" She stopped, glancing anxiously around the table, her gaze landing on the severe viscount. Everyone in the dining room understood why the baronet's family was visiting, although no one had mentioned the wedding or proposal. It was as if they were all tiptoeing around it, hoping someone else would do the dirty work and bring it into conversation.

Anna glared at Jacob, hoping her anger would pierce through that obstinate head of his. *How dare he put such a damper on a momentous occasion?* She nudged Beatrice. "Go on, dearest," she said soothingly. "What were you saying about David and the *wedding?*" She stressed the word strongly, knowing that Jacob would redirect his irritation to her. She was not disappointed. The gaze was so acute it almost took her breath away. Again, something inside of Anna tingled when his full attention latched on to her, something hot and deep pinging insistently against her ribcage like a dinner bell. His brow furrowed in consternation as he rubbed the back of his hand across his jaw, back and forth, back and forth, like a clock counting down to an execution.

Beatrice's stammering brought Anna back to the conversation. "I … I was just saying that we're all very lucky that David will be back in time." She lowered her head, her voice coming out strangled and low. "For the wedding."

"Yes, the wedding!" Violet sang, brandishing her wine glass in the air like a musketeer with his trusty sword. "We cannot wait!" She lunged forward, her chest back on the table. "We always knew these two would find their way back to each other. Didn't we?" she asked Iris.

Rose tittered adorably from her end, sharing shy, youthful blushes with Sir John. "Stop it, V," she said. "No one wants to hear those old stories."

"I do!" Beatrice replied.

Rose covered her face with her hand, the blue-green veins spidering from her skin juxtaposing brilliantly with her pink cheeks. However, it was telling when her protests fell off quickly. Not a word was heard from Sir John either. Anna couldn't believe how positively smitten her father sat as he watched Rose flush and laugh at her sister's teasing. At that moment, Anna's heart felt four sizes too large, gloriously unhindered by the flesh.

"Please? Tell us more," Beatrice pleaded. "I don't know anything about Father as a young man. What was he like? Was he dashing?"

Violet's eyes gleamed. "Oh, the most dashing. All the girls were infatuated with him."

"Hardly all," Sir John cut in.

Violet disregarded him with a mischievous smile. "*All* of them."

Beatrice was practically hanging over her dessert plate. "And was he gallant and kind?"

"He was a regular prince from a fairy tale," Violet answered wistfully. "All the girls in the village did everything they could to gain his attention whenever he rode by. They primped and fluffed their hair, pinched their cheeks, wore their newest dresses, but none of it mattered." Violet took a sip of her drink, her smile faltering along the lip of the glass. "He only had eyes for one."

The words lingered in the air, hanging and roving around from ear to ear as if they had a life of their own. When they finally fell, they didn't seem to land, like they were traveling down a deep, dark well with no bottom. And as they drifted, the joviality of the table morphed into something more somber. Digging up the past might be fun at first, but one's hands inevitably came away with cuts and bruises.

Oddly enough, it was Jacob who recovered first.

"Oh, come now," the viscount said, sliding his seat away from the table. Casually, he slung one leg over the other. "Call me a bore, but I'd much rather hear about David and his exploits in India. How long has he been gone?"

Sir John, who had been lost in thought, staring at his untouched raspberry blancmange, perked at the mention of his only son. "Um … yes … David … He's been gone"—he squinted at Anna—"three years now?"

She nodded. "He sailed right after my sixteenth birthday," she added.

Jacob *tsked*, and the sound felt like lashes on her back, each one opening old wounds. "Not the best birthday gift, I take it?" he replied, picking a piece of lint off his knee and flicking it to the side. "India is an odd choice for a peer to make, isn't it? Especially a first son set on inheriting. I must commend you, Sir John. If my only son told me he was escaping to India, my first thought would have been to chain him to his bed until he got over the idea." Jacob chuckled to himself, and while the remainder of the guests tried to echo him, the effect came off paltry and cautious.

Anna curled her fingers into the tablecloth. Where was he going with this?

Her father's grin was forced. He shook his head in a self-deprecating manner. "You got me, my lord," he replied. "I am soft when it comes to my children. Always have been, I'm afraid. I wanted to chain my son to his bed, believe me, I did. But a man must make his own decisions in life."

Jacob smiled. His teeth reminded Anna of something feral, an animal playing with its meal before killing it. "I know all about men and the bad choices they make. But surely … India?" He slapped his knee and shrugged his shoulders, playing up his confusion. "From what I've heard from my colleagues, many men make the voyage, but not many make it back. It can be a dangerous place for those who aren't used to the environment and customs. You must have great confidence in your son."

Sir John's neck straightened, all sense of levity gone from his countenance. "I have the utmost confidence—"

Jacob cut him off. "And he's coming home after three years? I thought the company required at least *ten* before they allowed their workers to visit their homes again. That's rather odd."

"You are incredibly informed, Lord Newton," Sir John said. "In his last letter, David explained that his friend, Phillip, wished to return to England, as his brother passed. He asked David to leave with him."

"That's a large request."

"Indeed," Mr. Williams replied. "I agree, but they are the closest of friends—"

Jacob continued, "I'm told there are only two types of peers who go to India, and neither of them are adept at surviving." He locked eyes with Sir John as he leaned toward the table. His long fingers closed around the stem of his wine glass while he swirled it round and round. "The first type has squandered his fortune and is in want of a new one. And the other is the man who has shamed his family so greatly he needs to hide before they accept him back."

"Jacob!" his mother said. Everyone swiveled their necks toward Rose—everyone except Jacob. His entire being was centered on the baronet.

Anna willed her father to stand up to this brutish tyrant, to put this false viscount in his place. Make him cower, make him apologize, make him rue all his ridiculous hints and insulting innuendos.

Then, suddenly, it came to her, why they'd been called there in the first place. Jacob Wright had no interest in getting to know her father or their family. He only wanted Sir John under his roof so he could embarrass him, demolish his character in front of Rose—ruin any hopes of the couple rekindling the love that had clung to its thin roots all these years. He planned to snuff out the fire before it had a chance to spread. It was so obvious. Anna should have known the second he'd deserted them on his doorstep.

As if she didn't dislike Jacob enough already, she had a completely new and valid reason.

Over the heady silence, Sir John choked out an anemic laugh, desperately attempting to recover the mood. Jacob didn't know him at all, Anna noted. If he was expecting an outburst, he wouldn't get it. The baronet had been raised on restraint and force-fed forbearance at every meal.

Her father opened his mouth to speak, but Anna beat him to it. "It's funny you only mention two sorts of men, my lord," she said coolly, as if this conversation's intent wasn't to embarrass her entire family. A shiver ran up her spine as Jacob switched his focus to her. She wasn't cold. If anything, her blood was blazing. "I've heard of another type."

"Oh, have you?"

Anna's smile was sickeningly sweet. "Oh yes, I have."

"Please"—Jacob raised his hands—"enlighten us."

"Thank you, I will." Anna lifted her goblet and encouraged the party to do the same. When everyone's crystal was in the air, she continued. "There's a third sort of man who travels where others are too afraid to go, who forges a path that benefits others more than himself." She turned to Sir John, granting him a true smile before zeroing in on Jacob. "It is this man who chooses duty above self, chooses obligation over want, chooses service over selfishness. David is a good, decent man, the very best"—her lips were pulled so wide she worried they might crack—"just like his father."

"I think we can all toast to that," Iris exclaimed, clinking her crystal with her sisters'. Soon, Anna was kissing glasses with everyone around the table—everyone except Jacob. He'd never lifted his glass. The only thing he lifted was the corner of his mouth—in amusement or annoyance, this time Anna didn't know.

Chapter Four

"YOU, YOU THERE, stop at once!"

Jacob lengthened his stride across the lawn, ignoring the wild summons behind him.

"I said, stop!" the shrill voice continued. "I know you hear me. Lord, you walk fast," it muttered. "I command you to stop!"

As if he'd run into a brick wall, Jacob slammed to a halt. And turned very, *very* slowly to face the arrogant woman. The incredibly *attractive*, arrogant woman.

Jacob feigned a bored expression as he waited for Miss Smythe to catch up to him. He needed her to hear his cutting words loud and clear so she would retreat to the house and out of his life forever. She'd stolen too much of his attention this evening as it was, and any more would not be tolerated.

The outrageous woman was visibly panting when she stood in front of him. "Your legs are much too long," she wheezed, planting a hand on her bare and heaving chest.

"Maybe yours are too short," he quipped, before shaking his head at his asinine comment. Why had he said that? Oh, yes, because he couldn't drag his gaze from the woman's creamy, ample breasts, and his mind had turned into a mound of pudding. "Why are you traipsing outside in this weather without a cloak? You should be inside with your family."

Anna glanced down at her gown as if just realizing her predicament. *Silly woman.* It had been a mild autumn thus far, but this November night was chilly enough to make Jacob wish he'd thrown on his coat before venturing to his cottage. Like him, Anna was still dressed for dinner. It was a respectable enough gown that shouldn't have affected him, and yet it managed to do just that. Every rustle of crimson silk at the dinner table had made him lose his train of thought and pull his focus back to her. That hadn't been the plan. *Anna Smythe* hadn't been the plan.

She hastened to fold her arms in front of her, blocking his view of her glorious endowments. *Damn. Be careful what you wish for.* "You, *my lord*, do not get to tell me how to dress, nor do you get to bark orders at me. I am not a child. I am your guest. And, by the way, I am not cold at all. Anything is warmer than the atmosphere you created in that dining room."

My lord. My lord. This wasn't the first time she'd addressed him in that way, all sarcastic and derisive. This daughter of a baronet was just like the others, thinking him a second-rate viscount who'd fallen arse-backward into a title.

Jacob mirrored her combative stance, folding his arms. He crept closer, taking advantage of his height. The brat's head barely made it up to his clavicle, even with her chin jutting so high and proud. "I was merely asking questions. I thought that's what this little visit was for ... getting to know one another."

Anna's eyes narrowed. They were as vibrant and cold as emeralds. Added to the shortness of her black hair, it reminded Jacob of the fairy stories his aunts had told him before bed each night. Tales of the tiny, dangerous creatures who appeared harmless and enchanting, but were always ready to lie and play tricks for their amusement.

But as much as he wanted to, Jacob couldn't match those tales of deceit with the women standing so commandingly in front of him. It was true, he didn't trust her family, but there was something about Anna Smythe that made him curious. For starters, the only women he knew with short hair had either sold it for money or had it cut off due to illness. Anna appeared healthy enough to him. More than enough. He had an insane urge to skim those short curls that ran rampant against her crown, see if they felt as silky as they appeared. Jacob had always been attracted to long hair, loved running his fingers through rivulets of tendrils. But the way Anna's short hair highlighted the curve of her neck, the indecent way it showcased every indentation and pulse of tendon … It *moved* him.

Could Anna sense his eyes on that swathe of skin? Because she unlocked her arms and placed her hands against her neck, seeming to hold it in frustration. "You know very well what you were doing at dinner," Anna replied. "I know your game."

"My game?"

"Yes, your game," she said, stepping forward. Challenging him. "You plan to make my father look like a fool in front of your mother. You're trying to ruin their relationship before it even starts."

"I think your father already did that when he dropped my mother like a used handkerchief years ago."

Anna gasped. At this vantage point, Jacob could make out every crease in her lips, especially the prominent one down the middle of her bottom lip that made it look abnormally sumptuous, like the kind of pillow that Jacob could rest his head on for the remainder of his life.

He shook his head, trying to rid his mind of the unhealthy thoughts. "Face it, my dear Miss Smythe. Your father was a blackguard. He used my mother cruelly in their youth, and now, for some reason I am still trying to fathom, he's back to finish the job. Well, I wasn't there before, but I'm here now, and I will not let it happen."

Anna's face mottled with hurt. A tinge of regret ate at him, but Jacob told himself it was for the best. It was anathema for him to hurt women—any woman. But *this* woman only had her father to blame.

Her voice wobbled. "My father is the best man I have ever

known. He loved your mother, and he loves her still. You will not come between them."

If Anna burst into tears, he'd be done for. Jacob couldn't wait around for that. He was a cold bastard, but he wasn't completely heartless. "I'm done with this conversation," he said, spinning swiftly. His legs ate up the ground again, but Anna's footsteps weren't far behind.

"Well, *I* am not done with this conversation! Where are you even going? The house is back the other way."

"I'm not going to the house," he said over his shoulder. "I have work to do."

"No doubt your office is in the house. Will you stop? I don't want to keep talking to your back."

"Then stop talking."

Jacob thought he heard her growl. *What an odd sound to come from a lady.*

"I will not stop talking," she continued. "Not until you agree to quit meddling. You don't know all the facts—"

At once, Jacob whipped around, almost slamming into the termagant. On instinct, he reached out, grabbing Anna's shoulders to steady her. His hands skimmed the downy skin of her upper arms, and he instantly realized he wasn't as strong as he thought he was. Because when he told himself to release her, he couldn't. Instead, Jacob pulled her closer, lowering his head so they were at the same level.

"When did your mother die?" he asked, balancing the harsh question with a soft tone. "Five years ago, yes?"

Anna nodded, her eyes as open and clear as the moon above them. He'd shocked her with the question, but there was a point to be made.

"Right," Jacob went on. "My father passed when I was ten. Almost twenty years ago now. Attack of the heart. It was instant. Collapsed right over on the floor. Alive one minute. Gone the next. He was lucky."

Anna's skin was warm against his palms. An electricity of

fellowship sparked between them. "My mother was not so lucky," she said thickly. "She died in childbirth. The baby was already gone when it came out; my mother followed it a week later."

Jacob increased the pressure of his fingers, soaking in the strength of Anna. The strength that he'd sensed from the beginning. Jacob had always been interested in people and their stories. That was why he'd gravitated to newspapers, even though his father had planned for Jacob to follow in his footsteps and be a solicitor. From years of experience, he could usually look at a person and know if there was something deeper lurking just below the surface. He'd noticed it the moment Anna walked into the room. Her younger sister may have been conventionally prettier with all the trappings of youth and expectation, but Jacob had barely given her a cursory glance. Anna was what he fixated on. As small as she was, fine-boned and doll-like, there was a thunder to her, a clash of life that hinted at loss and grief. A stony knowing to her countenance that spoke to wisdom. One could not fake that. And it was incredibly difficult to mask.

Jacob was glad that she didn't try to with him.

"I am sorry for your loss," he said genuinely. "But try to understand my point of view. Your father has been alone, just as my mother has been these last years, and yet he waited so long to reach out to her. Why? Is it a coincidence that he came calling *after* her son miraculously found out he was a viscount? She wasn't suitable before, but now she is?"

"That's not it. You mustn't think—"

"But it's my job as her son to think that! Wouldn't you? Why didn't he contact her before?"

Anna shrugged his arms from her shoulders; however, Jacob didn't retreat. Now that he was this close to her, creating more space seemed impossible. He liked the fire that roared within her, the way her flames flickered and mixed with his own.

"Our f-family has had hardship," Anna stammered, her lush lashes beating hectically against her cheek. "My father has had to deal with many things—things that are none of your concern."

Jacob's mouth curved into a merciless smile. Now they were getting somewhere. "But they *are* my concern. What is he hiding? Money troubles? Because if he thinks he's going to leech off my mother—and me—he is mistaken."

Anna scoffed. "Please."

"Then what?" he pressed. "It's your brother, isn't it? What scandal did your father help him run from? All you peers are the same. Iniquitous and flagrant."

"You have some nerve!" Anna screeched. "Aren't you a viscount?"

"Yes, but not a real one in your eyes. Isn't that right?"

Jacob knew he'd hit the mark when her cheeks burned the same shade as her dress. And that little piece of acknowledgment stung him. More than he cared to admit. Finally, he took a step back, shoving his hands into his pockets.

"Well, that's beside the point. The fact is that your family once thought it was too good for ours, and now I must inform you that ours is much too good for yours. The sooner your father gets that into his skull, the sooner we can all move on. I will not let him drag my mother's good name into the muck."

Jacob attempted to leave again; however, his feet had a will of their own. They were stuck in place, just as his gaze was glued to the woman before him.

Anna stood there, squinting at him as if she couldn't understand a word he'd just spoken. She was naturally hurt, but entirely resolute. Taking a deep breath, she pulled her shoulders back. Her voice was low and hauntingly fierce. "I don't know what exactly happened thirty years ago between our parents." She threw up a hand, hushing Jacob before he could argue. "And neither do you. No one does except them. Coming here, I was wary at first. I didn't have stars in my eyes like my sister. To be honest, I didn't know what to expect. But the moment I saw your mother and my father look at one another, I knew. I saw love. Only a blind man could say any different. Are you blind, *my lord*?

Or are you just choosing to be?"

Jacob gritted his teeth. Another *my lord*. "I see nothing of the sort. If anything, I see lust, which is another animal altogether. I can tolerate lust. I understand lust. I *know* lust. And your father is lusting after something he wants. But love ..."

Anna flinched. "Lust?" The word dropped from her mouth like rotten meat. "Lust? Are you deliberately being obtuse? People said you were intelligent."

People? Was she talking to others about him? Jacob found that he liked that idea. "Obviously, you have an intelligent man before you," he returned dryly, lifting his arms at his sides. "Intelligent and worldly."

She snorted. "Not worldly enough if he mistakes lust with love. It's clear to me that you don't know the first thing about either."

And just like that, the audacious woman turned her back on *him*. Anna flung a hand over her shoulder. "Now, *I'm* done with this conversation. Good night, *my lord*."

Once more, Jacob's feet wouldn't listen to him, because they actually ran after her. *After. Her.* Like a simpering puppy. "Oh no you don't. We're not finished yet."

"We are," Anna said. "I thought I was speaking to a real man, a man who understood things, who could be reasoned with, but I was wrong. Lust ... Ha!" A rude sound came from the base of her throat while she continued to mutter to herself. "Lust is like a child who needs to be constantly fed and tended to. Love is infinitely stronger, more resilient. Only love has the strength to withstand years of loneliness and solitude. Lust might burn bright, but it fizzles quickly. It is sophomoric that you believe lust has kept our parents' hope alive all these years. Lust is a weak substitute—"

Jacob snatched her hand, twirling Anna back around. This time he didn't stop them from colliding into one another.

"What in the world do you think—?"

Jacob silenced her the best way he knew how. He took control of her mouth in one quick move, sweeping his mouth over hers in a thorough kiss that forced a blankness in his mind that he'd never experienced before. For once, his thoughts didn't swirl; his commitments didn't hammer him. He could only feel Anna—the softness of her full lips as they pressed against his, the way she sucked the breath from inside him and whimpered into his throat.

It was a gentle kiss, much gentler than Jacob would have preferred, considering the lady appeared to have firsthand knowledge of lust, and yet he experienced it down to the soles of his feet. Jacob would be ninety years old and he would never forget that Anna Smythe tasted like red grapes and rosemary and that that mixture was now as much a part of him as his soul.

He released the dip of her waist and hung his hands ready and willing near her head, poised to cradle her closer, waiting to dig into her velvety, dark curls. But something held him back. Intuition maybe, self-preservation most likely, because the time wasn't right. Yet. However, it would come. Jacob knew, as surely as he now knew the shape of her two front teeth as he ran his tongue over them, that their time would come.

It simply had to.

His momentary bliss was shattered when Anna yanked away, one hand covering her pillowy, swollen lips.

Silently, she considered him with an expression he couldn't read. Not condemning, but awfully close. Her eyes were heavy and troubled, with one lid hanging lower than the other.

"Was that weak?" Jacob asked, catching his breath, claiming his composure. He moved to take her into his embrace once more, but she grimaced out of his reach.

"Don't …" Anna pinned her gaze away from him, cradling her torso in her arms. "Don't ever do that again … kiss me." Jacob blanched at her flat, hollow tone. The lady that had responded so ardently to his kiss was no longer there. "I am fully aware that we are going to have to tolerate each other's company for the next month, but I will not be your plaything. I am not a new toy."

"I never thought you were—"

It was like she didn't hear him. Anna continued to stare just over his shoulder, like looking at him while speaking was too much of an effort. "And you will leave my father and your mother alone. If you cannot do that—if you cannot be a gentleman and must continue to thwart their progress—then rest assured that I will do everything in my ability to foil your efforts."

Anna rubbed her hands up and down her arms as if the bitter night air had finally registered. She nodded a few times to herself before she turned, gingerly making her way back to the house.

Numb, Jacob watched her go, not understanding what had just happened. Had he read her so wrong? Surely she'd felt the fervor between them as he had? Was he too aggressive? Too forward?

"I apologize, Anna," Jacob said before she ventured too far. "I shouldn't have done that. I was just ..." He ran a hand through his hair before dropping it aimlessly at his side. He shrugged, knowing his words were pathetic before they even left his mouth. "I wanted to prove you wrong. That the lust erupting between us wasn't weak."

Anna's steps faded. Her face was shiny under the moonlight, incandescent, and he wondered if tears were the culprit. "Nothing is erupting between us," she returned quietly. "And that wasn't lust."

With that, she left Jacob alone on his lawn. Just as he'd wanted, though it felt infinitely different now.

Because being alone was how he usually liked it. It was how he could think and work out the puzzles of the day. But Anna had left him with one that nagged at him all night.

If their kiss wasn't lust, then what was it?

Chapter Five

"OUCH! THAT HURT. Will you please stop kicking up the rocks?" Beatrice stopped on the path and leaned down to inspect her ankle, shooting her older sister a murderous glare. "Might I remind you that you're the one who dragged me out of bed for this walk, and you don't seem to be enjoying yourself at all."

"I'm sorry," Anna grumbled. As she waited for her little sister to check for bruises, Anna rolled her neck back and raised her face to the sky, hoping the early morning sun would soak into her skin and leach out the consternation that had plagued her all night. After little to no sleep, she'd decided a walk would do her good, only it wasn't helping. Nothing was helping. For all her effort, Anna couldn't seem to get Jacob Wright out of her head. Nor his unexpected kiss.

Beatrice returned standing and resumed down the path with Anna stepping lightly in her wake. Everything about her was lagging today, her head, her heart—it was like she was stuck in a maze, and she kept taking the wrong turns. Every hedge appeared the same; every corner tricked her into going in circles.

"You usually love our walks," Beatrice said, slowing her pace until the women were side by side again. "What's ailing you? Is it Father?" Her grin was demonstrably sly. "Or is it someone else?"

Beatrice may only be sixteen, but no one could say she wasn't a quick study. Still … Anna wasn't in the mood to talk about Jacob. What was there to say, anyway? She was flummoxed at how to even put her feelings into words. But there were feelings. So many feelings. Like raindrops falling from the sky, Anna tried to grab hold of them, but they always dripped from her palm, never staying still long enough.

"Of course it's Father," Anna grumbled. It wasn't a *complete* lie. "I'm worried about him."

"Why?" Beatrice asked. "I think everything is going wonderfully. Did you see how Mrs. Wright looked at him last night? So many emotions were flying across the table that I thought I might get singed. Don't worry about Lord Newton. He's just being a protective son. He'll come around. I'm sure of it."

A soft smile came to Anna's face for the first time that morning. *Oh, Beatrice.* She was so young and naïve. She still believed that love conquered all. Anna wished she could do the same. But experience had taught her that love was something to be feared. It was too powerful, unpredictable, and unyielding, like those raindrops in her palm. Uncontrollable.

But who was she to douse Beatrice's excitement? The last thing she wanted was to tarnish her little sister's innocence. No one had taken Anna's girlhood—she'd given it away willingly—but she'd be remiss to allow the same to happen to Beatrice.

A quiet acceptance passed between them. Anna figured the best thing to do was to remain silent on the matter. It had frosted overnight, and she made the effort to admire the way the sun rose to its heights, making the lawn appear like a carpet of diamonds scattered out before them. How fresh, how new dawn made everything seem, like anything was possible. Like the past could stay in one place forever.

"Do you mind if we go back now?" Beatrice asked, breaking the idyllic solitude. "Miss Iris said I could join her in the kitchen today. She's making hot cross buns and asked if I'd like to join her. She prefers to do it early before Jacob can catch her. Iris says he doesn't approve of her spending time baking, and she hates upsetting him."

Anna blinked. "Hot cross buns? What do you know about making bread?"

"Nothing," Beatrice replied jovially. "That's why I want to learn. Miss Iris says baking is a wonderful hobby, good for the soul. She says kneading is also perfect for a vexed mind. Apparently, one can take out their aggression on the dough. You should join us. You might need it today."

Anna was at a loss. She didn't even know if Beatrice could locate the kitchens in their own home. Since when was she interested in such manual labor? Again, Anna wondered if Jacob's aunts were a good influence on her impressionable sister.

Nevertheless, she hated to dissuade Beatrice when she was so excited. Over making hot cross buns. Usually, the girl was only that enthusiastic when she was eating them. "I … suppose we can go back," Anna answered unevenly. "As long as you mind the cooks. I don't want you to get in their way. They have a job to do."

"Oh, I know," Beatrice said. "Iris said they don't mind. She says they're used to it. The family isn't anything like the old viscount's."

But was that a good thing?

Beatrice rambled on. "Miss Iris said that they caused a stir at first when they moved in, but the staff got over it quickly enough. She said they couldn't be blamed for behaving differently because they hadn't the faintest idea how to behave anyway."

A laugh crackled from Anna's chest. "Yes, I suppose that makes sense. But there's different and then there's *different*."

Beatrice's face was bright and clear as she laughed at her sister's comment. Not one freckle marred her perfect complexion. "I like it here," she said firmly, catching Anna off guard.

"You do? Why?"

Beatrice shrugged, gazing across the grounds toward the house where a commotion was building. Horses were being guided out from the stables to a waiting phaeton.

"It's just so easy," the younger woman explained. There was a verve in her voice that Anna had never heard before, something growing and expanding right before her eyes. "I love our home, you know I do, but it's been so dour. So much has happened. Mother dying, your illness, David leaving. It wasn't your fault," she rushed on, "but joyful moments were few and far between. Here, I don't know—there just seems to be so much laughter. Everything feels so … free."

An ache settled in Anna's chest. She'd always prided herself on her relationship with Beatrice. She kept secrets, of course— they were for her sister's sake—but she'd had no idea Beatrice kept them from her as well. Was their home so anemic? Anna hadn't thought so, but then again, she'd been lost in herself, bottled up with self-preservation. Perhaps her vision was skewed.

She couldn't afford to keep it that way. Not when this fresh start was being handed to her family. They deserved it too much.

A blush darkened Beatrice's cheeks. She made it a point not to meet Anna's eye. "I'm glad you told me," Anna replied evenly. *No one should be embarrassed for telling their truth.* "All right, let's go back at once. Make the most delicious hot cross buns we've ever tasted. And be sure to memorize everything so that you can continue to make them when we're home."

"Are you sure?" Beatrice asked, peeking up through her lashes.

"Of course! I can't wait to try them."

Beatrice lunged at her sister, kissing her ecstatically on both cheeks. "Thank you, Anna. I'll be sure to put extra icing on yours!"

"You better," Anna said, laughing.

The ladies changed course for the house, Beatrice picking up speed, and Anna managing not to kick any more rocks. By the time they were within shouting distance of the phaeton, the grooms had already secured four horses at its front. As if on cue, Sir John exited the house with Mrs. Wright on his arm. She was a lovely sight bundled in a deep purple cloak and white muff, with a matching bonnet perched precariously over her head. White puffs of air surrounded them along with their excitable chatter.

"Looks like Father also has plans for this morning." Beatrice giggled as Sir John lifted Mrs. Wright grandly into the phaeton.

"Indeed—" Anna started, but just as the word left her mouth, a third figure charged from the house.

Jacob.

The viscount wasted little time climbing into the phaeton along with the couple, arranging himself in the back seat without a care in the world. Sir John and Mrs. Wright parked themselves into the front seat and were too polite to share any uncomfortable glances about the interloper, though Anna could tell that was exactly what Jacob was. The couple's body language became too stilted and stiff when he joined the merry party. She had a sick suspicion that the man had invited himself. And he had only one goal in mind.

Well, it looks like I won't spend the morning reading in front of a fire, Anna lamented to herself. *No matter. This is much more important.*

"And where are you all off to?" she called out as she and Beatrice came up on the phaeton. She kept her tone light and pleasant, not wanting to alert the couple that she was onto Jacob's nasty game.

Sir John seemed visibly relieved as he greeted his daughters. Safety in numbers, and all that. "Mrs. Wright asked me to accompany her to the village. She said there are a few shops that I might enjoy. Maybe even stop for tea."

Like the night before, Anna could feel Jacob's gaze encroach upon her. It was rough and hot like a tongue against the skin. "Sounds lovely."

"Would you like to join us?" Mrs. Wright asked. Anna could have sworn that the lady rolled her eyes as she tilted her head slightly toward the back seat.

"Oh, I'd hate to intrude on the happy day," Anna said, finally fixing her attention on Jacob. The ridiculous man was clearly not used to waking up this early. His face was pale and humorless, and his clothes were ruffled and unkempt, as if he'd dressed himself in the dark. Naturally, his temperament matched. His expression was bland, emotionless as he waited for her answer, but she could tell he was aware of her every word. He played the relaxed man without a care in the world; however, he couldn't fool her. If he could have jumped out of the phaeton and thrown her in the house, he would have.

"It's no intrusion at all," Mrs. Wright said. "As you can see, we have just the spot for you."

Was it Anna's imagination, or did Jacob widen his thighs, usurping even more space on the seat?

She clicked her tongue against the roof of her mouth, making him squirm. Her smile could have melted butter. "Oh, all right, then," she relented. "You've twisted my arm. It sounds delight-ful."

"Splendid," Sir John crowed. He stood at once, intending to get out and help Anna inside, but Jacob was quicker.

He offered his hand, though Anna was hesitant to take it. She hadn't thought things through. She had decided to spend the day with Jacob without realizing that she would be forced to touch him from time to time. It wasn't something she relished. Not after their encounter last night.

As she placed her hand in his, Jacob lowered his head so only she could hear his words. "You can't really be surprised to see me?" He squeezed her fingers before letting them go, holding her a second longer than needed. Anna flushed as she settled herself in her seat and the groom whipped the horses into a start.

Over the commotion, she felt confident enough to whisper back without being overheard by her father and Mrs. Wright. "I'm not surprised, merely confused. I wonder why you are going to such great lengths to stop the couple when you've said yourself that this isn't love."

Jacob flashed her a dangerous grin, and suddenly, he didn't

seem so exhausted anymore. On the contrary, he looked wide awake … and determined. "Oh, it's not. It's war."

⟫⟫⟫✖⟪⟪⟪

THE PARTY WAS halfway to the village before Anna could muster the courage to speak. Annoyance had struck her so insidiously that she was afraid if she opened her mouth any sooner, she would've screamed. War? Truly? What kind of reprobate was she dealing with here? From their conversation before, Anna understood that Jacob would be difficult, but she'd underestimated his tenacity.

Her maelstrom of thoughts wasn't helped by the fact that Jacob was intentionally crowding her. His thighs were splayed on their seat, forcing her to hug the side of the carriage even though the phaeton was of medium size, with ample room for four people.

Before Anna could contain herself, she shoved her elbow into Jacob's ribs. "Will you please move over? You're doing this on purpose."

The obstinate man didn't budge. "Doing that?"

Anna's laugh was as bitter as dandelion tea. "You know exactly what you're doing. Don't play dumb."

"I'm not playing anything."

She sucked in a breath, praying for composure. She was a lady; she would not elbow him anymore! "You're asserting your dominance, trying to cower me. It won't work. Just like your other ploy."

"Other ploy?"

Anna cocked the brim of her bonnet to the couple in front, grateful they were too enamored with each other to hear the ridiculous conversation in the back seat. "You won't win, you know. I'm an excellent competitor."

Her head was forward, but all too well Anna could sense

Jacob inching toward her, feel the heavy weight of his breath before he spoke just above her ear. "And why is that?"

She closed her eyes, willing away the effect he had on her. If it was just her body, it would be one thing. Animal attraction was a simple biological occurrence. Common. But she couldn't lie to herself. Anna was enticed by him. Pure and simple. From the musky woodiness of his smell to the tight aggressiveness of his body, she was helpless in her reaction. But the way he captivated her mind bothered Anna to know end. She was constantly in tune with him—from the way his finger traced little circles on his knee to the way his foot tapped anxiously on the floor, every move he made was seared into her consciousness. It made no sense! And it made piecing sentences together damned difficult!

"I … um …" What had she meant to say? Anna shook her head, hoping Jacob couldn't see the blush she knew was permeating her cheeks. She elbowed him once more.

"Oof! Careful there," he said, rubbing his ribs. "I'm not one of your gentlemen. You bite me and I might bite back."

Why did that make her stomach flutter? It was a warning, but from the wistful way Jacob said it, it almost sounded like a promise.

"I'm not afraid of you," Anna countered, steeling her voice with as much force as she could. "And as I said, I am onto your game and will counter your move at every turn. Obviously, you didn't want to go shopping this morning. You're only here to be a thorn in the side of the couple. What are you planning to do? Walk between them the entire day? Hold your mother's hands so my father can't? It's so childish."

Jacob flashed that grin again, his one dimple making him appear almost charming. What an odd man. It was as if he were amused by all her condemnations. Anna had a laundry list of them; she surmised he'd be belly-laughing in no time. "It may be childish, but it will be effective," he replied.

"But to what end?" Anna slapped her hands on her lap before hiding them under her cloak. Not planning on this excursion, she'd left her muff in her room. Even with the sun, her hands were morphing into icicles. "Your mother is a grown woman with a grown child." She cut him a dry look. "Although how grown you are is debat—"

"Oh, I'm very grown."

"I'm not even going to acknowledge you said that," Anna quipped, ignoring his mischievous chuckle. "Back to my point— your mother does not need a guardian or another man to tell her what to do with her life. It's bad enough that women have fathers and then husbands, now they must contend with the whims of their sons? No thank you."

"For Christ's sake, give me your hand." Before Anna could jerk out of the way, Jacob snatched her hand from under her cloak and brought it up to his mouth. With wide, incredulous eyes, she watched as he shielded it with his own and proceeded to blow hot air on her fingers. Heat flamed against her skin, simultaneously shocking and prickling her. "How dare … What are you … You shouldn't be—"

"Oh, be quiet," Jacob said in between breaths. "Your hands are freezing. Don't be all proper when you're miserable."

"I … I'm not miserable," Anna replied.

Jacob merely lifted a brow in response. Then he did something even more ridiculous: he shoved her left hand into his coat pocket while cradling her right one on the top of his knee. Anna was plastered against him. And very, very warm.

"See?" he said as if they were indulging in a friendly game of cards. "I'm not such a bad chap."

It was like Anna was in the middle of a fit—she couldn't stop shaking her head. "This … this isn't right. We shouldn't—"

"How is it not right?" Jacob countered. "You were cold. I had the ability to change that. Problem solved. I'm not the devil you think I am. I like solving problems. I like helping women in distress. Believe it or not, I loved playing knight when I was a child."

Anna snorted. "You're hardly a knight. And no woman is in

distress. Not your mother, and certainly not me."

Jacob swiveled his neck to her. The prickly hair along his jaw attracted her attention, and she wondered why he hadn't shaved that morning. She lowered her gaze. Looking into his eyes at this range wasn't a good thing. They were like a fog to her, and she couldn't risk getting lost in those varying shades of gray.

"But I'm not the villain, am I?" he asked. The words drifted upon her face. Intimately. Indecently. Anna could smell the mint of his tooth powder, the bitterness of his coffee, and had to actively curb the desire rising within her to taste him again.

Luckily for her, reality came to call. From the periphery of Anna's mind, she heard voices and remembered that they weren't alone. She yanked herself back to the matter at hand. "You are the villain if you continue on this path to keep our parents apart. Warming my hands doesn't change anything."

"Pity," Jacob said. He was staring at her lips. "I'll just have to keep trying."

"Do your worst, *my lord*."

His nose crinkled. "Oh, I intend to, my dear. I intend to."

Chapter Six

U GH, COURTSHIP IS *intolerable.*

If it wasn't for the vexing back-and-forth with Anna, Jacob would have escaped the couple hours ago. The constant flutter of inane conversation threatened to do him in. How many times could people remark on the fineness of the weather? Or the fineness of the knickknacks in the shops? Or the fineness of the crowd on the road? Was that what love did to a person? Make everything seem perpetually fine? Well, count him out, then.

On an intellectual level, Jacob understood that one day he would have to settle down with a wife, especially since he held a title now and his seed was, apparently, too important not to spread. Nevertheless, if it meant spending countless hours remarking on the fineness of the world, then he could afford to wait a few years. His sanity depended on it.

Not that he was asserting this decrepit suitor, Sir John, held such strong affections for his mother. No, Jacob was still not sold on the baronet's genuine devotion, but he had to hand it to the man—Sir John Smythe played a very good game. Almost as well as his daughter.

True to her word, Anna continued to be the fly in Jacob's ointment. In her ladylike, graceful way she outmaneuvered Jacob throughout the morning, pulling and prodding him so that he was never quite where he wanted to be, namely in between his mother and Sir John. In each shop she stuck to him, finding new and advantageous ways to keep their parents' attention on one another and not his sulky comments. It would have infuriated him to no end, if not for the fact that it meant he had her glued to his side for the majority of their time. Jacob found that he rather liked that … liked it all too well.

Even now as the foursome gathered around the table at the Naughty Monk, Anna spun her magic on the situation, orchestrating the seating arrangements, dictating that Jacob sat next to her and across from his mother—as far away from Sir John as possible.

What he would have given for a rich, dark ale, not this worthless, limp tea that managed to make him more parched the more he forced it down his defeated gullet.

Anna's smugness didn't help matters. She was positively giddy as Sir John and his mother retreated to the bar to converse with the tavern owner, a barrel-chested man who liked to gossip more than a sewing circle.

"Sulking doesn't become you," she teased, handing Jacob an oval biscuit from the tray at the center of the table. "If you put your pride aside, you might realize that you've had a *fine* day." Her emphasis on the word managed to bring a resistant smile to his face. Fine. So she'd noticed the overuse of the banal word as well.

Jacob accepted the peace offering, shoving the buttery treat into his mouth. It didn't taste as good as Anna—nothing ever would—but the little sweetness was better than nothing. He washed it down with the remainder of his tea and grimaced. "I'm never going through with it," Jacob stated firmly. "All of this cloying 'yes, please' and 'oh, thank you' and 'isn't that lovely' nonsense. It's too much."

Tiny lines fanned out from the sides of Anna's eyes even as she pursed her lips in disappointment. "You will forsake the marital yoke, will you? Brave man."

"Not at all. Marriage is a business arrangement, no more so than in the peerage. I will merely find a wife and make my intentions known. If she's agreeable, then that will be that."

The adorable little creases evaporated from Anna's face—the disappointment, however, did not. "That will be that?" she spat. "How romantic of you. You better be ready, my lord, because with words such as those, all the available young ladies of good breeding all be swarming you in no time."

"Don't give me that look," Jacob said, reaching for another biscuit. He was hungry; he'd missed breakfast this morning when he found out about the excursion. He'd had to hurry to catch up to the couple before they left. "You think it's ridiculous too, all this nonsensical talk. It's offensive."

"I think no such … thing." Anna's words dropped off as if she regretted them the second that they left her mouth. Jacob waited for her to continue, though she seemed perfectly content to twirl her teacup around on the table, fixated on the little blue flowers painted on the side. "Well … maybe it is a *tad* dull, but they're new to this—new to each other. They're trying to see how they fit together without bashing around too much. It's lovely. It's how love is."

"Ugh, please. There's that word again." Jacob shoved himself away from the table so he could stare at the woman without putting a crick in his neck. "You seem well versed on the subject—is there something you're not telling me? Is there a man at home just biding his time until he whisks you off to his castle?"

Anna's brow furrowed. Jacob almost muttered a curse. *Stupid man.* He wasn't sure if her reaction was due to his comment or the harsh way he'd said it. Where had all this emotion come from? Still, his shoulders strained as he waited for her answer.

When she began to shake her head, Jacob barely had the strength to stifle the relief in his breath. Anna Smythe wasn't his woman. But he didn't want her to be anyone else's either. Especially since he planned on kissing her many more times during this fateful little visit.

Speaking of kissing …

"No?" he asked when no comment followed. "Huh. I figured that was the reason you almost slaughtered me last night after our kiss."

Anna's eyes snapped up from the teacup, brimming with anger and … hunger? Either worked for Jacob.

"You shouldn't have done that," she said, making sure to twist the knife when she added, "and it will never happen again."

Jacob grinned. He skimmed the top of her hand with her finger, laughing when she pulled away. "Why? I know you liked it."

"You do not."

"Oh, yes, I do," he continued, resting his forearms on his knees. Jacob bent toward Anna, his head perched just about her shoulder. "By the way, what did you mean when you said that my kiss wasn't lustful? I can assure you that it most definitely was."

Anna's gaze shot to their parents at the bar. They were still out of earshot and happily engaged with the owner. "From my experience, kisses are not a form of lust; they are beautiful, poetic symbols of love."

"Christ," Jacob scoffed, falling back into his seat. "You've been kissing the wrong people."

Anna raised her chin, her round face serious and resolute. "Not at all. The kisses I've experienced have been quite perfect, actually. And I feel sorry for you. Sorry that you will never encounter anything like it."

"Who was he?"

"No one," Anna squeaked, answering much too quickly.

"He wasn't no one," Jacob pressed. "Tell me."

She was back to staring at her damn teacup. "No one that you know."

"Yes, because I was a filthy newspaperman, I understand," he said with a mirthless laugh. He sobered instantly. "And he's gone now?"

"I'm not talking about this with you." Anna sighed. "I only mention it now to prove to you that I have life experiences. I'm not some sheltered little girl of the *ton*. I've tasted love, felt it, lived it, which makes me adept at seeing it now. Life isn't a game. Rarely does one have second chances at happiness. The fact that my father and your mother have this possibility is something to be celebrated, not derided."

Jacob had an insatiable urge to kiss her again, if only to wipe the sad, wistful look off her face. He wished that they'd never broached this ridiculous subject in the first place. The last thing he wanted to hear about was Anna's first love. The man had obviously died or jilted her, and she was still hung up on the dreamy devil. "Do you honestly think I want to hold my mother back? I want her to be happy."

"But?"

Jacob rolled his eyes. "I want it to be with someone who isn't trying to fleece her."

Anna flopped her hands on the table. *Good.* That forlorn expression was gone and replaced with irritation. He preferred that any day. "How many times do I have to tell you? My father's intentions are pure. You must think your mother a pathetic, weak woman if you believe she would fall for a con man."

"Certainly not," Jacob scoffed.

Anna went on, speaking over him. "All those years she kept food in your belly and a roof over your head after your father passed must have been a happy accident, then. She must have been lucky that providence was looking out for her so well to be able to take care of not only her son but her sisters."

"Oh, stop being so dramatic," he said, his spine popping as he straightened in his seat. "You know very well how highly I regard my mother. She is one of the strongest women I've ever met."

"But you don't trust her to know her own mind. You don't trust that she can guide and shield her own heart."

Jacob granted the vixen an appraising smile. He'd walked right into that one. His father would have adored Anna—her debating skills were unparalleled. Nevertheless, Jacob was down, not beaten.

He'd started to issue his retort when the sound of his mother's laughter cut him off. It was girlish and effervescent and still managed to delight him despite the situation. Anna sent him a winning grin, as if the laughter was actually proving her point. It was not.

"I do trust my mother," he explained in a measured, condescending tone. "But women are …" How could he put this without the dangerous chit breaking her teacup over his head? "Women are soft."

"Soft?"

"Weak.

"*Weak!*"

"In affairs of the heart," Jacob rushed out. He planted his boots firmly on the floor as he watched Anna's knuckles glow white around the cup. "It's nothing to be ashamed of; it's just the way they are—the fairer, more delicate sex and whatnot."

Anna's mouth puckered up as if she'd just eaten an entire raw lemon. The action served to make her bottom lip look even more ripe for the tasting. "Ridiculous," she muttered. "Absolutely ridiculous. I should have known."

"Known what?" Sir John asked. Jacob had been so wrapped up in Anna that he hadn't noticed that their parents had meandered back to the table. "Anna?" her father asked, eyeing her carefully. "What should you have known?"

Anna closed her eyes, inhaling deeply before she reopened them. She issued a fake smile that fooled no one. "Oh, it's nothing, Father."

Jacob's mother tittered nervously. "It doesn't seem like nothing, my dear. Jacob? What did you say to the poor girl? Apologize at once."

He threw his mother an incredulous look. "I didn't do anything. I just said that—"

"Women are weak," Anna replied, beating him to it.

"In matters of the heart," he amended.

"Anna," Sir John drawled with no small hint of warning. His spindly auburn eyebrows reached up to the top of his hairline. "I told you not to go on about cricket."

Cricket?

"Oh, cricket!" Jacob's mother exclaimed, visibly relieved that the conversation wasn't as serious as she'd assumed. "Your father says you are quite the player, Anna. He says you've even joined a club. How fun that sounds, being able to get all that fresh air and express yourself in that physical way."

Anna pressed her fingers into the grooves of the table, following a split in the wood. "We weren't talking about cricket," she said, her voice low.

"Good," Sir John said.

Her head popped up and whipped toward Jacob. "But now that you mention it, maybe we should."

"Anna …" Sir John cautioned.

Jacob put up a hand. "No, no. I think I want to hear this. Go on, Miss Smythe. I'm all ears."

In an instant, Anna reached into her cloak and pulled out an old piece of paper. She took her time unfolding it, smoothing out the edges before placing it on the table in front of him.

"Do you *actually* keep that on you at all times?" Sir John said, cradling his head in his hands.

She gave him a blank stare. "Yes. It's not odd. Don't make it odd."

Jacob peered at the document. "This is a newspaper. *My* newspaper."

Anna nodded energetically. "Indeed." She tapped her fingertips on the bottom right side of the page. "You wrote this article, did you not? About the matrons versus singles cricket match that took place last summer?"

Jacob frowned. Why was the woman so incensed? "Yes."

"Please, Anna," Sir John implored. "Drop this at once."

"I will not," she replied icily. "The man just said that women are weak—"

"*In affairs of the heart,*" Jacob railed. Christ. They were like a carousel, going round and round in circles.

Anna wasn't listening. "I just wanted to ask Lord Newton how he could write this drivel when he watched talented women play cricket. With his own two eyes, he witnessed my team pummel the matrons. I hit for twenty-three runs! I smacked the ball so hard that my palms hurt the next day. And after all that, he still has the audacity to believe that women are soft and weak. It is beyond my comprehension."

Weak in matters of the heart! Jacob knew better than to say it this time. Instead, fool that he was, he tried to defend himself, because the woman obviously hadn't read the article properly. He'd praised the players. The match had been a resounding success. Thousands had come out to enjoy it. What more did she want? *More* recognition?

"Are you angry because I didn't mention you by name? I had no idea you were so hungry for fame," Jacob said dryly.

Anna sucked in a breath. "You said we were a fad. You said that because we couldn't hit as far or bowl as fast, people would eventually lose interest in us. You said there was no place for women's cricket."

Jacob shook his head before she finished speaking. "I said nothing of the sort. I said that people would probably lose interest. Probably. That's an important word. Because it's true. Women can't hit the ball as far or bowl as fast. It's just the way it is, and people spend their hard-earned money and time to watch a spectacle. They enjoy speed and dynamic feats in the field."

"And women can't provide that? Even if we practice and train and work harder than the men, you still don't think we have a chance at succeeding?"

Jacob shrugged, feeling cagey and out of his element. He was no stranger to confrontations; many a person had hounded him on the streets, hollering about something he'd written. It was a hazard of the trade. But the way Anna was regarding him, as if he'd ripped out her heart and stomped on it with his boot, made him reconsider ever picking up a pen again.

"I'm sorry," he said quickly, glancing at his mother for help. She wouldn't meet his eye; it was obvious whose side she was on. "I don't wish to dissuade you. If you enjoy playing, then play. What does it matter if you don't have the same number of spectators as the men?"

Anna's eyes narrowed viciously. "It's not about the crowds."

"Then what?"

Anna didn't answer. "I'd like to go now," she told her father, rising from her seat. "I didn't get much sleep last night. I'm … I'm very tired all of a sudden."

"Of course, my dear," Jacob's mother replied, gathering her things. "We'll go at once. What was I thinking keeping you out so long? You've only just arrived yesterday."

Jacob couldn't leave it at that. He simply had to know. "Then what, Anna?" he persisted as the others rose to their feet. "Tell me."

Her face was hauntingly baleful. "You wouldn't understand."

Jacob reached for her hand, ignoring Sir John's ferocious scowl. "Why wouldn't I understand?"

Gently, Anna extricated herself from his hold. "Because you've never had to."

Chapter Seven

DESPITE CRYING OFF, Anna did not go back to her room that afternoon for a nap. Instead, the instant the phaeton returned the party to Newton Place, she made a beeline for the kitchens.

Reaching the entrance, she peered around the busy workspace with wild eyes. "I need dough," she announced.

Beatrice lifted her head from her place in the far corner of the madness, interrupting her absorption on a tray of freshly baked buns. A grand smile sprouted on her face as she took in Anna's obvious distress. "That's the girl I love."

Iris stood at Beatrice's side, her apron covered in flour. She eyed Anna appreciatively.

"I won't be in the way?" Anna asked, creeping near the table. "I don't know the first thing about baking, but I have an indescribable need to hit something, and to hit it hard."

She assumed that Iris would be mortified by her statement, but the woman nodded in apparent understanding. "You've come to the right place, my dear," she said. She wore an old, tattered blouse that looked like it was older than Anna and had rolled her sleeves up to her elbow. She placed her toned bare arm around Anna's shoulders. "Welcome home."

AFTER AN HOUR of sifting and measuring, rolling and kneading, Anna concluded that she showed very little signs of becoming a confident baker. She wasn't even a big lover of sweets. However, that wasn't to say she didn't enjoy pummeling the life out of the gloopy mixture Iris placed in front of her. Beatrice had been right: handling the dough was awfully cathartic—even more so than playing cricket. She loved the sport dearly, but it was nearly impossible to play by oneself. It was a game that relied on relationships. With baking, Anna could take out all her anger, her frustration, her energy on that sad, elastic, and remarkably resilient ball of dough. It was a revelation.

At first, the servants showed small signs of being concerned at yet another body taking up space in the kitchen, but soon they turned a blind eye, concluding that she was just another eccentric peer, no different than Iris or Beatrice. The cook, Mrs. McGuan, reminded Anna of her cricket captain, Myfanwy, by the way she yelled out commands to her underlings. The squat, round woman was positively frightening, though Anna learned she was more bark than bite. The leader also offered many kind words to the servants who needed a boost of confidence.

As Anna worked, something broke inside her, a dam of emotion that gained speed and alacrity along with the surety of her hands. The environment surely helped. The air in the active room was just as filled with conversation and gossip as it was with spices and herbs. Laughter and whispers permeated the space, making Anna feel undeniably safe enough to eventually divulge what was bothering her.

"I just don't understand men," she said, eyeing the way Iris manipulated her dough from the corner of her eye. Jacob's aunt pulled off chunks of the mixture and rolled them into little, smooth balls against the table with the palm of her hand before placing them back on the tray. They looked impeccable, like little shiny billiard balls lined up into straight rows.

Anna blew out a long sigh of frustration. "The world is changing. Every day women are doing exciting and new things; how can he truly believe that we're weak?"

"I don't think he's saying that, sister," Beatrice replied gently, balancing a large bowl in her arm while madly whirling a whisk inside. She had been promoted to icing duty. "I think you're only hearing what you want to hear."

"What does that mean?" Anna snapped.

Beatrice whisked harder, avoiding her sister's glare. "It means I think you want to condemn him. And I don't know why."

Anna scoffed. "That's ridiculous." Her nose itched and she didn't have one clean finger to scratch it. Oh well, if she left this room with flour all over her face, so be it. "He's a tyrant. He thinks he knows best about everything; he won't even trust his own mother to make up her mind. He's the kind of man who believes that women are too emotionally fragile to handle difficult choices. It's asinine."

"I suppose," Beatrice replied.

"I'm right. You know I am," Anna said, gaining speed. "Just look at Iris and Violet."

Violet sat across from them, acting as *supreme taste tester*. "I would prefer not to get involved in this spat," she remarked between chews.

"You're not involved." Anna laughed. "He's your nephew and I know you love him. I'm sorry for speaking poorly of him, but you have to admit, he's acting like a child."

"He's acting like a man," Iris returned dryly. "Sometimes there's very little difference."

"Exactly!" Anna said. "And that child doesn't approve of your coming down to work in the kitchen from time to time. He makes you dance around his feelings so as not to upset him. How is that fair? You are a grown woman; you should be allowed to do whatever you want without worrying about his *emotionally fragile state*."

Iris chuckled, now rolling one ball in each hand against the tabletop. *Show-off.* "You might be condemning him a little too harshly," she said diplomatically. "Jacob is one of the good ones, I promise you. His life wasn't easy, you know. His father … Well, his father could be difficult. There was a reason Violet and I didn't move in with Rose while she was married."

Beatrice stopped whisking. "What do you mean, difficult?"

Iris frowned at her work and shared a look with Violet. When she placed a ball on the tray, Anna noticed the round shape was slightly off-kilter. "Rose didn't know Jacob's father, Wallace Wright, for very long before she married him. We told her to wait and not rush into things, but she was so upset when Sir John said he couldn't marry her. She cried straight into the arms of Wallace. She thought he could fix her broken heart, and he did for a time before …"

"Before?" Beatrice asked.

Iris sighed, wiping her hands on her apron. Her face appeared impossibly long, like butter melting in a pan. "Before his temper got the best of him. There was nothing any of us could do about it. Poor Rose would try to hide the bruises as best she could."

"And Jacob?" Anna said. Her chest seized as she asked a question she wasn't sure she wanted to know the answer to. "Did he have to hide bruises?"

Iris's smile was sad but kind. "Not many, thanks to his mother."

Even with the hustle of the servants rushing around the trio, the room felt impossibly quiet, like they were all watching a scene that Iris had painted for them, filling in the details with their imaginations. It was difficult for Anna. She couldn't fathom being afraid of her father. Even in her darkest hour, Sir John had restrained his condemnations and only been sympathetic. She doubted many others in his position would have done the same.

Iris broke up the contemplation when she backed away from the table, slapping her hands together to rub the flour off. "I didn't tell you that to make you feel sorry for Jacob—or Rose.

What's done is done and over with. But it might help explain why the boy is so possessive of us. He was helpless to help her—us—for so many years. And now he's a viscount, and a rich one at that. By scolding me not to break my back over this table, he's telling me how much he loves me. I know that, which is why I let him do it. There's no harm in it, truly. I don't dance around his feelings, but I do try to respect them." Iris moved over to Beatrice's side to inspect her work. The sweet buns glistened on the tray, each topped with a generous amount of Beatrice's snow-white frosting. "I think we've had enough talking for one day. What do you say we do some taste testing?"

"I'm way ahead of you." Violet chuckled, spraying a puff of powdered sugar from her mouth.

"Oh, thank the Lord!" Beatrice announced, tearing off her apron. "I was beginning to worry Violet would have all the fun!"

"Story of my life," Iris teased.

As the ladies enjoyed their buns and tea, the topics involved lighter affairs. The atmosphere couldn't have been more relaxed as the women sat in the servants' dining area, sharing their desserts with whoever had a break in their day. There was no more talk about Jacob or Rose or the man who had left scars on both.

But even as Anna tried to laugh and engage with the others, Jacob was never far from her mind. Perhaps she had been too harsh on him. Perhaps he *was* only trying to help, albeit in a ham-fisted way. One could hardly expect anything different from a man who'd grown up in those circumstances. After all, Jacob had told her that his favorite game as a child was playing knight. In his mind, every woman needed rescuing, even if they were perfectly capable of rescuing themselves.

What Jacob needed was a friend, not a foe, someone who could show him the error of his thinking with a soft, delicate touch. And Anna was just the person to do it. Maybe then he would stop seeing her father as a villain.

Yes. That's it.

Anna relaxed back in her chair, her anxiety and anger draining from her body. Finally, she reached for the sticky bun on her plate and took a generous bite. The sugar immediately coursed through her veins, causing her spine to straighten back up again with lightning speed.

Iris was reading a newspaper but caught the act. "Good, aren't they?"

Anna nodded because she was too busy chewing. It was like eating a soft and spongy cloud. She wiped her mouth. "Almost too good. It would be hard to stop at one."

The newspaper shook along with Iris's scoff. "Who said you have to stop at one?"

The vibrations of the paper snagged Anna's eye, and she caught the headline at the top. Unceremoniously, she leaned across the table to read the small black print. She had to restrain herself from snatching the whole thing out of Iris's hands.

"What's the matter?" Beatrice asked, her sweet bun lifted just outside her mouth. "Is everything all right? Please don't tell me it's another article about cricket. I don't think I can take it."

"No … not at all," Anna replied, reclaiming her seat. With a smile on her face, she took another delicious bite. "It's something better."

Because Anna finally had a plan.

⇥⟫⟪⇤

WHEN THE HOUSE was quiet and everyone was busy getting changed for dinner, Anna ventured down a corridor she hadn't been down before. She'd never had a reason to go into this wing of the house until now.

She gathered her courage one final time and knocked on the very last door at the end.

"Not now," a deep voice bellowed from inside the room. Anna rolled her eyes. For a man who wasn't born a viscount, he sure had mastered the tone in no time.

"Just open up," she called back.

Immediately, the door flew open. Jacob stood before her, his black hair dripping at his nape and his white linen shirt unbuttoned. A patch of dark, curly hair peeked out from underneath. Anna didn't dare lower her eyes any further because she was almost positive his trousers were equally unclasped as they hung loosely from his hips.

"Yes?" he asked. He sounded irritated and entertained at the same time. Anna couldn't understand how one person could place so much emotion on one short word.

"Um … right…" she stammered, shutting her eyes. It was the only way she could gain control over her faculties. What was wrong with her? She wasn't some innocent. She'd seen a naked man before. But that man wasn't Jacob Wright.

"Are you going to make me stand here all night?" he asked. He leaned against the doorframe, folding his arms across his chest, sadly blocking her view of his skin.

"No, of course not," she hurried out.

Jacob bent over the threshold, craning his neck to look past her down the hallway. "This isn't some trick, is it?" he asked. "Someone isn't going to jump out and see you undressing me with your eyes outside my bedroom and force us to marry, correct?"

Anna cocked her head, unleashing a sardonic smile. "Don't *you* think so highly of yourself, my lord? Have no fear, your virtue is safe with me. I have no nefarious plans. I'm not the marrying type."

Jacob's wariness vanished. "Why?"

She flicked a hand in the air, dismissing the topic. "Never mind that. I … um … I came here to apologize for how I behaved earlier."

"Think nothing of it."

"No, don't do that. Don't brush it off. I want to make it up to you."

Jacob's brows lifted. He glanced back into his room. "Make it up to me," he replied slowly. "How?"

His meaning hit her like an arrow to the chest. "Not like that!" she said, feeling her knees weaken at the invitation.

The cad had the audacity to appear disappointed.

"I was hoping … I was …"

Anna's thoughts died a quick death. Jacob uncrossed his arms and reached for her hair. She could only watch as he gently ran his fingers through the curls at her crown, too flabbergasted to even jerk out of his range.

"What are you …?"

Jacob lifted his hand in front of them, rubbing his fingers and thumb together. He squinted at the tiny granules that fell to the floor. "Have you been in the kitchens?"

Flour. Anna was mortified. Jacob hadn't massaged her locks, overcome by desire. He was picking dried dough out of her hair.

"Never mind that," she repeated irritably. "I want to know if you will accompany me tonight. After dinner."

"Where?"

"Some place educational."

"No. That sounds terrible."

She groaned. "Not educational. Informative, then."

Jacob tugged his pants to his hips. "Equally terrible."

"The circus! All right? I want to take you to the circus!" Anna clamped her hands over her mouth. She'd screamed so loudly she was sure the entire house now knew of her clandestine plans.

Jacob's eyes narrowed. He scratched his jaw as he contemplated her. "Your father will never allow it," he said.

"My father doesn't have to know."

"You'd lie to your father?"

"I'm lying *for* my father."

Jacob's chest rumbled in laughter, showcasing the thick patch of hair again. *Don't look. Don't look. Don't look.* Anna looked anyway. "I think it would be difficult explaining that to him," he said. "Ladies do not go out with gentlemen after dark, especially to pleasure gardens. Even I know that."

"But you're not a gentleman, are you?" Anna asked.

When Jacob didn't reply, she knew she'd received her answer. She hid her smile as spun away, retreating down the hall.

He would come. The writer in him was too intrigued not to.

As was the man in him.

Chapter Eight

Handel's Traveling Circus was different than any other circus Anna had visited before. For one thing, it used a giant, tarp-like tent for its enclosure. Up until that point, most circuses had used existing structures and old warehouses to put on their shows. In the newspaper article Anna had eventually wrestled away from Iris, she read that Handel had just returned from a visit to America, bringing the tent innovation with him. It was an ingenious idea, allowing the entertainment group to set up shop in new locales throughout the country. No longer limited, the traveling circuses could go wherever there was a large swath of land and demand—and England had both of those in abundance.

"I have to admit," Jacob began as he helped Anna down from the carriage, "this wasn't at all was I expecting."

She clicked her tongue in response and took the lead trudging across the field toward the main tent along with the gathering crowd. The excitement was palpable, and she found that her footsteps were lighter and quicker the closer they came to the flimsy-looking structure. Thank the heavens that rain clouds were nowhere in sight. Anna didn't know if she'd dare enter the tent when a storm raged outside. Would the winds pick up the tarp and take them all with it?

"I suppose you assumed I was taking you to Astley's?" she replied with a knowing lilt to her voice.

"Naturally."

Anna *humphed*. Astley's Amphitheatre was a popular venue in London where most of the upper classes went to see and be seen. The grand structure was surrounded by boxes and galleries where people could sit comfortably and watch equestrian performances, the latest plays, and even mock-naval battles.

Needless to say, as they were pushed and prodded in line, waiting to give a man with a mouth full of golden teeth their coin to enter, this was a far cry from Astley's.

"Please don't tell me you do this often," Jacob remarked regretfully when they finally reached the man at the entrance. Half of his face was tattooed in designs that one might find in the Book of Kells. Jacob had to yank Anna out of her gawking. The colors were uncommonly beautiful on the man's skin.

"I do not," she replied absent-mindedly, handing the man her coins. He gifted her with a wide, golden smile along with her ticket. "I read about a performer tonight that I didn't want to miss. Why?" she asked, twisting her mouth. "Are you nervous? Have you flown so high as a viscount that you can't enjoy simple country pleasures anymore?"

A deep sound rumbled from Jacob's throat. "Hardly," he scoffed. "Though I've never been to one with a woman. I'm just trying to think of what I'll tell your father when he finds out."

"He won't find out," Anna assured him. "Stop worrying. It will ruin the night. Now, come—I want to make sure we get a good seat. It's starting soon."

It would take more than that to erase Jacob's frown. Honestly, the man was like a nervous mother hen, clucking all around her. Whenever anyone ventured too close, he used his body as a shield to make sure nothing got in her path. It would have been chivalrous if it wasn't so unnecessary.

He curbed his botheration long enough to squeeze them into a place in the grandstand a few rows up from the bottom. The gallery followed along the perimeter of the tent, surrounding the dirt-floored oval in the center. Gas lamps were placed at various intervals, giving the atmosphere an ethereal quality, as if magic was accumulating for the performers to grab and use at their disposal.

The seats let out groans as they sat, though Jacob's was louder. "If this entire place falls to pieces around us, I will contend that it is all your fault."

"Naturally," Anna agreed before turning a critical eye on her companion. "I'm surprised at you, my lord. I would have thought a writer such as yourself would enjoy being among real people. What could be more real than this?" As if on cue, the two men sitting to their side tossed a handful of nuts into their mouths and took turns seeing who could spit the shells the farthest past the heads of the people in front of them.

Anna usually adored competition, but even that particular game was too much for her.

Jacob ripped off his hat and scratched at his temples as his eyes narrowed on the rude offenders. "I do enjoy being around *real people*, as you call them. But ..." He stifled his words and returned his hat to his head. "It's nothing. Never mind. Let's just watch the show."

"No, tell me." Without thinking, Anna placed her hand on his thigh, imploring him to continue. It startled her, how small it looked in his lap, and she had an odd urge to spread her fingers wide to feel all that lay undiscovered underneath.

Jacob's brow furrowed as he stared at her hand, but he didn't remove it. He released a low, simmering breath. "I was just going to say that my life has changed in ways I couldn't ever have imagined. I hate to say anything, because it sounds like I'm complaining or ungrateful for my good fortune, but I can't help but feel that I'm constantly being pulled in two directions, expected to be two different people—the person I thought I was and the one I now should be ..."

"Keep going," she prodded when his words thinned into

nothing. The man was obviously not used to speaking about himself.

Jacob continued to stare at her hand. "After I was given the title, I thought nothing would change. Well"—he cocked his head, granting her a rueful smile—"some things would change, but not me. I thought I could keep working at the newspaper, go about my business like before ..."

"But?"

"But I was wrong. Horribly so. I quit the newspaper. I was told it *wasn't the done thing.*" He rolled his shoulders, stretching his neck back and forth. "There are so many things to be done all the time. I have estates that need to be tended to, renters that need my attention, servants to tiptoe around, parties to host. I know I need to trust my managers, but I have a difficult time leaving my work to others. I have this incessant need to want to keep abreast of everything, but it's maddening. Did you know I had a garden party at Newton Place a few months ago? My mother thought it would be a good idea."

Anna answered with an awkward smile, "Yes. You invited me. I came."

He chuckled sheepishly. "Sorry. I should have known. Did you see me?"

Anna shook her head.

Jacob rolled his eyes. "That's because I hid most of the time. I didn't have the faintest idea what to do or say when I met people. The *ton* already thinks I'm a fraud; the last thing I wanted to do was prove them right."

Anna removed her hand from his leg and straightened his tie. It had been off kilter ever since they sat down and had driven her mad. Jacob's Adam's apple bobbed during the slight motion. Was he so affected by her touch?

She lowered her hands, feeling a warmth rush over her body. "You're not a fraud, Jacob. You're just different. It doesn't make you wrong." She squared her shoulders toward the center of the ring, where performers in flashy colors and various stages of undress were beginning to congregate, placing props where they needed them for their acts. "This is a new world we're living in, where amazing discoveries are happening every day. If you want to be a viscount newspaperman, then be one. You're luckier than you think, because there's no one to stop you."

Jacob made a noncommittal noise as he followed her gaze to the ring. She didn't want to point out that his frown was gone, in fear that it might return. "Is something standing in *your* way, Anna?" he asked.

Perhaps it was the way Jacob asked it, but the question bothered her more than she could say. When had the night taken such a turn? They were supposed to be amusing themselves while Anna showed him a spectacle. But now she had a vague hollowness in her heart, one that could only be solved by a decent cry. And she wouldn't be doing that anytime soon.

Tears would only be seen as another sign of weakness.

"Now who's tight-lipped?" he teased.

Anna's eyelashes flickered as she willed herself to keep her emotions in check. "I'm not tight-lipped," she said breezily. She turned to him with a confident smile, though it felt false, like she was lying. She told herself she wasn't; she was merely withholding all the truth for her father's sake. For *her* sake as well. "I didn't need anyone to stand in my way. I did it all by myself. I ..." Anna shut her mouth.

Jacob's eyebrows pinched. "What does that—"

"Oh! It's starting! Finally," she said, hopping to her feet along with the crowd, clapping loudly

Inside, she castigated herself. Had she almost told him? No ... but it had been close. What had she been thinking? Her secret was hers and hers alone, and it needed to stay that way. Divulging it would only hurt her father, and she would never do that. It didn't matter if Jacob continued to look at her in that way, forehead down, gray eyes searing with curiosity and compassion.

She didn't deserve it.

⟫⟫⟫✕⟪⟪⟪

"STOP PULLING ME. I'm simply not leaving until I know for sure," Jacob railed, dodging the other spectators out of the tent. "I don't care what you say. I don't believe it."

Vexed, Anna sighed and hurried to keep with him. She'd known Jacob would be a hard sell, but she'd had no idea he would carry on in this way.

He stole out of the entrance and marched toward the covered wagons and smaller tents scattered alongside the main enclosure, in search of where the performers congregated. Anna lunged forward to grab hold of his arm, allowing him to tow her along. His legs were too long for his own good. The man was a menace.

"Haven't you ever heard the saying 'seeing is believing'? Why must you always think everyone has some nefarious plan?"

"Don't make this about your father," he growled over his shoulder.

Anna growled right back. "How can I not? You always think someone's trying to trick you."

Suddenly, Jacob halted, and Anna rammed right into his back with a yelp. Did he not have an ounce of fat on him? Rubbing her cheek, she navigated around him and realized why he'd stopped. Outside a navy-blue tent, a placard was staked into the ground. In bright red letters, it announced that inside was the *World-Famous Strongwoman, Helga Bitterman. Enter at your own risk.*

"Ha! Strongwoman," Jacob muttered before reaching for the tent flap. A man sitting on a bale of hay struck his leg out right as Jacob was about to charge inside. With a piece of hay hanging out of his mouth, he proceeded to whittle at a piece of wood with a knife the size of Anna's forearm. "A man can't just barge into a lady's dressing room. Helga's overcome from the exertions from the night," he said, not bothering to look up from his wood. How could he even see what he was doing in the dark like that? Anna worried that he would chop a finger off in front of her.

"My apologies," Jacob said at once, stepping away from the leg. He reached into his pocket and took out a handful of coins. "My wife and I merely wanted to meet the lady in person. She … ah … put on quite a show."

My wife. The words shocked her more than the guard's knife—scared her just as much, too. The whittling paused. The guard lowered the knife and took Jacob's money, weighing it in his hand. "Go on in. Helga loves visitors," he said jovially, even standing to lift the flap for the couple to enter.

Jacob placed his hand on Anna's lower back and guided her into the tent. It was a bright and cheerful space, cluttered with colorful pillows and trunks that looked like they'd traveled a great distance. At least five barbells were stacked in the corner, along with other cumbersome objects that Anna could only assume were additional weights of some kind. A small child, presumably Helga's daughter, sat next to them, ignoring the guests. Anna guessed her to be close to ten years old. Her light brown hair was pulled back into a charming braid while she played with the only two things in the room that Anna was familiar with—a miniature cricket bat and a red leather ball.

"Do you like cricket?" Anna blurted, causing the little girl to drop her toys in her lap. Instantly, her gaze went to the opposite side of the tent, where Helga Bitterman appeared from another entrance.

"Cricket? Is that what you call that game?" the strongwoman said. Helga strode into the tent and winked at her daughter before posing in front of a full-length mirror. As she was still clad in her paltry performance outfit, Helga's well-formed body was on full display to the couple. Over six feet, Helga was the tallest woman Anna had ever seen—as well as the most muscular. Strike that. Helga was the tallest and most muscular *person* she'd ever seen.

"Yes," Anna replied. "That's a cricket ball and bat. Does your daughter play?"

"Only with me," Helga said, contorting her body in funny shapes in front of the mirror, highlighting different areas. With one swift sweep of her arm, her thighs erupted into lines and bulging muscles that reminded Anna of giant fissures in the ground left over after an earthquake. "My husband told me to buy her dolls, so I bought her dolls. But she didn't like the dolls. Then she found the bat and ball left over one night after a show. She hasn't let go of them since."

Helga switched positions, causing large muscles on the sides of her back to widen and expand as if she were sprouting wings. Did everyone have muscles in those places? Anna wondered. Could *anyone* be this strong with the right amount of dedication and perseverance?

"My husband wonders if it is a wise idea to let Inez play with them, but I don't think it will harm her. I wasn't much interested in dolls when I was her age either."

"Neither was I," Anna said, smiling encouragingly at the girl. "And I know it won't harm her."

"I asked some of the men around here to teach Inez how to play, but ..." Helga shrugged. "Circus life is a busy life."

Jacob cleared his throat. "Yes, Miss Helga, we understand you are busy, and we're terribly sorry to bother you, but we have a question we'd like to ask."

Helga paused in another pose and slowly turned around. Her face was square and angular, and she wore her light brown hair in a fussy, feminine bun with two long curls bookending her face. She grabbed a thin, gauzy pink robe from her chair and flung it over her body, though it was short and barely covered more than her costume.

"Not at all," she said grandly in an accent Anna was having a difficult time placing. It sounded vaguely Germanic, with an unlikely hint of London's West End. "You are in awe of Helga, are you not? You came to witness more of my physical greatness."

Anna smiled at the woman's confidence *and* the way it made Jacob stutter. "Ah ... yes ... Well, about that," he said. He glanced at Anna, but she ignored his entreaty. He was on his own. Jacob rubbed his palm over the back of his neck. "Your physical greatness is apparent," he began, his eyes bobbing all over the tent. Was he blushing? "But … if you wouldn't mind, that is … I wanted to inquire if I could admire your … cannonballs. Hold them … actually."

Helga paused, hands on her hips, stretching her spine to her full height. "You want to hold my balls?"

Goosebumps flared on Anna's skin.

"If you don't mind," Jacob repeated, his face beet red. He also straightened his spine, but it didn't have the same effect, in Anna's humble opinion.

"Why do you want to hold my balls?" Helga asked.

Jacob ruptured into a fit of coughs. The poor man, Anna thought. He was positively beside himself. She pounded him on the back.

The strongwoman sauntered toward the couple, visibly throwing her weight around, owning every inch of her surroundings. "You don't believe that I juggled three of them? You think I'm one of those second-rate performers who relies on trickery?"

"Indeed not," Jacob answered, retreating a step. "It was just such a spectacular performance, and … and …"

Anna slid in front of him. "And my husband wanted to prove his strength to me," she finished. When Helga looked directed at her, Anna could understand Jacob's trepidation. She felt like David to Helga's Goliath, and sadly, she didn't know the first thing about slinging rocks. "You see, my husband has always been ridiculed for being a skinny, small man—a beanpole, my brothers used to call him. Good for nothing. A weak wastrel. Cowardly, really."

Helga scrutinized Jacob, looking him up and down. "Yes … yes, I see this in him."

Relieved, Anna flashed a smile. "Exactly. But what was I supposed to do? Love has a way of blinding us all."

"My husband is also a small man," Helga said. "More feminine, like this one."

"Now, wait a minute—" Jacob started.

Helga kept going. "But I, too, fell in love. The heart is a strange creature."

"Indeed," Anna said. "Indeed. But now my husband wants to prove himself as a man to me, and I love him too much to try to stop him. It's sweet in its own pathetic way, isn't it?"

"Yes, pathetic ... but sweet," Helga said. "But more pathetic."

Anna grinned at Jacob and cupped his chin in her hand with a playful tug. "I told him that if he managed to lift one of those cannonballs in each hand then I would make his favorite fish pie tomorrow for supper." She lowered her eyes, playing coy. "I know I shouldn't encourage him, but a man's ego is a weak thing. It needs to be tended like a fragile garden."

Helga nodded, spinning away from the couple. Next to the mirror she opened a trunk and brought out two cannonballs as effortlessly as Iris had handled her sticky buns.

Helga held them in front of Jacob, one eyebrow arched in a frank challenge. The cannonballs were each the size of a fat baby's head, and Anna couldn't guess how much they weighed. Helga lifted them above her head, clearly showing off. "I know all about men's egos," she said, tossing the balls from one hand to the other, all while keeping Jacob's stare. "I've had to battle them my entire life. But soon I will go to America and have more money than I know what to do with."

"And then you'll retire?" Anna said. "How lovely. Congratulations."

Helga snorted. "Never. My work will never be done. There will always be women who challenge me, people who need to come into my dressing room. There will always be men who want to hold my balls. And I will allow them because I owe it to all the strongwomen who came before me."

She gave Anna a smirk. "Now, let's see how this one does."

Chapter Nine

JACOB SULKED ON his side of the carriage. "I don't even like fish pie," he grumbled. "I'm quite contented that you don't have to make it for me."

Anna was glad her smile was hidden in the shadows, though she wondered if the white of her teeth was visible. She tried to be a good winner, but it was so difficult when Jacob sat across from her like a petulant child. "Well, that's good, because I have no idea how to make it anyway." She drummed her fingers against her lap, needing to fill their silence. "You shouldn't be so down on yourself. It was a good try."

"Don't patronize me."

"I'm not! Besides, it's your own fault. You were only supposed to hold two cannonballs. No one asked you to try to juggle three."

"Oh really?" Jacob huffed, pinning her with a long-suffering scowl. "You and your new friend were goading me the entire time. I thought if I replicated her act then *your brothers* wouldn't think of me as such a pathetic, cowardly beanpole."

Anna couldn't hold back her laughter. She giggled until her stomach hurt. "As I said, it was a valiant effort. You're lucky you didn't break your foot when you dropped them."

"I've never hopped so fast in my life," he said, his voice

warming despite the pouting. "How would we have explained that to your father?"

"Oh, I'm sure I would have thought of something."

"I'm sure you would have," he said. Moonlight danced across his face as it filtered past the curtain. His words were like a caress, and he held her gaze so long that Anna had to look away. Maybe *she* was the coward tonight.

Jacob sighed, rubbing his hands back and forth over his thighs. "So, this was all a part of your plan, yes? You brought me to the circus to embarrass me, show me that a woman can, no doubt, crush my skull with her fist."

"Not quite," Anna said. "But when I read that Helga was touring nearby, I thought it important for you to see her."

"I don't understand why. I already told you that I know how strong women can be. This was entirely unnecessary."

She regarded him curiously. "I'm sorry that you didn't enjoy yourself."

"Now, I didn't say that. I just don't understand this obsession you have with proving something to me that I already know. It has me thinking ..."

"About?"

"About how maybe you're trying to prove something to yourself instead."

Anna scoffed, ducking her head to peek outside the window. They still had a half-hour before they reached his home. She'd hoped they'd spend it laughing and discussing the extraordinary members of the circus, not investigating her motives. Yet again, the incorrigible man couldn't accept anything at face value. Jacob always had to dig deeper. Hadn't he learned *anything* tonight?

"Come here."

Anna had been so locked up in her inner turmoil that Jacob needed to repeat the command before it registered.

She tittered nervously. "I'm quite comfortable where I am."

"Oh, come now. You've made enough of a fool of me tonight. The least you can do is come sit next to me when I ask."

"You didn't ask."

"I'm asking now."

Anna nodded, taken aback at the shyness that flooded her—and her willingness to do as he wished. She migrated to Jacob's side of the carriage, though continued to keep her distance, being mindful to keep their thighs from touching.

He watched her awkward dance closely; his eyes tormented her, almost insisting that she open to him like a flower to a honeybee.

As the seconds dragged on, the silence—and the fact that they were pretending this situation was normal—became unbearable; the air inside the carriage was thick and stuffy with restlessness and calculation. Jacob cut into it first.

Anna almost jumped out of her seat when he palmed the nape of her neck. Like a scientist finding a new, exciting discovery, he curled a short piece of hair around his finger and studied it pensively. Everything in her body told her to order him to stop, but she didn't want him to. It had been so long since she'd been touched in such a way. She was like a sunflower stretching for the sun, filling herself with its rays before the night inevitably took over.

"Why did you cut your hair?"

Anna focused on her hands in her lap, twisting her fingers together until her knuckles burned. "I ... um ... I was sick."

"When?"

"Three years ago. It was a fever. I don't remember much," she said. "Father said I was raving, thrashing about until I lost consciousness. I woke up days later, and by that time the doctors had cut off all my hair."

"Why?" Jacob asked. His voice was so tender, as soft and distracting as the way he ran his fingers across her neck.

Anna shivered. "They told my father that I would die if I didn't. I had long hair; it went past my waist. They said it was keeping me too warm, prohibiting me from fighting the fever."

"I'm sorry," Jacob whispered.

"It's fine."

"No," he said firmly. "I'm sorry."

The words left her in a breath. "Thank you."

"How long did it take you to recover?"

"A few months. My body was always strong," she replied. It was her mind that had kept her in bed for much longer. "I'm perfectly fine now."

His smile was genuine. "Fine enough to play cricket."

"Exactly."

Jacob's fingers continued to weave magic against her skin, caressing her neck in a way that made her want to ball up into his lap and fall asleep until they reached his home. However, the taciturn viscount was in a mood to talk. "Why hasn't it grown?" he asked. "After three years I would imagine it would be longer than this. Not that I don't like it," he added, shaking his head at his blunder. "I like it very much. Very much indeed."

Maybe it was because he asked the question in such an innocent, undemanding way, but Anna had no qualms about answering him truthfully. It was almost a relief to release this side of her instead of always holding back. "I ask my maid to cut it whenever it starts to get long again," she said. "You probably think it's ridiculous, but so much happened and I have no desire to look the same as I did before. I'm the same person, but I'm not. It's important that the mirror reflects that."

In response, Jacob applied pressure at a spot behind her ears that miraculously made the tension in her back release. Or was it her admission?

"I don't think it's ridiculous at all. I understand you perfectly."

Anna smiled shyly. She believed him.

"It suits you, you know?"

"You don't think I look like a boy?"

Jacob's laughter was deep and masculine. "Nothing about you reminds me of a boy. You're the loveliest woman I've ever seen. That's why I let my lust guide me when I kissed you that day." He paused, gazing at her lips. His jaw hardened as he weighed his next words. "That's why I want to let it guide me once more and kiss you right now."

Anna bowed her head. "There it is again. *Lust.*" The simple sound felt wicked sliding off her tongue. Sensual and forbidden. Evocative.

Jacob canted his body toward hers. "Lust isn't the weak-willed emotion you believe it to be. I could show you if you'd let me."

He placed a finger under Anna's chin, lifting her back to him, and then ran it to her mouth, skimming it along her bottom lip, tracing it back and forth in a languid trance. "I could stare at this mouth forever," he said, his tone silky, reverential. With a smirk, he angled his head to catch her eyes. "But not kiss them, correct?"

Anna was dizzy. She was taking so many breaths, and yet it didn't feel like nearly enough oxygen was getting to her brain. "Correct," she replied.

Jacob's finger paused. He pulled her lip slightly away from her teeth, dotting his skin with the wetness inside. "Because kissing is an act of love?"

He was playing with her again. Testing to see if she would break. "Y-yes, Anna stammered. "I've already told you."

Jacob's smile didn't reach his eyes. They were somber and severe … wicked. "And we are not in love."

"No." Anna vowed to respond with more than one word soon. She came off like a simpleton engaging with him this way, a child. Immature when she was anything but. However, the whirling feelings he elicited from her felt entirely different than what she'd experienced in her past. They felt raw and dangerous, brimming with vivid promise.

Jacob trailed his finger smoothly down her chin, settling once more on her neck. Anna's heart thumped erratically against the lonely digit. The carriage seemed to amplify the pumping. It was dark, cavelike, a hidden grotto designed for bad decisions and wayward intentions.

"Not in love, but maybe lovers," he whispered in a suggestive, gravelly tone that made Anna's toes curl in her snug boots.

She knew the correct answer. It would be another one-word response, but it was the right one. She had let herself get swayed once before in life, and the consequences of that would stick with her forever. Shaming herself and her family once more was not possible.

But she wasn't the child she once was. If she chose to dive into this liaison, it wouldn't be anything like the first. Stars weren't anywhere near her eyes. Love was not what she wanted—or expected—from a man like Jacob. And it never would be.

Just because Anna had declared that she would never marry did not mean she could not experience pleasure.

It was something to think about. Another time.

However, Jacob wasn't in the mood to wait for her to come to grips with her thoughts and worries. He was close enough that his breath tickled her neck; when it skated across her lips, she panicked.

"No," she said, jerking away.

Jacob chuckled. His hand came back to her chin, urging Anna to look at him once more. "I wasn't going to kiss you on your lips," he said.

Slowly, he lowered his head and placed a single, gentle kiss against the same heartbeat that he'd held under his finger. His whiskers rasped along her sensitive skin as he lingered there, flicking the tip of his tongue to taste her. It was a devilishly quick movement, over before it began, though it still elicited a gasp. And then he released her.

All of her.

Anna's chest caved in as she surrendered a breath. She had been kissed before—many times in childish exploration and fervor—but that was the single most thrilling moment of her life.

She wondered if Jacob could say the same.

He settled back in his seat, his legs no longer touching her, while he swiped the curtain out of the way to peer outside.

Disappointment coursed through Anna, and she'd opened her mouth to speak before she stopped herself. From the corner of her eye, she noticed Jacob drawing circles on his knee. It was a small motion, but the hand was obviously shaking. Because of her.

Because of how she made him feel.

No more needed to be said tonight. Even one-word responses were completely unnecessary.

Chapter Ten

W AS THERE ANYTHING worse than a picnic? Whoever first initiated the idea of eating outside was a criminal of the highest order, Jacob concluded morosely. For starters, lazing on the ground—even with the aid of pillows and blankets—was terrible for the knees and disastrous in terms of optics. Respectability and manliness were impossible to maintain.

Then there was the case of the elements. True, it wasn't raining this afternoon, unlike most afternoons; nevertheless, the wind was a constant nuisance. One's hat or napkins were always blowing away. And one mustn't underestimate the ant situation. Their destructiveness was certainly not aligned with their size. Enjoyment was simply untenable with all these nonstop variables.

And lastly, but most importantly, there was a significant lack of tables. Tables were monstrously important to enjoying one's lunch. Without them, chaos ensued. Who wanted to hold their plate and their glass of champagne at the same time? How positively barbaric!

This was why Jacob would never understand the upper classes. Why would they applaud and encourage this type of rustic behavior when they had perfectly good castles, fortresses, and palaces to eat in? Did they know who ate outside? Street urchins!

80

Homeless people! Miners and farmers gulping down Cornish pasties because they were too busy and back-bent to enjoy their homes.

And yet here Jacob sat—he refused to laze—on a thin, scraggly blanket that, for some reason, the servants had decided to place over a craggy patch of lawn that made him feel every bone splintering in his arse. Fewer ants here, they'd said. Since he'd already dusted two off his sandwich, he would beg to disagree.

But he would have to deal with the injustices of his life. He was getting rather good at it, since the recent days had been loaded with them.

The week hadn't started as a complete cesspool. Jacob's adventure to the circus with Anna had put him in high spirits. However, his mother and Sir John had shown singular devotion to ruining that with all their quaint activities. If Jacob had known how mild their phaeton trip to town was, he would have attempted to appreciate it more.

But that was only the tip of the iceberg. The next day his mother insisted on showing off Newton Place, guiding Sir John through every piece of artwork hanging on its illustrious walls. Strolling behind them, Jacob had been bored to tears. He had no interest in bland landscapes and didn't give one farthing about the austere ancient relatives scowling painfully down from their frames as if bloody piles ran in the family. Luckily, Anna spotted the trio and decided to tag along. She even conjured voices for each of his ancestors and invented conversations between the portraits.

Most of the back-and-forths involved their displeasure with him. Indeed, Jacob *was* in tears at the end of the mind-numbing tour, but from snickering so much. So, in the end, he had to admit, the impromptu tour wasn't a complete waste of an afternoon.

Next was the music night, which primarily consisted of Beatrice regaling the household with her piano-playing prowess. Jacob allowed that that portion was tolerable enough. However, when his mother and Sir John insisted on singing poorly advised duets of insipid songs from their youth, Jacob spent the remainder of the night taking breaks to his office, where he choked down enough brandy to sedate a small elephant. He couldn't remember what Anna had said to keep him calm during that particular episode, though he recalled that she'd sat next to him the entire time. Jacob wouldn't have stayed if she hadn't.

And then there were the god-awful daily walks on the grounds. Jacob didn't want to think about those ever again.

The real problem was that he was getting nowhere. Sir John and his family had been under his roof for over a week, and he had no real dirt on the man. The baronet was a shite singer—and a proponent of picnics—but those terrible characteristics weren't enough to sway his mother's heart. Even the investigator that Jacob had hired was coming up woefully short.

And it didn't help matters that Jacob's growing infatuation was distracting him to a worrying degree. Half the time when he trailed behind his mother and Sir John, he was more intent on Anna than the couple. He didn't even bother listening or butting into their monotonous tête-à-tête during the last walk. He'd been too wrapped up in whatever Anna was saying at that moment ... and her succulent lips, which continued to be a source of limitless fascination.

It occurred to Jacob that maybe that was Anna's plan all along ... flirt with him, occupy him, seduce him while Sir John slipped a ring on his mother's finger.

And damn the woman, because it was working.

Even now, uncomfortable as all hell on the flinty, unrelenting ground, balancing his plate in one hand and a fork and a champagne flute in the other, Jacob's entire being was focused on Anna with her simple bonnet and strawberry-colored gown. What had made her laugh (Aunt Iris's story about the time Jacob hid a dog under his bed for a full week after it had followed him home, and it had repaid him by eating the pages out of his Latin school books). What had made her smile (Sir John telling Jacob's mother that he loved the color of her dress). What made her clap her hands in delight (Aunt Violet asking Anna to teach her cricket). And, lastly, what made the perfect shade of red infuse the tops of her round cheeks (Jacob. Every time he glanced at her).

It was a wonder he could stand or walk without tripping over. His need for Anna was absurd and only getting worse. He simply had to find a way to get her to himself again. Kissing her neck the night of the circus had been damn near perfect. But that was the folly of man. One could never be satisfied. When one tasted the sublime, one always craved more.

⟫⟫⟫✕⟪⟪⟪

FORTUITOUSLY, A SITUATION presented itself to Jacob the day after the picnic, and he pounced. He left a note in Anna's room, instructing her to meet him at his carriage after dinner, insisting she "make the same arrangements she did for the circus."

With her sense of fun and natural curiosity, Jacob harbored no doubts that she would accept the summons. And that night, as he paced in the dark for her, nervously his feet tapping against the dirt path outside the stables, he was rewarded for his efforts.

Anna slipped along the long shadows of the house, wrapped in a deep purple cloak and matching turban. Jacob laughed. She looked ready to accept a position at Whitehall and spy against the French.

"We have to hurry," she whispered, taking his hand without hesitation and hopping into the carriage. "This is the second time I've cried off playing cards this week with the group. My father gets agitated whenever I tell him I'm feeling unwell."

Jacob followed her inside, eschewing his usual seat to settle beside her. He ignored the sigh, and the elbow she lodged in his ribs to create more room between them.

As before, he tucked his finger under Anna's chin. Jacob maneuvered her cloak out of the way and placed a single kiss against her creamy neck. "I'll just have to make it worth your while, then, won't I?" he said, enjoying the way she failed to hide the quiver his kiss created.

A smile tugged at the corner of her lips—another thing she was helpless to prevent. "Yes, you will."

⤛⤜

HOURS LATER, ANNA granted Jacob an appraising look. "You've come a long way, my lord. I was positive you were going to ask the poor man if you could lift him over your head."

Jacob grinned sheepishly. They were back in the carriage again, returning to Newton Place. It had been a successful outing, just as Jacob had hoped it would be. Anna had been fascinated by the Curiosities Exhibition at the music hall in London. For nearly two hours they'd toured the displays, admiring them and speaking with the performers, who ranged from a young lad who was barely taller than Jacob's knee to a grizzled banshee of a woman who declared herself to be one hundred and thirty years old.

However, the figure who'd claimed to be the strongest woman in the world had naturally been the star attraction for Jacob. Agnes Worthington didn't disappoint. Born "somewhere in the wilds of America," the strongwoman wasn't as tall as Helga Bitterman but was just as bulky. In rapt fascination, Jacob and Anna marveled as Agnes picked up her husband and twirled him round and round above her head. She hadn't even broken a sweat. And Jacob had made sure to check.

"I learned my lesson with Helga, believe me," he said, laughing. "Agnes's husband barely reached her chin, but he was sizeable enough. I didn't want to break my back challenging her strength. I don't know if she is the strongest woman in the world, but she is stronger than me, no question."

"I was nervous by the way she was looking at you that she

was going to pick *you* up next!" Anna giggled, wiping a tear away from her eye.

She saw that, did she? Jacob had wondered if Anna noticed how Agnes was batting her lashes at him despite her husband's proximity. "Believe me, I was nervous too. Why do you think I grabbed hold of your arm?"

"Oh, I don't know," Anna drawled, her laughter chirping out. "I just think you like touching me."

"Very astute of you, my dear," he said. Without thinking, he swung his arms around Anna and picked her off her seat. She landed firmly on his lap.

"Jacob!" She squirmed, fighting his hands at her waist. "This isn't … You shouldn't …"

"What?" He chuckled. "I was just proving your point. Besides, we'll both be more comfortable this way, trust me."

Anna's eyes narrowed, but once more the corner of her lips twitched up. "I am not more comfortable."

"But you could be."

"Is this the *only* reason you asked me here tonight?"

"No," he answered with a roguish grin. "Not the *only* reason."

Anna slapped his chest. "You know, sometimes I wonder if you're only giving me all this attention because you want to distract me from our parents. I was barely able to circumvent your nefarious plans all week."

Jacob huffed, juggling her on his lap. Lord, it was torture for his cock, but he wouldn't have moved her for the world. "It's funny you say that, because I was thinking the exact same thing about you."

She frowned and rearranged herself again. It was Jacob's fault, as he was rock-hard underneath her; however, it wouldn't be solved anytime soon, especially since she continued to stare at his mouth like she was starving for it. "I suppose we will just have to live with the uncertainty. After all, you were the one that said this wasn't love, but war."

"So true," he answered diplomatically. "But even in war,

there are stalemates from time to time."

"Is that what this is? A stalemate?" Anna licked her lips, making Jacob want to scream. He tightened his hold on her hip. He wanted to make her scream too.

"It is the only civilized thing to do."

"Civilized?" Anna smiled sweetly. Was Jacob imagining things? *Did she just flex her pelvis into mine?* "I don't think I would ever use that word to describe you."

Jacob had to close his eyes. All the blood was rushing from his brain. It made making forming coherent sentences difficult. "How would you describe me, then? As a good and decent man?"

Anna laughed, though it came out more like a purr. She shook her head slowly. "Never."

"Dashing? Devilishly handsome?"

She bent toward him, folding her arms across his chest, her head just above his own. "You're getting closer."

There was no mistaking it this time. Anna began to rock her hips suggestively, causing sweat to break out on Jacob's forehead. Holy hell, how had she turned into the aggressor? Wasn't that supposed to be his job?

Jacob dashed that thought from his mind. If a woman could pick up her husband and spin him around over her head, then surely one could grind his cock to submission without a by your leave.

Suddenly, the lips Jacob so desperately wanted to suck between his teeth pouted adorably. "You know … I don't like that they call them freaks."

"What was that?"

"The performers at the exhibition," she said.

"Oh well, yes … I agree," Jacob replied, trying not to ruminate on how wonderful it would be to feel Anna's breasts in his hands. "But you know as well as I that anything considered different is usually considered wrong."

Absent-mindedly, Anna moved her hand to the back of his neck. She played with a piece of his hair with a far-off look in her eye. Jacob began to tap his foot on the floor; he couldn't seem to contain his nerves with the seductively innocent touch. "But most of them weren't even that different," she continued. "Take Agnes … She was just muscular and strong."

"But not ladylike. Not like Helga."

Anna's gaze made its way back to his. "I don't know. She looked like a lady to me. Did you see the way her husband looked at her?" She brushed Jacob's hair off his forehead. It was such a casual motion, effortless, but the familiarity it evoked threw him off balance.

His voice sounded completely foreign to him. Needy. "How did he look at her?" he rasped.

Anna's smile was secretive and sultry. "Like the way you're looking at me now."

Jacob couldn't stand it anymore. He leaned forward to take her lips, but just as before, Anna veered out of his path. He signed. "Still?"

"Still," she answered.

Then, like she was placing salve on a cut, she lowered her mouth to his ear. Her nearness, the cuddly softness, almost did him in. Jacob's entire body felt stretched thin, entirely too sensitive. "But isn't there still fun to be had?"

"Christ, yes." That was all the confirmation Jacob needed.

His fingers trembled as they pushed Anna's cloak off her shoulders. One simple kiss on her neck wouldn't be enough tonight—not for either of them. She giggled as he worked the buttons on the front of her gown, starting at her high neck. He took his time, wondering at which button she would stop him. But the lower he dared, no words came, only deeper, faster breaths.

Jacob reeled himself in as he ventured just below her breasts. There would be time to go further. Tonight, in his carriage, was not the night.

He paused on the edges of her gown, spreading the fabric like a curtain on a famous stage. Shakespeare's plays had nothing on what Jacob was about to experience.

He could feel Anna's eyes on him. "I'm not a ... voluptuous woman," she said softly. The edge of embarrassment in her voice struck something inside him, something he never wanted to feel again.

Jacob wasn't an untried lad. He knew what to expect when excavating underneath a woman's dress; however, Anna, as ever, surprised him. There was no corset, only a thin chemise that hung low over the swell of her breasts, exposing more than they hid. Even with the paltry moonlight stretching in from the curtain, Jacob was given a lovely view of the nipples that pointed prominently through the gossamer fabric.

He had to tear his eyes away from the succulent view. The little points were like an oasis to a man dying of thirst. "You're perfect," Jacob said, his voice embarrassingly hoarse.

"No one is perfect," Anna said shyly. She attempted to cross her arms, but Jacob stopped her. *Fuck!* His hands wouldn't stop trembling. He held her breasts in his palms, slowly massaging them, letting the weight of them make everything inside him feel impossibly right.

"You are," he replied, rubbing his thumb around her nipples, tickling the sharpness of her skin against his fingernail. Anna arched her back and wrapped her arms around his neck; the motion had an air of desperation to it that Jacob loved.

Dipping his head, he captured a velvety nipple in his mouth, swirling the bud with his tongue. Kissing her in that spot wasn't the same as kissing her lips. It wasn't better or worse, just different. And as they'd ascertained this night, there was nothing wrong with different.

Jacob drenched the chemise with his mouth, sucking and rolling his tongue along Anna's breast, emboldened by the sweet, desperate noises she made. He traced the valley between her orbs with the tip of her tongue, all the way to the tendons of her neck, heating her skin with his breath, paying homage to the gift she was giving him.

But Jacob hadn't forgotten that he'd wanted to make Anna scream, and while the carriage wasn't conducive to some things, it *was* very helpful for that. As he found her ear, sucking on her lobe with a mindful intensity, he dipped his hand under her skirts, landing first on stockings and then rich, silky skin.

Anna clawed around his shoulder, where she simultaneously pushed and pulled. Jacob understood her perfectly. The feelings were overwhelming, almost too much to handle. Her sweet bottom on his cock rocked him gently in a motion that felt utterly natural and yet out of this world. The friction of his trousers rubbing along his shaft was hell, and yet bliss.

"I … I think we're almost home," Anna stammered, craning her neck to the side to give Jacob more room to nuzzle.

He smiled against her dewy skin. "We have all the time in the world." He kissed a slow, meandering path back down to the breast he hadn't loved yet.

She released a blustery sigh. "Time for what?" There was indecision in her voice, a lilt of fear. It was contradictory to the way her pelvis continued to encourage him, searching, foraging for appeasement.

Jacob would give it to her. He would stay in the carriage all night until he did.

"Time to give you want you want. What you need." Anna shivered as he ran his hands up her thighs, swirling along the skin, marveling at the beauty he knew was there but couldn't see. She tensed as he reached the hollow between her legs, but since she was spread over him, there was little she could do to halt his invasion.

Anna hugged his head against her chest now, her bottom rising and falling over his cock in tiny movements that would drive a weaker man crazy. "Are they the same?" she panted, canting her pelvis toward his roaming fingers.

Jacob's laughter was shaky—just like the rest of him. He palmed Anna's sex like it was his and only his, swiping his fingers along the folds, grinding the hood at the top with an insistent rhythm. "For you they are," he said before taking her breast into his mouth again, more aggressively this time. A man had only so much willpower, and a wildfire that was becoming more and more difficult to control had emerged inside him.

Nothing was safe. Nothing wasn't at play. From their heads to their toes, their bodies undulated against one another as Jacob petted her velvety core. Anna's sounds became louder and wilder as their intensity climbed. His cock was at the precipice. He would release in his trousers like the untried lad he prided himself on not being, but it didn't matter. Nothing mattered except hearing this luscious woman scream in his arms while he sucked her nipple and fingered her cunny.

He gave her a moment to accept him. Dipping one finger inside her sheath, Jacob felt her inner muscles resist. "Let me in," he said. "Don't fight me. Let me give you this."

He felt Anna nod her head and release a steadying breath. Instantly, her walls relaxed, and he could fit another finger inside. Her spine arched abruptly as he stroked her, working her passage along with the little ball of nerves along the top of her entrance.

"Oh God," she said through her teeth, bouncing on Jacob with single-minded determination. "Oh God, please!"

How much Jacob wanted to hear those words in his mouth, suck the pleas off her lips. Instead, he continued to pull and tug on her nipple, the last little bite leading to a sharp, decisive keen that would echo in his ears for years to come. He answered with a howl of his own as he let himself release, all the tension and strain instantly evaporating into an erotic cloud of euphoria.

Seconds passed as they panted against one another. Jacob didn't withdraw his fingers. The way the walls of her core pulsed against him was another gift, a sign that he had done his job and done it well.

Eventually, Anna peeled herself off his chest, her hair delight-fully messed and sticking to the sheen on her forehead. There was a glorious, self-satisfied vibrancy to her skin. "Well, that was different."

Jacob chuckled, pulling her back for a hug. "Different good or different bad?"

The vibration of her words murmuring against his chest made his heart skip a beat. "What do you think?"

Chapter Eleven

"THAT'S PERFECT, VIOLET. Swing like that again. You'll get a hit soon, I promise!" Anna crouched just behind the wicket, waiting for Beatrice to bowl the ball. Violet bent her knees in front of the wicket, her stance awkward and clumsy as she clutched the cricket bat.

"It didn't feel perfect," she grumbled while Beatrice nodded, indicating she was about to begin her approach. "It feels like I might pitch over."

"Take the weight off the balls of your feet," Anna instructed her. "Stand on your whole foot."

"I've never heard of anything so ridiculous," Iris remarked off to the side, where she was waiting her turn to bat. "Doesn't everyone always stand on their whole foot?"

"Ignore her," Anna said to her pupil. "Just focus on the ball. Follow it with your eyes."

"What else would she follow it with?" Iris laughed.

Beatrice's arm slumped to her side. "Excuse me? Can we please stop talking? I'm bowling!"

Anna rose from her crouch. "You shouldn't let people distract you. Real players have to be able to drown out everything but the game."

Beatrice stuck out her tongue at her sister. "But I don't want to be a real player. Iris and I want to go inside and work on a plum bread, but you forced us to be out here."

"It's too fine of a day for that," Sir John exclaimed, sharing a laugh with Mrs. Wright. "Stay outside with us. You're a fine bowler." The older couple reclined next to each other on matching chairs situated on the outskirts of the makeshift pitch, enjoying the younger people and their games. A small table was set up between them, topped with a tray of cheese and fruit as well as two glasses of red wine. Sir John's cheeks looked like they'd been painted with rouge, and Mrs. Wright was uncommonly giddy.

Anna rolled her eyes as Mrs. Wright broke into another round of hiccuping giggles. She and Sir John acted more like love-struck children as the days went on. Anna glanced at Jacob, who was the only fielder. His usual sneer of disdain wasn't readily apparent. He merely appeared mystified by the older couple's antics. Maybe even entertained.

"How much more do I have to throw?" Beatrice demanded with a distinct sulk.

Anna glowered, lowering into her spot again. She had a new appreciation for the coach of her cricket team. Samuel Everett was curmudgeonly at the best of times. Anna had always assumed it was just his nature; she'd never believed that his players could have been the reason for his recurring irritated state.

"Just a few more," Anna answered, spying a wobble in Violet's knees. The older woman's thighs must be burning. She hadn't wavered from that position once Anna had placed her in it. Her legs would certainly be sore tomorrow. "Hurry up now. I want to make sure Violet and Iris get a decent hit."

Beatrice stabbed her hands on her hips. "I'm not the one holding everyone up!"

"Just bowl the ball!" Violet yelled. "I have no idea how much longer I can stand like this, but it doesn't look good!"

"You better not faint," Iris warned. "The last time I had to carry you somewhere, my back was sore for a week."

"You're hardly as light as a dandelion flower!" Violet returned.

Anna's gaze was stuck to the woman's knees. They were trembling like a tuning fork at this point. "Bowl the ball!"

"I am!" Beatrice hollered back—but not from where she was supposed to be. The ridiculous girl had meandered over to the refreshment table and was stuffing her mouth with a piece of fat cheese.

"That's it! I'm leaving. I can't wait here anymore," Jacob yelled, swiping his arms in front of him like he was clearing the dishes off a table. "It's too much for any man to abide."

Mrs. Wright stood up from her seat, the little blanket she wore on her lap falling to the ground. "Oh, come now, Jacob. You're doing so well out there!"

Halfway off the field, he stopped, his expression incredulous. "What are you talking about, woman? We've been out here for an hour, and no one has hit the ball once." He gestured toward Beatrice, who was now tucking into the grapes. "She's only bowled three deliveries."

"It's not my fault!" Beatrice argued, her hip stuck out in indignation. "Anna's the one who keeps taking forever to teach this insufferable game."

All eyes soared back to Anna, some sympathetic and some riddled with condemnation. "I thought it would be fun!" she snapped, straightening her knees once more.

She took the bat out of Violet's hand, helping the poor woman relax out of her stance. Violet stumbled slightly, maintaining her dignity just in time. She patted Anna's arm. "It's not your fault, dear. I'm sure it's a wonderful game once you get to the hang of it."

Anna smiled weekly. "Thank you," she said. "It is."

Sir John followed Mrs. Wright's lead and crept up from his chair, his knees cracking as he placed his empty glass back on the table. The servants hurried to round up the food and blankets and take them back inside.

Anna watched as the party retreated toward the house, her ego deflating more and more with every relieved step. Perhaps she wasn't destined to become a coach or a captain. It wasn't something she'd said out loud, this idea of being more than a player one day. The thought had been at the periphery of her mind, a fleeting notion. Although she was sure that a position would be open soon enough. With Samuel Everett playing professional cricket again—and his fiancée, Myfanwy, most likely spending more time at home when a family came—the Single Ladies Cricket Club would be forced to change its current iteration. As one of the early members of the club, Anna had thought that possibly, maybe, eventually, she could take a more prominent role … a leadership role. However, with the afternoon's events, that concept seemed out of her reach.

"Oh, now it wasn't that bad."

Anna jumped, clutching her heart. She spun around to find Jacob behind her, giving her a ruefully sympathetic smile. She lowered her head. Ever since their time in the carriage, she'd found it difficult to match his stares without blushing. What on earth had come over her that night? It had been days, and she still couldn't explain it to herself. She'd never allowed herself to act so wanton before, so free. It had been liberating—and frightening.

"Not so bad?" she retorted, collecting herself. "Weren't you the man who just stormed off the field?"

"You can hardly blame me for that," he replied. "It was getting rather tedious." He stole the bat from her and took one of her hands, blowing warm air into it before placing it in his pocket. He directed her toward the house without remarking on this sweet gesture, like it was just the kind of thing that civilized people did in civilized company.

Anna knew better than to agree; nevertheless, she wouldn't be the one to break the façade. Not when it continued to exhilarate her. "So, was it *rather tedious* or *not that bad?*"

Jacob answered by reaching across and squeezing the hand that wasn't getting toasty in his pocket. "I was trying to make you feel better."

"I think you may need practice."

Jacob chuckled. Anna loved that sound, so rich and intoxicating coming from deep inside his chest. It reminded her of hearing a shock of thunder from the safety and warmth of her bed. For a second, she wished Jacob was a man that always chuckled, but then took that back. If he was one of those gregarious types, these moments of bliss wouldn't be as special, and he wouldn't be the Jacob that she was growing to … growing to admire.

"I'm sure you're familiar with the saying that you can lead a horse to water, but you can't force it to drink?"

Anna frowned. "Who is the horse? Am I the horse?"

Jacob answered her with an exasperated sigh. "Just keep trying. They'll come around. The aunts have never let anything defeat them in their lives. Cricket will be no different."

"Perhaps I'm not explaining it well enough."

"You're explaining it just fine. These things take time. You have to remember that not everyone grew up playing the sport like you did."

She tugged on his arm, forcing him to stop. "I didn't grow up playing. I didn't start until I heard about the Single Ladies Cricket Club three years ago."

A crease formed between Jacob's eyes, and he shrugged. "You told me your brother loved playing. I just assumed that you played with him."

A caustic laugh burst from Anna's throat. "David? He never let me play. I had to sit off to the side and just watch him and his friend bowl to one another like a good little girl."

Jacob's gaze fixed on her for a long moment, his expression inscrutable. Eventually, he nudged her toward the house again. "In any case, most young women don't grow up understanding the game like you did. You have to admit that it can be a bit confusing."

"Of course."

"So," he went on, squeezing her hand once more, "give it

time."

Anna nodded, getting lost in the sensation of her hand in his. His fingers explored hers, always moving and circling, constantly making her body react under all her layers of clothing.

They lapsed into silence, quickly gaining ground on the others. Anna could hear the excitement in her father's voice as he discussed a card game he was eager to play that night after dinner. She reluctantly dragged her hand from Jacob's pocket, but he wouldn't release the other despite her tugging.

His head dipped low to her neck. Anna's ears had become so chilled from the cool weather that the hot breath of his words gave her a certain frisson of pain. "I want to see you tonight," he said.

She wrangled her lips into a tight smile, although her mouth wanted to widen from ear to ear. "Another outing?"

Jacob scrunched his nose. It was so unlike him, so ... adorably youthful. "Afraid not. The rest of the strongwomen must be lifting their barbells and husbands somewhere on the Continent."

"Then what do you suggest?"

For the first time, Jacob appeared moderately disconcerted, unsure of himself, *unsteady*. He shifted his weight between his legs. If he played on Anna's team, she would have told him to stand equally on both of his feet.

Jacob gazed down at his boots. "Maybe," he drawled, "you could come to my room tonight? We could talk."

Was he asking what she thought he was asking?

"Talk?"

Jacob pulled back his shoulders, puffing out his chest, a Roman legionary offended that his honor was being questioned. "Of course talk."

Anna angled her head. "Talk?"

He deflated and rubbed the back of his neck. "I would be open to other things ... if you were agreeable."

This was the oddest proposal of a tryst Anna had ever encountered. And the politest. Although, to be fair, she hadn't had many.

A mischievous thought occurred to her—to lengthen out the process, make the man squirm until he received her answer. He was the blackguard who'd walked off the pitch today, after all. Unfortunately, Anna didn't have the time. The party was almost indoors, and she would have to decamp to her room to dress for dinner.

Her lips fought with her, again wanting to fan out into an impossibly large grin. If she had told herself a week ago that she would enjoy spending time with Jacob Wright, she wouldn't have believed it. But this viscount continued to surprise her.

Anna snuck a peek at the rest of the group, judging whether they were paying any attention to her, but they were busy speaking in animated tones with the butler, who'd just come out to meet them.

She placed her hand on Jacob's chest. Over his coat, she couldn't feel his heartbeat, though she let herself imagine that its tempo had increased from her touch. "I think that can be arranged—"

"It's David! Anna, come quick! It's David!"

She jerked her hand off Jacob like she'd been stung. She turned to see Beatrice running toward her, skirts picked up in her hurry. She threw her arms around Anna, knocking Jacob further out of their circle. "It's David! He's here. He's home! The butler just told us. And he's not alone."

Anna was stunned. Her brother was early, which was terrific news. But he wasn't alone …

"Who did he come with?" she whispered. Her heart felt like it had tripled in weight and was now pumping from the confines of her lower belly. "Is it him?"

Beatrice backed away, clutching Anna's cheeks in her palms. "Yes," she squealed. "It's him. It's Phillip. He's returned!"

She released Anna as quickly as she had tackled her, kissing her cheek before running back to the house. Anna stood in her wake, her knees locked, her mind reeling. This reassured her that this news wasn't entirely a surprise. She'd always assumed that Phillip would come back with David one day. They were boyhood friends, after all, more brothers than anything. And yet … and yet now that the moment had arrived, Anna was not as prepared as she'd thought.

Jacob cleared his throat. Anna lifted her gaze to find him shoving his hands in his pockets.

"I—"

"We—"

Their words clashed.

Anna tore off her bonnet, raking a hand through her curls. She wanted to tear at them until she could feel something again besides bewildered surprise. And fear.

"We should go inside," Jacob said. His somber tone was a far cry from what it had been minutes before. As was his chivalry. With his head bowed, he took long strides back to the house, leaving Anna behind.

Her hands were cold.

Chapter Twelve

THE ENTIRE TABLE rumbled. Wine bobbed precipitously in crystal goblets. Forks and knives clanked raucously against China. Laughter was shared from person to person, ricocheting off the walls.

A merrier dinner could not be had. The prodigal son was home.

As was his friend.

Jacob wasn't usually the kind of man who would force a smile to make others feel comfortable—that was one of the better things about being a viscount—but to brood at his dining table when everyone was having such a splendid time seemed juvenile. Nevertheless, he couldn't quite place his distemper. Why should he be upset that David had returned? It wasn't like they weren't expecting him.

And the boy seemed pleasant enough, polite, even—though wastrels usually were. David had that look about him, the kind of look that said he enjoyed arriving at parties early and leaving late. The kind of look that made fathers throw them on ships bound for India in the hopes that it would evaporate in the heat and hardship.

Sir John wiped his eyes—no doubt at a tear of laughter—and then smacked his son on the shoulder. "I should be furious with you, dear boy. You should have sent a note the instant you got off the ship. We could have met you in London."

David basked in the glowing admiration. He was tall and handsome like their father, though his red hair was more discreet like Beatrice's, his cheekbones and chin chiseled with youth and vitality.

"I didn't want to ruin the surprise," he said. He drank his wine and stared at it appraisingly before gifting Jacob a nod of approval. Jacob responded with a wince of a smile.

"I tried to get him to write, Sir John. I did," Mr. Phillip Williams said, leaning across David to catch the older man's eye. "But he wouldn't have it. Boys will be boys, won't they?"

Sir John sat back in his chair, making it difficult for David's friend to address him further. In the short time he'd been forced to share his home with Sir John, Jacob hadn't known him to be rude, but that curt action was decidedly so. "Yes, boys will be boys," the baronet mumbled just loud enough for Jacob to hear.

There was something there. Jacob was sure of it.

The problem was that he was losing the heart to care. About that potential intrigue or the one involving David. Because all he was truly focused on was getting Anna to look at him again. She'd stopped doing the simple gesture the moment David's arrival had been announced. And now, hours later, she sat at his table, pushing around his food on her plate, taking tiny sips of his wine with her neck bowed.

Anna's anxiety wasn't so very obvious. She laughed on cue and smiled in the face of every innocuous quip, but Jacob knew her well enough to recognize her discomfort.

And all signs pointed to the obnoxious dullard at David's side as the reason. It was unfortunate that no one else in his family concluded the same about the newcomer. Jacob's aunts and mother had practically fallen over themselves to make the dashing man feel as welcome as David. And Mr. Phillip *fucking* Williams had soaked up the attention like a fat seal sunning itself on a beach. Not that Phillip was fat—sadly, he was not. He was the exact opposite. Tall and trim, he filled out his dinner attire better than most, as if he were born wearing it. His strong nose and high forehead were better suited to a Roman coin than Jacob's dressing room—that was to say, the man was attractive by conventional standards. By anyone's standards, really.

And Phillip knew it.

"I just can't get over Beatrice," David said, admiring his youngest sister from across the table. Beatrice covered her face in shyness, blushing prettily. "She grew up when I was gone. Three years seems like too short a time for something that monumental to happen."

Phillip nodded aggressively, his big eyes glistening. He *also* seemed to approve of Jacob's wine, though he didn't give off the affect of a drunkard, more like a famed naval captain who drank in between saving England from its enemies. "We came back just in time, David," he said, a warning lilt to his voice. "I'm sure all the boys have been crowding around and giving Sir John trouble." Phillip's smile faded as he switched his gaze to Anna. "No doubt the same could be said for her sister."

There. Jacob saw it. Clear as day. Something tugged between Phillip and Anna, who finally lifted her chin to meet his gaze, an invisible string of knowing that no one else was privy to. Her lips parted slightly, her lungs inflating. A patch of color saturated her cheekbones as she wiped a barely there sheen of perspiration above her mouth with the tip of her finger. She looked both lost and found.

It came to Jacob in waves, the stories and hints Anna had dropped like cookie crumbs at his feet. She'd always been opaque, scant on details, but Jacob had been paying attention. No one else could be the man she'd spoken of, the man that she'd given her heart to. But had she also given her body?

To this bombastic man-child?

The convivial conversations continued to churn around him, in concert with his upset stomach. Phillip kept the table enraptured with death-defying, quixotic tales of India. Everyone laughed at them, but Anna's giggles pierced Jacob in the skin like tiny shards of glass.

But why? Why the pain? Because Anna wasn't his. And she was never going to be. Despite her protestations of marriage, she was always meant for someone like Phillip. Someone who looked and acted the part better than Jacob ever would. Someone who didn't give a damn about printing other people's stories, and only cared about making his own.

In his grand home, seated at the head of his absurdly long table, drinking his fashionable wine, Jacob felt alone. Anna was three seats down, and she'd never seemed so far away. He wanted her at his side. Somewhere deep inside, he believed that he might have had a chance … but the possibility of that had just slipped through his fingers.

JACOB COULDN'T SLEEP, which was difficult to understand, since he'd drunk enough brandy to fill a horse trough. Why did he continue to lounge in his office when he could have retreated to his cottage? Solitude was always best when he was in these types of moods, but he hadn't been able to pull himself away. After dinner he'd remained close to the rest of the party, skulking in the drawing room, sipping glass after glass, while the others engaged in frivolous merriment. Card games, more of Beatrice's piano playing … even dancing! It was a celebration. And although Jacob couldn't bear to take part, masochist that he was, he also didn't want to miss another look between the star-crossed lovers.

Anna had played her role, doting on her brother and sticking close to his side. At least Jacob could be thankful for that. She had taken mercy on him and not run off with Phillip to the nearest empty bedroom at the earliest convenience. To her credit, she shied away from the bastard.

From his seat in the corner, Jacob had watched Phillip like a hawk while Phillip watched Anna like a hawk. She pretended not to notice. The whole damn room pretended not to notice, which made the stab to his gut infinitely worse.

He stumbled out of his office. It had been an hour since everyone else went up to their bedrooms. His world wasn't spinning yet, but it was getting awfully close. He was just about to climb the stairs to (hopefully) locate his bedroom when he heard voices coming from the library.

Could it be them? Could Phillip have wrestled Anna from her bedroom to profess his undying love? Well, not in Jacob's house! If the handsome blackguard was intent on taking Jacob's woman—why did he like the sound of that so much?—then he was going to have to go outside and deal with the uncomfortable chill in his balls when he did it.

Jacob kept a steady hand on the wall to guide him toward the library. His steps were light, quiet, his ears open to intrigue. And he was rewarded. It soon became apparent, even to his inebriated brain, that the voices were male, and this wasn't a secret, happy rendezvous. There was very little cheer between Sir John and his son.

Jacob plastered himself against the wooden paneling in the corridor, stilling his heart so he could hear the conversation over the roar of his blood.

"I just don't understand why you didn't stay," Sir John admonished his son. A glass rattled against a tabletop. "Leaving after so short a time seems like a waste."

David's words slurred. His voice was difficult to pick up, hollow, as if he were speaking into his glass while he was attempting to drink. "Phillip's brother died ... didn't need India anymore."

The words were muffled. Clothing rustled; footsteps sounded over the carpet. Were they embracing?

"You are not his keeper," Sir John said with a long sigh. The man's weariness was evident, and it had nothing to do with sleep.

David was slurring again. Jacob couldn't make heads nor tails of it. "… didn't want to take the journey alone … needs to marry. His father … debt."

Sir John urged him to his bed. Jacob had to leave. He couldn't risk getting caught. He rushed down the hallway back to his office while the men made their way to the stairs. In the end, it was David—drunk, incoherent, cordial David—who confirmed everything that Jacob didn't want to hear.

"Phillip would never hurt her," he said. David hit his toe on the lip of the step and caught himself on the banister before landing face-first. "… don't know why you're worrying so much."

Jacob could hear the anguish in Sir John's voice. "Because you've never had to."

Chapter Thirteen

ANNA COULDN'T SLEEP. She'd been wandering around her room listlessly the second she'd been able to beg off. She'd done her part, smiling and nodding, giving her brother all the attention she'd longed to give over the past three years, but the stress of it took its toll. After two hours in the drawing room, she couldn't stomach it any longer and had to say good night. It was self-preservation.

The roots of her hair ached. Anna had twisted the ends around her fingers for so long that there was no longer a hint of curl. Did Phillip approve of her hair? He'd noticed it, she was certain. During dinner, she'd caught him watching her with that old gleam in his eye. Immediately, it transported her back in time. She was that girl again, preening for his attention. The side of his mouth would arch up, a knowing smile. Anna's body had gone from cold to hot in a flash, making the hair on the back of her neck stand up. At any other time, it would have felt like a warning.

As she wore out the carpet in her room, the knock on the door didn't surprise her, though who might be on the other side of it was a mystery. With her heart in her throat, she walked tentatively to the door, trying for some semblance of composure. Her sweaty palms slipped on the doorknob twice before she could twist it open.

Her father chuckled at her expression. "I think I understand why you're disappointed to see me," he said lightly, edging himself past the door into the room. "But I hope you don't truly mind that I'm here."

Anna shook her head, digging herself out of her stupor. "Not at all, Father. Never."

He ambled around her space, making the tracks that Anna had created on the floor even deeper. "Should I be worried that you are still up at this hour?"

Anna shrugged. "It was such an exciting day. It's hard to wind down after such a surprise."

"Indeed," Sir John said. After a moment's pause, he sighed and sat down on the bed. Giving Anna a fatherly look, he patted the spot next to him.

Anna's slippers shuffled on the floor. She didn't have the energy to pick up her feet. "I know why you're here," she grumbled, plopping down. Sir John threw his arm around her shoulders in a half-hug. "You don't have to worry."

"I'm your father," he said, kissing the side of her head. "I'll always worry. Until my dying breath. It's my lot in life."

Anna's laugh was harsh and distinctly bitter. "Then I suppose I should be grateful that I will never have children."

Her fists clenched in her lap as if she were withholding the urge to jump out and grab her words and stuff them back in her mouth. She'd never said them before, and she didn't know why she said them now. After the emotionally taxing day, her willpower was at its lowest.

Sir John's soft tone—even more than his words—brought fresh tears to her eyes. "The doctor didn't say you couldn't have children. Only that it was not likely."

"Not likely," she repeated.

"Your body suffered so much, my dear." Sir John's hand trembled on Anna's shoulder. It tickled her.

"I'm strong. You know that."

"I'm not worried about your body, Anna. I'm worried about your heart."

This was foreign territory for both of them. Their relationship was the kind that normal fathers and daughters in the *ton* couldn't dream of. Their openness and acceptance weren't built in a day but rather forged by years of trial and error. Sir John had never balked at trying to understand his children's individuality and giving them what they needed despite what society dictated.

But in the three years since Anna had been ill, he'd never once mentioned Phillip. Not since the night he almost lost his daughter.

Anna wiped her nose with the back of her hand. The time for propriety was long gone. "My heart is strong too," she said.

"He should have come back before."

"He couldn't leave his post," Anna said, frowning at her father. "He had to complete his duty. I wish you hadn't written him that letter. He didn't need to know I was ill."

"I had to tell your brother ... and him."

Anna raised her head. Rivulets of tears ran down her face. "But why? I didn't die. It probably caused him unnecessary worry—" Anna blanched. "You didn't tell him the real reason I was ill, did you, Father? Please don't tell me you did."

"Of course I didn't," Sir John huffed, shifting his weight on the bed. "I told you that I wouldn't, and I didn't. But if the man truly cared for you—like he told you he did—he would have come back for you. Done the honorable thing."

"We were young, Father."

"And that's an excuse?"

"No. But it is all I can say."

Sir John leaned toward Anna, both hands on her shoulders now, forcing her to hold his gaze. "Just promise me that you will be careful. I don't know why he's here. I don't know what he wants."

You don't think he wants me?

Anna couldn't form the words in her mouth. The embarrassment and shame were too strong.

"He's just the boy we used to know," she said, placing her hand over her father's arm. "He's David's friend."

Sir John closed his eyes, shaking his head. "He's a man, my dear. And since his older brother died last year, he's his father's heir now."

"What does that matter?"

Reluctantly, Sir John released his daughter. "It means his priorities have changed."

Later, after her father had left her room, Anna stood in front of her full-length mirror, her pointer fingers and thumbs touching as she laid her hands on her abdomen. The last few years had been filled with tears, but she surprised herself by spilling more.

How could life be so unfair? Why did someone always want something the moment they could no longer have it?

➤➤➤✕◀◀◀

ANNA WAITED AT the edge of the lawn, her fists on her hips. "Oh, so *now* everyone wants to play cricket."

The afternoon was windy and cool, but the clouds had remained thin enough to allow the sun's rays to streak over the grounds, giving the day a feel of spring even with winter close on the horizon. Knowing that months of gloomy days were ahead sparked another venture outside, with blankets and chairs for those who wanted to watch and cricket bats and balls for those intrepid few who wanted to take part in the game. Unlike the day when Anna had headed the event, the aunts and Beatrice were the first ones out on the makeshift pitch, bright-eyed and hungry for information regarding the sport. The only sour tones to be heard were from Anna.

"What are you complaining about?" David asked as he sailed by his sister, jogging out to the center of the lawn. He spun around to face her, his grin infectious as he ran backward. "It's the best sport in the world. Who doesn't love to play cricket all the time?"

"You'd be surprised," Anna muttered. She searched around for Jacob, but he was mysteriously absent again. She hadn't glimpsed hide nor hair of him in the two days since David's return. She missed their bantering and adventures. She missed other things as well. Anna had searched for him around the house but couldn't figure out where he was hiding. And he *was* hiding—she was sure of it.

"You remember how to hold a bat, don't you, sister dear?" David called from his end. To Beatrice's glee, he'd decided that he would bowl, giving the others a chance to work on their batting skills.

Anna rolled her eyes at his patronizing tone, bending over to retrieve the cricket bat. "I think I can manage."

David tossed the red ball up in the air, catching it behind his back. *Such a show-off.* "Don't worry. I'll go easy on you. I don't want you to hurt yourself."

"Yes, we wouldn't want you to hurt yourself, Anna," Iris scoffed as she meandered toward the wicket.

"Women are so very delicate, you know," Violet chimed in. From the invisible sidelines she was busy contorting her hips this way and that, stretching before it was her turn. She stopped to scratch her head, her eyes dreamily cast toward the field. "I have to say, though, if I were you, I think I would miss the ball every time if it meant Phillip might come up next to me to *show me how it's done.*"

Anna blushed beet red. "Oh, stop," she said over Iris's guffaws. "It's not like that … between us."

Violet reached for her toes and only made it halfway. "Maybe not to you, but your sister doesn't seem to mind." She straightened and pointed her fleshy chin down the field, where Beatrice was *quite happily* engaged in a batting tutorial with Phillip. Their conversation was too low to hear over the breeze, though her giggling wasn't. Anna's stomach knotted as she watched Phillip position himself behind Beatrice, folding his arms around hers to place them on the bat's skinny handle.

"That's ridiculous," she said to herself, lost in the scene. A headache began to take root smack in the middle of her eyes. "Beatrice already knows how to hold the bat. She's an expert batswoman."

Violet snorted. "Looks like she forgot that fact."

Iris moved to Anna's side. "Attractive, helpful men like that tend to make that happen," she quipped.

Anna inflated her lungs. The aunts were like the angel and devil perched on her shoulders, constantly providing their opinions.

Phillip stepped away from Beatrice, giving her room for a practice swing. It was so terrible she almost fell over. At the last second, he lunged forward to pluck her elbows before they went crashing into the grass.

Violet clicked her tongue, stretching her arms high over her head, her bountiful chest wedging under her chin so aggressively that her voice came out muffled. "All we're saying, Anna dear, is if your memory becomes a little faulty today, we won't blame you. Shame to let your sister win. That young beauty has years of conquests ahead of her."

Anna averted her gaze, focusing once more on her bat. She wrapped her palms around the handle, strangling its poor neck like a starving man with his last chicken. "He's not a conquest," she replied, wincing at the irritation in her tone. She lowered her voice, but the irritation was still apparent. "Phillip is like her older brother."

From the corner of her eye, she saw the aunts give each other a look. Such nosy women!

Iris whistled. "Well, we don't have a brother. So perhaps we don't know about these things."

"Yes, perhaps," Anna said. She flashed the ladies a smile, hoping it would put a period on the ridiculous conversation. "But as I was saying, I don't plan on missing any balls, so it doesn't matter."

"Hey! Are we going to play or gossip?" David yelled, his tanned face becoming mottled in frustration. "Honestly, this is why women don't play sports. You wouldn't be able to get in a whole match with all their talking—"

"I'm ready, David!" Anna barked back, taking her place in front of the stumps. "You're the only one talking now!" She turned back to the aunts. "Watch and learn, ladies, because I'm about to show these boys how to play cricket."

"THREE YEARS? YOU'VE only been playing for three years?" David asked, rubbing his upper arm as he walked with Anna off the lawn. A table of refreshments had been set out near Sir John and Mrs. Wright, who were, as always, seated in their chairs and lost in a deep exchange.

Anna would be too embarrassed to admit it to her cricket club teammates, but her ego soared from her brother's astonished praise. "Well, I watched you all those years playing at home. That helped."

David squinted as if he'd never seen her before. "I doubt that could have done much. I just can't believe it. I leave for India, and I come back to find my sister is better at cricket than I am. Now we just have to work on Beatrice."

"Oh, I don't know," Anna said, shooting Beatrice a reproachful glare. Her little sister ducked her head to avoid her. "I think Beatrice was just having a bad day. She's usually much better when I practice with her." Anna accepted a glass of punch from the servant. She drank it like a conquering hero. "In any event, don't be so hard on yourself. I doubt you had much time to play while you were in India—more important things to do and all that. Keeping safe."

David's chuckle was awkward. "You'd be surprised," he said,

his expression mired in chagrin. He shared a look with Phillip, who sidled up behind her. Anna didn't have time to question the odd exchange. The moment Phillip came near, all her thoughts and senses centered on him. He swayed back and forth, his arm casually brushing hers. It was an unnecessary touch and threw her off balance.

She blinked rapidly as if something were in her eye. But it was his smell. Minty and citrusy, like an exotic tea. The scent was as significant to Phillip as his name. It *was* Phillip.

"S-sorry," Anna stammered. "Why would I be surprised?"

Phillip laughed, causing her to blanch. Surely her question wasn't that funny, not enough for Phillip to laugh so loud that the entire party stopped to stare at them?

"Oh, Anna," he said breathlessly, placing his hand on the middle of her back. Her entire body froze at the intimacy—and audacity, considering they were not alone. "We played cricket more than we worked in the offices," he said, not moving his hand an inch. It had a proprietary feel to it, like he were re-staking an old claim. Anna didn't know what to make of her nerves. She used to melt into that hand, twist and contort her body so that she could always fit. Now, she could barely breathe. The act felt intrusive.

Phillip went on, his voice assured and loud. It was the voice of a man who always assumed that everyone wanted to hear him. "We came to India too late; it's quite subdued now. After the last skirmish, the Indians had learned their lesson. There were a few issues here and there ... You know, some middling maharaja getting a few hundred followers worked into a state over ridiculous claims about taxes and injustice. Can you imagine that? *Those people* should be kissing the ground we walk on. That place was a barbaric wasteland before we came to it. If it wasn't for the empire dictating how *those people* should live, they'd still be living in caves and huts."

Those people. Anna flinched each time Phillip spat the words.

"Surely there's no harm in living differently than we do in

England," she said. Phillip's hand dropped from her back. "If people are not content under English rule, then perhaps it is best to let them go. It's like any relationship, really. If it only benefits one partner, if it takes so much effort to cohabitate, maybe it's not meant to be."

"I'm sorry, Anna, I don't think you were paying attention," Phillip said, arching an amused brow at David. Luckily, her brother didn't chuckle in response. By the cautious look he gave Anna, he surely knew better. "It's fine. This sort of politics is not for women's ears. It is simply too much to understand. Because I am an old friend, I will sum it up for you, though. Those people love us there. They look up to us like children look up to their parents, and we act as benevolently as we should. But every place has bad apples that must be dealt with. And we dealt with them"—he slapped David on the shoulder—"when we weren't playing cricket."

"I'm just glad you're safe," Anna said to her brother.

"And *those people* weren't completely without favor," Phillip went on, missing the siblings' exchange. "Damn fine cricket players. They don't have the respectability and inner restraint of British players, no class, obviously—however, they are an energetic people. Willing, as it were."

"I wish you could have seen it, sister," David added. "Some of the Indian players were extraordinary. I don't know how to explain it … the way they can whip the ball. It's explosive—joyful, even."

"Ha!" Iris guffawed from the refreshment table. "Well, no one could ever accuse the English of being joyful."

Phillip pressed his lips thin. "As I said, they're childlike. Games come easy to them."

Beatrice huddled close to Iris, picking out a square of pale yellow cheese. "Well, that must have been exciting. Playing with people from the other side of the world. How small the world can seem sometimes. You don't even speak the same language as the Indians, and yet you both know the rules of cricket."

Anna's annoyance with Beatrice vanished. Every once in a while, her younger sister said something so poignant and beyond her years. Anna wished she wouldn't temper that intelligence whenever an attractive man walked by. She made a mental to mention that to her.

Phillip's top lip curled away from his teeth. Anna had never seen him look so harsh before. He'd always been such a carefree boy. "Oh, we don't play with them … we play against them."

David's tone hinted at frustration when he explained, "The British have their teams, and the Indians have theirs. We don't mix."

"Why not?" Anna asked.

"Why not?" Phillip repeated. He cast an incredulous, dramatic expression around the group. "Because we just don't, that's why. They're different."

"And different is bad?" Anna asked weakly.

Phillip huffed in exasperation. "Isn't it always?"

Chapter Fourteen

"WHAT DO YOU mean he isn't coming for dinner?"

The harsh note in the voice stopped Anna as she descended the staircase. She leaned over the banister to find Mrs. Wright and the butler in the corridor, each with expressions that said they would prefer to be anywhere else.

"That's just what he said, madam," the butler answered stoically, though there was a modicum of apology in his grave voice. It was uncommon for Anna to hear it. English butlers were heralded for their steadfast grace under pressure when dealing with their employers. However, Mrs. Wright wasn't an ordinary chatelaine, and either she wasn't taught or simply didn't care that she was visibly rattled by the unwanted information.

"But it's been days," she lamented, wringing her hands. "What will they think?"

The butler waited the appropriate amount of time in case the question turned out rhetorical. "They will think the viscount is busy, madam."

"Busy?"

"Precisely, madam."

"Busy or just plain rude?"

The butler sniffed. "If you'll permit me, ma'am ... To a viscount, it shouldn't matter."

Mrs. Wright slammed her arms down to her sides. She gave the butler a sharp look before hurrying down the hallway, muttering, "I didn't raise a damn viscount. I raised a man."

Anna continued down the steps, hoping to veer off to the drawing room to wait for the dinner, avoiding the butler. Good servants knew everything that happened in a house, especially when guests eavesdropped. She was almost at the entrance when the polite clearing of a throat stopped her in her tracks.

"Miss Smythe, I have a message for you."

Anna's heart thudded against her ribcage. Was the butler relaying a message from Jacob? For her?

"Yes," she said, turning. Why had her palms become wet all of a sudden? Why did her dress feel impossibly tight?

"Yes, Mr. Williams told me to tell you that he would like you to join him in the library." The butler raised an eyebrow. "Before everyone else comes down."

Anna frowned. "Oh, I see."

"Should I tell him that you have other plans?"

Anna waved a hand in the air. "No, no, that's fine. I'll go at once." Her laughter was hollow. "I suppose I've been summoned."

With a bow, the butler left her to make her way to the library. Perhaps Phillip was reading a book he enjoyed and wanted to show it to her. Although the more Anna thumbed through her memory, she couldn't find one instance of his reading. He'd never been an erudite man. He preferred being outside to sitting in a library any day. She'd always preferred him that way as well. His body was always best admired when it was in motion.

As Anna entered the room, Phillip didn't have a book to close; rather, he placed his crystal snifter on the table next to his chair. Anna hadn't spent much time in the library, but it was a charming space, with the top half of the walls covered in forest-green paper and the bottom half with oak batten board. A fire roared generously in the hearth, casting fans of light against the dark brown wood.

Phillip sat in his tall-backed chair, one leg crossed over the other, a note of scrutiny on his face, as if everything in the room belonged to him—even her.

"I'm sure you don't mind," he said, gesturing to the seat next to him. "I hoped you'd be down before the others. Get you all to myself. I wanted to take advantage of a little peace and quiet."

Anna tripped slightly at the comment. Collecting herself, she took the seat he offered, folding her hands primly in her lap. "It certainly hasn't been quiet these last few days."

"Joyous occasions are rarely somber."

"No. I suppose not."

Anna's head was bowed. She heard a rustling noise and then saw Phillip's hand come into view and fold over her own. A sensation to squirm out of his reach rushed through her. It made no sense. Nothing about how she was feeling made any sense. Because she'd expected more. More of everything. More of how it used to be. More of how she used to feel. Was she dead inside?

Had the illness killed all sources of joy inside of Anna as well as the baby she'd carried?

No, it hadn't. Her limited time with Jacob had shown her that.

"I have to admit, I expected you to be a little more … joyous."

Anna's eyes shot up. Guilt filled her as she encountered Phillip's put-upon expression.

"I'm so happy you're home; you know that," she rushed out. "I … I'm sorry I'm not expressing it better. I think I'm just so shocked that you're back."

"Of course I'm back. You knew I would come. We have history, you and I. It can't just be erased by a few paltry years."

Paltry wasn't how Anna would have described them.

Nevertheless, Phillip was right. They did have a history. But Anna couldn't shake the notion that she'd had to contend with most of it on her own. Their liaison had only gone on for three months. Before that, it had mostly developed from her end—

childish love from afar. But Anna would always remember that summer before he left for India. The way Phillip's limpid eye had finally landed on her, and he noticed what she had to offer in the bloom of her youth. A once-in-a-lifetime event, like witnessing a comet shoot across the night sky.

And then it had ended. And Anna—only Anna—had had to pick up the pieces of the heartbreak.

She bit at her lip, willing the words back in her throat, but they were determined to come forth. "I … Well … My father, that is, thought you would have come back earlier."

"Earlier?"

Anna desperately wanted Phillip to let go of her hands. Her palms were uncomfortably sweaty, and she yearned to wipe them on her skirt. "After you received his letter … You did receive it, didn't you? David said you both received them."

Phillip frowned. He uncrossed his leg and bent at his waist, leaning closer to her chair. With the fire at his back, his shadows ran long and heavy over Anna, casting much of her body into darkness. "Of course I received it. Dear girl, what kind of a man do you think I am? I was beside myself with worry. But my hands were tied. I had just landed in India. I couldn't just come home."

Anna was strong, but even she was surprised by the strength she mustered to keep questioning him. Phillip never liked being questioned. He was a gentleman, he'd informed her once. And a gentleman should always be taken at his word.

"Your father is a baron," she countered, her voice growing more strained. "He helped you gain a position with the company. He could have cleared the way to come home."

"And risk everything? Anna, seriously, who have you been speaking with? You know I needed to go to India. It was the only place I could make my fortune. I wasn't always my father's heir."

"And did you? Make your fortune?"

Phillip hesitated. "There were some minor hiccups. But I don't want to talk about those right now. I want to talk about us."

"Us?"

"Yes, my dear Anna! Us!" Suddenly, Phillip was out of his chair. On his knees, he perched in front of her, like a supplicant at her feet. The sixteen-year-old Anna would have fainted at this show, this grand display of affection. Not this Anna, though. The grimace on Phillip's face as he scooted toward her only made her want to laugh.

Once more, he covered her hands with his. Did he think she was going to run away? "Is this why you've been so distant with me? You're upset I didn't automatically return when I heard about your illness. You know I blame myself. How could I not when I see what it has taken from you?" He lifted his morose gaze to her hair then reached for a lock, running it through his fingers. "It will grow back. And you will be beautiful again."

Anna was stunned. Did the man not know how long it took to grow hair? She was more perturbed over that idea than the notion that she needed hers to be longer to be considered beautiful. "I like it short."

"No wife of mine will have short hair."

Wife. There. He'd said it. A word that Anna had spent countless nights and days dreaming about. A word that had once held more importance than her sense of self. A word that she'd thought had been lost forever.

But again, the impact was disappointing. The butterflies that had always camped in her stomach whenever Phillip was near were long gone.

Shame was the only thing that persisted. Because he deserved better from her, didn't he? Or was it Anna who deserved better?

Regardless, the man deserved to know. She couldn't move forward in any way without his hearing the whole truth from her lips.

"Phillip, I have something to tell you," Anna started. "I wasn't just ill. There was a reason."

"Of course there was a reason."

"No." Anna sucked in a breath. "It was because of us … you." Her knee began to shake. After all this time the words were harder to find than she'd imagined.

"Me?"

"No, me … us … what we did." She was butchering this. Anna had to get it out. The truth was pressing from inside her, stretching her skin until it hurt. "There was a baby," she blurted. "I lost the baby. I didn't know until it happened."

Anna paused. And waited. The word *baby* seared her tongue. She'd never used it before. The doctors … her father … everyone had called it *the accident*. But it had been a baby. Phillip's baby. *Her* baby.

The sounds of the fire popping and crackling and the servants wading back and forth to set the table for dinner battled against the ominous silence. Anna kept her eyes closed. She couldn't look at him, didn't want to read into any expression on Phillip's face, because she hadn't the faintest idea what she wanted him to feel. Remorse? Sadness? Relief? Were any of those emotions the right ones? Anna didn't know. Since the miscarriage, she'd shuffled through them all like a stack of playing cards.

"Well, of course it was the baby. What else would it have been?"

She felt like her entire body was submerged under water, the pressure growing the farther she sank. *The baby.* Phillip said *the baby.* Only he didn't say it like she had. He spat it out like he'd just discovered a bug in his food.

Anna had always believed that she was the only one with a truth to tell, but she'd been wrong. And, as ever, she was the only one to pay the price.

"You knew?" she rasped. She swallowed a lump in her throat. "How did you know?"

Phillip scowled at her like she was an unruly child who couldn't keep track of the conversation. "What are you talking about? I just told you that I received the letter."

The letter that her father had written. The letter that was supposed to have no mention of the miscarriage.

Phillip bristled, uncomfortable with the position and Anna's loss for words. "I explained it all to your father. I apologized for the little indiscretion, but seeing as how the accident took care of itself, there was no reason for me to cancel my plans and hurry back."

"*Little indiscretion.*"

"I stayed for us, Anna! I stayed so our life would be better."

But her life was already better, and it had nothing to do with Phillip. The love and compassion of Anna's family, and her strength of will, had seen to that.

"My father could have thrown me out of the house," she murmured. "I could have been ruined. I could have lost everything."

Phillip dashed a hand in the air as if he was shooing away a gnat. "Your father wouldn't have done that. He's not that kind of man. Generous to a fault. I knew he would take care of you."

Anna slipped her hands out from under his. His nonchalant touch was making her sick. "But you couldn't have been sure. You didn't know. You didn't check. You didn't ask. Not once in three years did you write to me. Why?"

Phillip pursed his lips and settled back on his heels with a huff, bored with the conversation. "I was working for the East India Company, *Anna*. It's practically slave labor. I didn't have time to write countless love letters—"

"But you had time for cricket," she snapped. Anna redirected her gaze to the books lining the wall. She could read every single one and not find a story more ridiculous than hers. Phillip had known about the baby. He'd known about the miscarriage. And he'd still stayed away. Even after her father's letter, no doubt urging Phillip to come back and marry her, do the honorable thing, he'd remained where he was. Searching for his fortune. Sucking India dry of its spices and silks as competently as he'd sucked away her girlhood.

No … Anna couldn't blame him for everything. He may have flattered and coaxed her, impressed her with his lavish bouquets, badly written poetry, and cheap trinkets, but she had eaten it all up like a glutton. No spoon had been too big. She'd swallowed every morsel of his affection.

And the cost would continue to plague her.

Phillip's face softened. He came back on his knees, clutching Anna's face in his hands, forcing her to look at him. "My dear, I understand you are upset. I do. However, all of that … *distastefulness* … is in the past. We can start anew. You say I wasn't there for you before, but I'm here now. Soon, I will be a baron and you will be my lady. Just as we've always wanted. We can start fresh, and you won't have to be so angry all the time, so … *forward*. You can be the girl I fell in love with who always had a ready smile for me. My heir can't be raised by a short-haired shrew, can he?"

"There won't be an heir."

Phillip cocked his ear toward her, his grin silly with disbelief. "I'm sorry?"

The trauma of this conversation must have taken its toll, because what she said next didn't hurt Anna half as much as she thought it would. She'd learned early on that her body was an amazing thing, only giving her as much pain as she could handle, and then numbing her for all the rest.

She actually smiled when she jutted her chin toward Phillip, daring him to condemn her for her physical failure. "You heard me. I can't have children. The doctors said the fever was too much. It wrecked any chance I have of conceiving again."

"You're certain? The doctors said this with absolute certainty?"

"Not absolute. But close enough."

Phillip toppled back on his heels once more. The hands that had just contained her own were now holding his head, long fingers massaging each temple.

Anna had to remind herself that she didn't want Phillip touching her. But as she watched him console himself, she couldn't shake the feeling that a real man might have considered consoling the woman who'd been told motherhood would not be in her future. Which would most likely mean that marriage wouldn't be in her future either.

And that was what her father had warned Anna about in her bedroom. That was what he'd been so worried about. He'd pegged Phillip for who he was. Sir John knew the man would never act honorably. If she were being honest with herself, Anna had known it too.

Nevertheless, she'd still harbored some distant, childish fantasy that Phillip might still profess his love for her. That, perhaps, even though they could never marry now, he'd still declare an undying devotion that would keep her warm and satisfied on all the lonely nights ahead. That, from across ballrooms, as he stood with his young, new, fecund bride, he would gaze over the heads of their friends and search for her. Catch her eye for a fleeting moment and give her a stare that said she was still the only one who'd known him at his best, who'd captured and guarded his soul so well that he would never ask for it back.

"That's the dinner bell," Phillip remarked, sighing as he lumbered to his feet. He glanced at the doorway, where footsteps could be heard cascading down the stairs.

Their time was up. Anna hid her disappointment and heartbreak behind a mask of composure. She stood and patted her dress in front, smoothing out the wrinkles. She might be a shell of a person at present, but she wouldn't look like one.

Phillip walked to the doorway and stopped himself, wincing as he turned back to her. "Do you want me to wait for you?"

"No," Anna replied before her throat closed up.

He nodded and left.

There would be no more waiting between them.

Chapter Fifteen

JACOB STARED AT the blank piece of paper. Any longer and he might go cross-eyed. Was that even possible? Where had he heard that ridiculous fact?

He leaned back in his chair away from his desk, tossing his pen across the room. It couldn't be helped. Focus was not to be had this night. It wasn't to be had last night either.

Perhaps he should venture off to London. He could call on a few of his old friends from the newspaper and make a night of it. He hadn't done that in months. For good reason. The last time he'd tried, the occasion had been filled with uncomfortable silences and a never-ending chorus of "Apologies, Jacob—I mean, my lord." For some reason, his old friends couldn't get it into their thick skulls that he was still the same Jacob Wright despite his title. They kowtowed to him in an obsequious, pandering manner. They wouldn't even allow him to pay for his own drinks. The absurdity! He was an obscenely rich man and, apparently, too high and mighty to touch coins with his bare hands.

Jacob had left disgusted. Not with his friends. They couldn't be blamed. The social culture and hierarchy of the empire had been beaten into them all as lads along with their daily Latin. One must always recognize and respect one's betters. But Jacob was far from being anyone's better, and even a title wouldn't prove it to him.

The lords from history books and myth were handsome and dashing, debonair and courageous. Like the Duke of Wellington and William Marshal. If anyone had ever been blue-blooded, it was men like that, and it had everything to do with the ice in their veins. A man's actions gave him character, not his position on some ancient family tree.

Jacob could use some of that character and courage right about now. It might save him from making a complete ass out of himself and hiding for the second night in a row. His self-respect was at an all-time low, and staring at this blank paper wasn't helping.

Writing had always been a source of solace for him. A way to collect his rambling thoughts, make sense of the world. Now all it did was dredge up memories of a life he could never have again. Because he was a *better*.

Funny, he'd always thought rising in the ranks would make him feel better about himself. As always, life laughed at those who believed they had it pegged. Because the only thing that all of his homes and money had made Jacob feel was heavy.

For Christ's sake. Was he feeling sorry for himself? For being a peer?

Jesus wept!

Wait. What the hell?

A noise came from outside the cottage, loud and unrestrained, like an animal in pain. Jacob walked over to his dirty window, finding a shadowy figure huddled outside in the garden. It appeared that Jesus wasn't the only weeping that night.

He threw open the door. "What the hell are you doing out here? Without a cloak on … again!"

Anna jumped in surprise. Quickly, she used her gloved arms to sop up the tears that were threatening to drown her poor face.

"I … I just needed some air," she said, spinning away. Her voice wobbled terribly.

Jacob was so delighted to see her that he continued to yell. "What you need is a cloak."

Anna clenched her hands at her sides. "Well, I didn't bring a bloody cloak!"

"For fuck's sake." Jacob shook out of his coat and walked it over to her shivering figure. She didn't turn as he draped it softly onto her shoulders, though she did mutter a reluctant "thank you."

Jacob stood there watching her, waiting for her to acknowledge him once more. It gave him time to appreciate her in his environment. Save his mother, not many people ever ventured to this end of the estate. Jacob had always attested that that was the reason why he liked this garden so much, in addition to the hermit's cottage that it housed. However, he would have loved it regardless. Unlike the rest of the grounds, this portion was designed with a Chinese influence. A red and black pagoda, topped with two golden dragons, rested on stilts in the center of a tiny pond. One intrepid fellow could probably jump to it from the banks, but there was a bridge on either side for the sensible person. Small, Asian statues were stationed throughout the remainder of the garden, in between plants and hedges that were confoundedly English in origin. Clearly, the architect of this garden had never been to China, nor did he care to stay solely authentic in his design.

Jacob still considered the scene captivating. The pagoda, so different and blatant out there in the middle of the pond, was disrupting. Its presence was proud and exultant not despite its differences but because of it.

Having Anna in this space caused an intense rightness to tug at Jacob's chest.

Until she spoke. "Where have you been?" Soft and undeniably battered, her voice soaked into him like the cold chill against his linen shirt sleeves.

"Here. I've been here."

"Your mother is furious. You're being horribly rude, ignoring your guests."

"I'm sorry."

"You're not sorry." Anna whipped around to face him. Her eyes were glassy and round, as big as the moon's reflection in the pond. "If you were truly sorry then you wouldn't have run away, taking your responsibilities for granted."

Jacob took small steps toward her. Her eyes narrowed, but she didn't back away. "I understand you're upset, Anna, but blaming me won't help."

She seemed to wilt, her shoulders slumping away from her ears. "It might."

"Who made you cry?"

"I'm not crying," Anna lied, before adding, "No one. Me, I suppose."

Jacob's smile was gentle. "You?"

She let out a short laugh, a pathetic and paltry thing, void of life. "I knew better. I knew *better*. But against my better judgment, I let myself believe that it wasn't all for nothing. I let myself think that what I went through was an act of love … commitment … devotion."

"And what was it?"

Anna's lips quivered; her face was impossibly young and pale. Jacob wanted to scoop her into his arms and carry her into the little pagoda on the pond and live there forever, away from pain and heartbreak and responsibility.

"It was a childish folly." She pulled his jacket tighter around her. "It was … I don't know. I suppose it was what I deserved. All of it." Overcome with emotion, Anna burst into silent tears, and Jacob couldn't hold himself back any further. He went to her, enveloping her in his arms, holding her captive against his chest.

Anna's tears soaked through his shirt as she sobbed. "Shh," Jacob said, swaying back and forth like his mother used to do when she held him. He remembered how hypnotizing that simple motion used to be, how it utterly soothed his breaking heart. "I have you now. You don't deserve anything bad to ever happen to you."

"I do. You have no idea," Anna whispered. She pulled at his waistcoat on his back, gripping it in her fists in her unrelenting grief. "I am a bad woman."

"You are not. Hush now," he replied. "You've been hurt."

Jacob could barely contain himself. He wanted to find Phillip Williams and beat him to a bloody pulp. He wanted to pound his fist into that pretty mouth so the blackguard would never be able to show off those dazzling teeth again.

But he wouldn't. Because Anna needed him. And *he* wouldn't let her down. Holding her, rocking her, providing her solace was his job, and he would do it for as long as she'd let him.

Anna trembled. "I've been stupid."

Jacob rested his chin on the top of her head. "You were young."

"I was ridiculous."

"You were naïve."

Her scoff was muffled against his shirt. "You don't even know what happened. You don't know the full story."

"I don't need to know it." He backed away, lowering his forehead so she could see him clearly. "I know *you*."

Anna stared at him wide-eyed, stuck in a daze. Jacob used the time to his advantage, wiping away the tears on her face with the rough pads of his thumbs. When they traveled to her lips, he lingered for a few seconds too long before eventually falling away.

Her mouth began to move but nothing came out. She tried again. "Jacob … I …" She grabbed his wrists, wrapping her hands around them—not pushing him away but keeping him in place.

"What is it, Anna?"

She blinked and more tears fell. They reminded him of diamonds. "I … I need to tell you … something."

Jacob widened his stance, fighting for composure. He kept his expression still and open. "Anything. You can tell me anything. I want you to know that about me. I will always be here for you.

Whenever you need."

She pressed her lips together so tightly it seemed painful. The lovely lines and grooves in her lips were lost in the tension. "You're a good and decent man, Jacob Wright."

Jacob chuckled, bending over to brush a kiss against her forehead. He shouldn't have done that. All he could taste was their time in the carriage. All he could taste was the gluttonous need for more. "Is that all?" he teased.

Anna frowned, flicking her head slightly in an exasperated motion. "I … I …" Her shoulders fell again as if she'd lost her nerve. "I'm cold."

ANNA WORRIED THAT Jacob was walking her straight into a giant shrub. Was this a mystical garden, where plants and flowers opened their leaves, allowing you to get lost in their flowers, sleep on their petals until the magic faded and you were restored?

She laughed to herself. What fanciful nonsense. But her mind was scattered, her concentration limp and decayed. She might have believed anything that night, with the moonlight streaking down on them, a bizarre Asian house held up on stilts at the center of a pond. What was this place? And how, after the last few chaotic days, was it here that she had finally found Jacob?

He held her hand, surely and solidly as he guided her toward the giant shrub. On closer inspection, Anna realized it wasn't, in fact, a large bush, though the thick emerald moss covering the exterior gave it the appearance of something living, something wild. Jacob stopped in front of the odd structure, using his arm to push a bundle of gangly vines out of the way to locate a handle.

A door. To a tiny cottage hidden in the labyrinthine enclosure of the garden. Anna had heard of these hermit's cottages, though she'd never seen one before. Her father had never included one on his estate, despite the fad. Perhaps the old viscount had been eccentric, she thought as Jacob escorted her inside.

Anna hugged Jacob's coat around her frame and surveyed the minuscule space. To call it a cottage might be an overstatement. He left her at the entrance and added another log to the fire. Anna took her time reading the room, which held a skeletal set of belongings that just hinted at life. A rudimentary desk and chair took up the majority of the space, along with a single bed wedged against the far stone wall. A cup of tea sat on the desk next to an oil lamp, along with a single sheet of paper and a pen.

Despite the austere surroundings, Anna was infused with contentment.

Jacob straightened from his crouch near the hearth, dusting his hands on the back of his trousers. He glanced around the room, a shy expression on his face. "Would you like tea?" he asked, his eyes falling on the teakettle that was hanging above the hearth. "Wait ... Do I have any tea left?" He went to his desk and looked inside the bottom drawer. "Yes! I have a little left. I'll have to remember to bring more from the house. Oh, damn. I only have the one teacup." Finally, he looked at Anna, his features comically anxious. He lifted the single cup off his desk. "You don't mind, do you?"

Anna didn't have the heart to tell him no. She had no desire for tea, but Jacob seemed to need something to do, something that would help her in some way. She nodded and let him get to his work pouring water into the teakettle from a jug that sat near the only window of the cottage, a dirty thing that was in desperate need of cleaning.

Anna meandered about the area, taking small steps to make the journey last longer. When she made it to the bed, she noticed the sheets were ruffled. "Do you live here?"

Jacob paused from dropping tea leaves into the kettle. "Some-times," he answered. "Though I wouldn't say *live*. I come here when I need to think ... when I need to be alone."

An overcoat was hanging from a hook on the wall, a robe next to it. "And how often is that?"

Jacob smiled wryly, hanging the teakettle back over the flames. "Enough."

She wandered away from the bed. As Jacob continued to fuss, they kept up a companionable façade. She didn't know it at first, but it was exactly what she'd needed. After the conversation she'd just shared with Phillip, she craved something different—a lack of confusion, of always wondering what something truly meant. Anna was tired of reading into words, searching for hidden messages. She needed something true and real. She needed Jacob.

Anna picked up the blank piece of paper from his desk, holding it up for him to see. "Was the muse not here for you tonight?" she asked, lifting an impish brow. "I hope I didn't interrupt anything."

He wiped his hands on his pants once more and smirked bashfully, two spots of pink on his cheeks. She hadn't meant to embarrass him, though she'd be lying to herself if she said she didn't enjoy the charming effect.

"I thought I would try to write something, and ... well ... you can see how that went."

Anna placed the paper gently back on the table. "Why is it difficult?"

Jacob frowned, moving over to the opposite wall—as far away from Anna as he could find. He leaned against it, crossing his arms. As always, he was uncomfortable speaking about himself, but he was the one who'd brought her here. This entire cottage was an extension of him, and Anna couldn't leave without attempting to understand more.

"I thought I would try my hand at writing ... fiction," he explained. "I've been told it isn't proper for a viscount to have a profession, but it's perfectly fine for them to dabble in the arts. However"—his face screwed up in distaste—"would it shock you to hear that I'm not terribly artistic?"

A bark of laughter escaped her. Anna's hand flew to her mouth to stifle any more. Jacob's brow rose at her response.

"But you were a writer for a newspaper. Surely you had to be artistic in that endeavor."

He shrugged. "I can't say, really. I never thought about it; it came so easily. I don't enjoy making up stories. I like telling them. I liked reporting on the world and all the changes and events. London is such a captivating city, enthralling. Anything and everything can happen here. Everything *is* happening here. I liked being a part of that."

Anna had never seen Jacob like this before. How beguiling it was to watch his eyes light up as he spoke. The passion flowed through his body, electrifying the very core of him. Anna was impressed ... and jealous. She wondered if she would ever feel that way about anything again.

She ran the tip of her hand over the wood, leaving no mark. No dust. Someone must come to clean it, but then, why was the window still so dirty? "Is it really such a crime for a viscount to work?"

"You tell me."

Anna bobbed her shoulders, and then it came to her. She grinned at Jacob, and for the first time tonight, it didn't hurt to do so. Because she wasn't pretending. "I thought being different wasn't such a bad thing."

Jacob sighed as if he'd had this argument with himself a million times before. He leaned his head against the stone. "You're right, I know you are, but ... having all this ... It just feels like I have so much more to lose now. And it's not just me. I want to make sure my family never needs anything ever again. I want them to have calm, safe, pain-free lives. I need to keep my focus here. Besides," he added with a sheepish grin, "my children will grow up in this life, so different from the one that I did. I don't want to ruin it for them, make it more difficult by being ... eccentric."

It was like Helga Bitterman had reached into Anna's stomach and twisted it with both hands. Children. Yes, of course Jacob would want children—*need* children. Every viscount desired an heir. But why did that fact make her want to lie down on the floor and hug her knees until she fell asleep?

"What's wrong?" Jacob asked. "Are you all right?" The kettle whistled, and he hastened to remove it from the heat. He poured the liquid into the cup but left it on the table.

"Anna?" he said, coming toward her. Without hesitating, he wound his arms around her waist. "What did I say? Tell me."

Lord, how could she be crying again? But she could feel the vexing tears coming, feel them building along her bottom lid. "It's nothing." She placed her palms on his chest. His heartbeat steadied her enough to hold back the tears. "I'll be fine, I promise."

Jacob nodded, but his gaze said otherwise. His wariness and concern were etched in the lines bracketing his mouth. "Do you want the tea?" he asked gently.

Anna shook her head.

"Do you want me to take you back?"

She could tell he wanted that even less than she did, which gave her the courage to say what she said next.

"No." She played with a button on his shirt. It was mother-of-pearl, impossibly smooth. "Can I stay here tonight?" she asked quietly.

Time expanded and lengthened between them, providing an infinite number of possibilities and an infinite variety of lives. They could be anybody in this little cottage, any couple needing time and space to just *be*.

Jacob swallowed. He slid his hand down her body to take hers, then led her to the bed and flung back the covers. Without hesitation, Anna sat down on the surprisingly comfy mattress and scooted over to the far side to make room, but Jacob didn't follow.

"I'll sleep on the floor—"

"You will not," Anna replied at once, shocked by the vehemence in her voice. The man wasn't understanding. She didn't want to go back to the house—that was true—but what she truly wanted was him.

He released a mirthless laugh, rubbing the nape of his neck. "There's barely enough room for one person—"

"We'll manage," Anna said firmly. She patted the mattress. "Please, Jacob. Please."

He eyed the bed for a long moment. "You need to sleep."

"I plan to."

Jacob whistled as he released a long, defeated sigh. "If you wake up with a crick in your neck, don't say I didn't warn you."

Anna hid a smile as he situated himself on the mattress, hugging his side so gallantly that there was a good six inches between them. Half of his body hung off the bed. She chewed at the inside of her cheek, tapping her fingers on her belly.

"You know you're not comfortable," she said.

"I'm fine."

"You're not fine."

"Go to sleep."

Anna slipped to her side to face him. Jacob's broad back was to her, and just as she'd expected, one leg was hanging off the bed. "You can touch me, you know."

"I don't think that's a good idea."

"What?"

Jacob turned on his back, staring at the ceiling. "I said I don't think it's a good idea. You need to rest."

She reached for the shiny button on his shirt again, but he captured her hand, flattening it upon his chest. "I can sleep with someone touching me. It can't be that hard."

Jacob's laugh came out of nowhere. He ran a hand over his face.

"What?" she asked.

"Nothing. Go to sleep."

"I told you—"

He flipped on his side to face her. They were like two halves of a heart, broken in the middle. "Maybe you can go to sleep touching me, but I will have a damned hard time sleeping while touching you. You know this."

Anna opened her mouth to speak, but he cut her off.

"You *know* this," Jacob repeated. His features softened. "I just want to take care of you."

"You *are* taking care of me," Anna said. She squeezed her hand out from under his and placed it on his cheek. His whiskers stabbed her skin. She adored the sensation. Anna had touched him so many other times, and yet this small brush of contact seemed so much more intimate. A conversation without words. An understanding. "I need more tonight, Jacob. I need you to hold me. I don't know why, and I'm sorry if this sounds needy and selfish, but I just do. I will never ask anything of you again, I promise. Just tonight. Just this."

Jacob's lips curved, though his eyes still held a degree of reserve. "And what if I don't want you to keep that promise?"

Anna traced his cheekbones, up between his eyes, following the shallow lines across his forehead before she skimmed her fingers across the pillowy expanse of his lips ... back and forth ... one, two, three times, before eventually breaking away.

There was an opening. Anna saw it on his face. An invitation, a hope for something more—but she couldn't take any more disappointment. She couldn't go to him knowing that nothing would come of it. She wouldn't take advantage of Jacob's good nature. She was not Phillip.

With a wistful smile, she turned to her other side, facing the wall. She reached back for Jacob's hand, draping it around her middle, encouraging him to mold his body to hers. It took a second for the coaxing to work, but she eventually heard him let out another strangled breath and follow suit.

When Jacob enveloped her, it felt so undeniably right. It was like lying on a warm patch of grass on a sunny day. He was the first sip of tea after coming in from the cold. He was the light that ships at sea searched for in the night. He was the ultimate. Jacob was abundance. Contentment. Peace.

Anna was the fraud. Her breath hitched as she attempted to hold back more tears, more disappointment.

Jacob must have heard her. He placed his head on top of hers. His arms maintained their gracious pressure.

"Now you know," she said weakly. "You know that I'm not as strong as I thought I was." Her maudlin thoughts traveled back to his cricket article that had incensed her. She thought about their silly excursions. Taking him to see strongwomen seemed worthless now. Anna wasn't anything like those women, and she would never be. She clasped his arms, holding them against her front. They were a life raft, and she was lost at sea.

"I told you. I was raised by women," Jacob whispered into the night. His body was the tiny cottage built to keep her safe. "And I know how strong they are. You are no different."

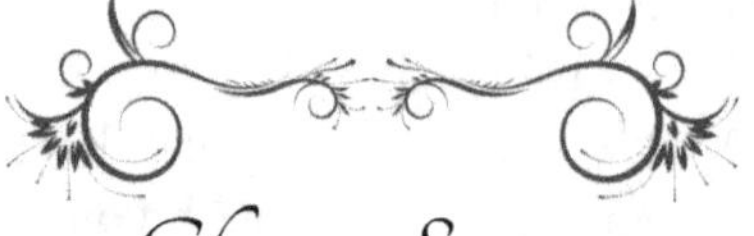

Chapter Sixteen

ANNA'S SNORING WOKE him.

Jacob blinked a few times, trying to remember where the hell he was and how the hell he got there. He stretched along the warm creature in his arms, causing Anna to stir. Her snores became softer.

He glanced at the window. It was always difficult to tell with the glass, but he suspected it was close to dawn. The faint music of birdsong could be heard just outside the cottage.

Fuck.

He hadn't meant to fall asleep. He had planned to lie with Anna just long enough for her to do so, and then pick her up and carry her back to her bedroom in the house. When her maids found her room empty, they would surely become distressed. He didn't need a search party combing the grounds to find them huddled together in his little enclave.

But he'd failed. Anna's body had been too enticing, her proposition too tempting. The moment Jacob had let his head lie next to hers on the pillow, he was done for. Her scent, an intoxicating blend of roses and lavender, had lulled him to sleepy bliss. He'd had no chance.

But there was still time. He had to move quickly if he was going to salvage this disaster.

Perception was such an interesting thing. Waking up with Anna in his arms certainly didn't feel like a disaster; however, she would probably think so. Her father most *definitely* would. Jacob had no great love for Sir John, but no father deserved to have his daughter taken advantage of. And although Jacob's motives had been pure, nothing about their current predicament could be perceived that way.

Anna's snores picked up again. Jacob smiled. He was in trouble. He must be the only man in history to think a woman's snores were adorable. He craned around to look at her. Anna's mouth was slack and open, a tiny trail of drool running onto her pillow. Her hair was plastered across her forehead and onto her pink cheeks. The cottage didn't retain heat well at night, but Jacob had done his job. Anna was pleasant and snug.

He could have gazed at her all day, memorizing the angles of her face, the way her nose was thicker at the tip than at the bridge. The way she had one small brown freckle at the corner of her eye and three moles on the side of her neck lined up like Orion's Belt. Her lashes fluttered as if she were in the middle of a dream.

Was she dreaming of him? *Or Phillip?*

Instantly, Jacob kicked that bastard from his mind. He couldn't imagine sharing an early morning with Anna ever again. He wouldn't ruin it by thinking of that son of a bitch.

"Go back to sleep," Anna said, her voice thick and gravelly.

Jacob grimaced. Did she know he'd been watching her? Should he be embarrassed about that? Should he apologize? He'd never stared at a woman in his bed.

"It's almost dawn," Jacob replied, though a few more minutes couldn't hurt. Besides, it was cold outside, and so very warm inside with her.

"I don't care," she grumbled, burrowing her face into the pillow. Jacob got a shock when she arched her lower half into his pelvis, inciting his morning hunger even more. He gritted his teeth.

"You'll care when everyone finds you here."

"No, I won't."

Obstinate woman.

Obstinate, tantalizing woman.

Anna was a horrible influence because Jacob's body was acting as stubborn as she was. His cock wouldn't calm down and his arms wouldn't stop hugging her!

Let go!

No. Never that.

Jacob needed to be harsher. "I will not compromise you."

Anna's laughter was much too acerbic for a woman her age. It cut him more than her words. "I've already been compromised, Jacob. Don't pretend that you don't know that."

He did. He didn't know the extent of Anna's relationship with Phillip, but he understood that it had gone too far in more ways than one. Was Sir John aware?

That was beside the point. Jacob was not Phillip. And he would not treat Anna like she was a new toy to be played with and then easily discarded.

"And you must stop worrying about your virtue," she went on. "I told you. Marriage isn't in my future. My father knows that. He won't force anything on you."

"I'm not worried."

Anna *humphed.* "You should be. You don't want to be stuck with a woman like me."

A woman like me. What was she going on about now? Jacob still hadn't a clue what had happened last night before he found her, but this wasn't the Anna that he was beginning to know. His Anna was forthright and sincere, courageous and proud. This morning, as she kept her eyes closed and attempted to disappear in the covers, she sounded so defeated and lonely. Beyond caring or trying.

Jacob took a deep breath, relaxing against her once more. His mind whirled with what he should do—the proper, right, decent thing to do ... but the longer he held Anna, the more he came to the conclusion that holding her was the answer. Especially since she responded so readily to him. Inside the cocoon of his body, her shoulders released their tension, her breathing grew slower, her short limbs became lax. It dawned on Jacob that she felt safe with him.

"You've ruined it," Anna muttered.

"What?"

"My sleep," she said. "I can't go back to bed now with you thinking so much."

"I'm not thinking!"

"Liar."

He squeezed her tighter. "I'm not *trying* to think."

"Well, you're not *not* trying to think, either."

Jacob rolled his eyes. He couldn't argue with such insane logic.

She let out a long, distressed sigh. "You'll just have to put me back to sleep, then."

"And how in the world am I supposed to—"

Oh.

Was she saying what he thought she was saying? Christ, his cock already knew the answer to the question. Jacob cleared his throat. "I already told you that I won't dishonor you while you're in this state."

Anna twirled around in his arms, facing him with a delightfully mischievous grin. Her eyes were full of devilment; the green was lighter than usual, more peridot than emerald. This was the kind of important information a man could only glean in the morning.

She placed her hands on his chest, throwing one thigh over his legs. "Yes, but you never said anything about my dishonoring you." Her voice was rich and husky and confident. This was the Anna he knew.

Jacob couldn't help but smile as her hands crept down his torso. He was still wearing his waistcoat over his linen shirt, and she took her time, releasing the buttons, each one like a tiny lock being picked.

"We have to return you to the house," he argued, but even as he said the words, his arms were circling her waist, his fingers pressing into the fabric of her gown, mining for a hint of skin.

"I told you," she said. Her smile evoked images of honey and silky-smooth whipped cream. "I'm not going back to the house."

Anna's attention was fixed low on her work. She had finished with the waistcoat and moved to his shirt. She pulled it out of his trousers so she could finally dip her hands underneath the linen and find his belly. Her touch scorched him.

He jerked back from the searing action, causing her to laugh. "You weren't this jumpy in the carriage," she said, her voice a siren song of temptation.

Jacob fought for composure. "I was in control that night."

"You could be in control now, but you refused."

Her fingers made small circles around his belly button, a hypnotic blend of innocence and desire. Jacob lowered his head, trying to catch her lips, but Anna ducked at the last moment. He growled and wedged his face into her neck, nipping her skin with his teeth.

Anna gasped. The sound made him crazy.

Her hands meandered to the buttons of his trousers, and the moment she began to work on them, Jacob concluded that he must still be asleep. He was in the middle of an erotic dream— that was the only thing that could explain this incredible occurrence.

But the taste of Anna's skin was too sweet. The smell of her sweat was too heady and spicy. Jacob flicked up her skirts and palmed the fleshy part of her thigh as he reached for her full behind. That … that was no dream. It was heaven, and unmistakably real.

Anna leaned into his chest, nudging his head to the side so she could kiss his neck. They were light kisses, soft and angelic, a stark contrast to her hands, which could only have the devil in their corner. Her hips undulated in a slow rhythm as she worked.

Jacob braced himself. He couldn't breathe as he waited for her to take him in hand. But nothing could have prepared him for the moment Anna clasped him in her grasp, the way she held him as if she owned him, the heroic way she made him feel as she explored his manhood.

"Oh, Christ, Anna, that's … that's …" Jacob couldn't find the words. He was lost, and Anna was the only one who could find him.

"I'm not doing anything," she whispered. The worry in her tone managed to pull him from the enchantment. "I've never done this before. I'm not sure …"

Jacob's laughter was haggard, stretched tight. He bucked in her hand, and Anna dropped him.

"I'm sorry. I'm sorry," she said, hiding her head in his shirt.

Jacob smiled through his pain, placing a hand on the back of her head, cuddling her close so she wouldn't think of fleeing. They weren't done yet.

"You didn't hurt me," he said, chuckling. "Why did you … do that … if you didn't know what to do?"

Anna's blush scorched through his shirt. "I assumed that …"

"Assumed?"

She sighed. "Assumed that you would know what to do and would take it from there. Stop laughing at me."

"Oh, sweetheart," Jacob said, rolling her back and forth on the bed in a giant hug. He couldn't remember the time he'd had this much fun. Certainly not in bed with a woman. Jacob had never thought of sex as fun before. It was a release—vigorous, enjoyable, *necessary* entertainment—but not exactly fun. But, as always, with Anna, everything was different. Different and better.

"I could show you," he drawled, growing even more excited by what he was proposing, "or you could explore. What would you prefer?"

Anna's face emerged from hiding. Jacob had been right. Her cheeks were as red as fire. "You'd let me explore?"

"Hell yes."

She grinned. That impish look returned.

Jacob rearranged himself, lying on his back. He folded his hands behind his head.

Anna's stare was comical. She squinted at him in disbelief. "I don't want to hurt you."

"So don't."

She snorted. "I only want you to feel as good as you make me feel."

"Yes, let's do that."

The sultry curve of Anna's lips made his heart slam into his ribcage. So beautiful. And only for him. So many grand things had been given to Jacob in recent years, but beyond a doubt, that smile was the one that meant the most. He would cherish it forever because he'd earned it.

This time when she gripped his rod, she wasn't completely devoid of confidence, though she *was* hesitant. She stared at him for a beat, biting into her bottom lip. She fanned her fingers out over him, her touch as light as gossamer, so soft that Jacob felt it all the way up his spine like a fuse that had just been lit.

His groan surprised both of them. But Anna didn't pull away this time. She squeezed harder.

"That's it," Jacob rasped, moving his hips for her. "Hold me like that, sweetheart."

But, true to form, Anna would not be dictated to. She matched his movement with punishing strokes of her own, pumping her fist up and down his shaft.

Jacob was like a puppet, his entire body held on strings under Anna's control. But it was his damned fault. He'd given her free rein to explore—and explore she did. She pumped him fast and slow, hard and soft, even using both hands at times. Jacob could barely keep up. Sweat drenched his forehead, his body was on a precipice, and the ground was shaking.

"Is this what you want?" Anna asked as she worked him, draping herself down next to him so she could plant more kisses on his chest. Her breath tickled his ear. "Or is this?" she said, her hand moving faster. She licked the cords on his neck.

Jacob's pelvis lifted off the mattress; his hands balled into fists at his sides. He was unmoored. Every time he reached for her, Anna inched out of his grasp. She was making this all about him. But the more she pumped him, the higher and farther she took him, he concluded that he didn't want to take this journey alone. Jacob needed Anna to fly with him.

Flooded with desire, he flipped Anna on her back and tossed her skirts up to her chest. "Keep going," he growled, shoving her hand back on his cock. Her eyes were wide, but she didn't falter. She only nodded, taking his rod in her hand again, rubbing the tip of it against her inner thigh.

But Anna couldn't hold back her scream as Jacob thrust two fingers into her hot passage, massaging her pearl with the fat of his thumb.

Yes. That was what he wanted. Anna stretched her neck to the headboard, her tendons straining into a V-shape. He caressed her pussy and dipped his head into that V, flickering the indentation with his tongue.

"We'll go together," Jacob said against her flesh. "Can you do that?"

Anna's mouth opened, but nothing came out. She nodded instead.

"No," he said, reaching deep with his fingers, caressing her swollen and tight insides with his expertise. His movements were fluid and sure, and he watched her now, as closely as she'd watched him, making sure that he was hitting the notes that would make Anna sing. He kissed her jaw, sucking it with desperation and disappointment because it wasn't her lips. "I need to hear you say it. Say you will come when I will."

"I will … I will," she answered. Jacob wasn't even sure Anna knew what she was saying. Eyes closed, forehead creased with lines, she was in the throes of ecstasy, wild with abandon.

Her hand had slackened, her grip loose on his cock, but it was still holding him, and that was all Jacob needed. He was so close.

Anna could touch the tip of him with her fingertip and he would still explode. He was waiting. For her passion to build. For her journey to reach its end.

They moved together. All hips and groans, ragged breaths and frantic need.

Anna arched into his hand, asking—nay, pleading—for more. Just a little bit more. She pulled on his shoulder, asking for everything, giving him infinitely more.

They came together, both screaming at the same moment, jolting and pushing into one another in a grinding, pulverizing manner that left them each boneless and exquisitely depleted on the bed. He fell on top of her, his seed coating her legs, her juices coating the length of his fingers.

Jacob laughed into the mattress. He could die a happy man. Or was he already dead? It didn't matter, not when he felt this alive.

With all his power, he swiveled his neck to find Anna. She still had that smile on her lips. "Do you think you can go back to bed now?" he asked.

But the lady didn't answer. The lady was sound asleep.

Chapter Seventeen

"WHAT DO YOU mean, she's in *your* cottage? What blasted cottage?"

Jacob winced. The drawing room felt impossibly small that morning as he stood across from Sir John. He'd taken the poor man from his breakfast so they might speak alone about the delicate matter. Jacob had never had to meet with a lady's father before, and he certainly never had to inform one that his daughter was still tucked away in his bed. Sir John was actually taking it better than Jacob had imagined. He'd imagined a fist to the jaw.

"On the grounds, near the pagoda."

Sir John's eyebrows rose comically high. "Pagoda? What pagoda?"

"It doesn't matter," Jacob replied. "It's not far. I found her crying last night. She said she didn't want to go back to the house."

"And you just thought you would take her to your cottage, then?" Sir John's comment was laced with innuendo, and it took a monumental amount of Jacob's strength to continue to meet the man in the eye. Faltering would only make him appear more guilty.

Jacob locked his hands behind his back, raising his chin. "I have to admit, sir," he said, "I didn't know what else to do. When your daughter makes up her mind, it can be difficult to change it."

Sir John's face was mottled; his shoulders inched closer to his ears. The man was on the verge, but of what, Jacob wasn't sure. Probably of killing him. Jacob hoped to hell that he never had a daughter. They seemed like a hell of a lot of worry.

He watched Sir John screw up his lips. They twitched back and forth, as if he were contemplating whether to let out any words before he beat Jacob to within an inch of his life. Jacob would have to let him. On the one hand, Sir John was his guest, and one must always be hospitable, but also … it wasn't as if Jacob was completely innocent. Anna had reached for him that morning, but his protestations had been halfhearted at best.

"I …" Sir John stepped to Jacob, who immediately took a step back. "You …" The man's face was as red as a poppy and quickly morphing to crimson.

Coward that he was, Jacob closed his eyes, waiting for the blow to come.

But as seconds passed and he remained standing, he reluctantly cracked one open. Sir John hadn't moved. He was still in that spot, the color slowly draining from his face. The older man stretched his fingers out at his sides—no more hint of a fist.

He exhaled. "You're right," he said. Jacob wouldn't normally describe the man as jovial; however, all the confrontation had simply vanished. "Anna has always had a mind of her own," Sir John went on. "If she didn't want to come back to the house, then there was nothing you could do to make her."

Jacob shrugged. A feeling of guilt nagged at him for getting off this easily. "I could have thrown her over my shoulder and dumped her in her room."

Sir John chuckled through a grimace. "I'm glad you didn't try. Something tells me that wouldn't have gone over well … for any of us."

Jacob tried to laugh, but nothing came out. The oddness of this exchange continued to hit him. Sir John had been a guest at Newton Place for the last few weeks, and this was the longest they'd ever spoken to one another. He was amazed at how natural it was. Then again, the baronet was an easygoing man, always ready with a smile and a placid remark. Jacob had thought him bland at first, though he wondered now if it was something different.

Sir John ran a hand over his face, brushing his light auburn hair off his brow. His gaze darted around the room. "You wouldn't by any chance have anything to drink in here, would you? Something befitting this type of information?"

Finally, something akin to a laugh escaped Jacob. He gave the older man an understanding look while he walked to the bureau and opened its doors, then brought out a crystal decanter of gin along with two glasses. He filled them to the brim and handed one to Sir John, who accepted the gin, raised it in thanks, and then tossed it back, swallowing all the contents in one go.

Jacob did the same. It stung going down like a hive of demented bumblebees had been unleashed inside him. He desperately needed to cough, but Anna's father was taking it like a man, and so he'd be damned if he couldn't as well. Sir John returned the glass, nodding that he'd need another. That meant Jacob would have to have another as well.

He filled the glass again—halfway this time—and handed it over. "She doesn't want to come back to the house today, either," he said.

Sir John's mouth pursed before he, once more, raised the glass in salute and tipped it back. Scrunching his nose, Jacob did the same. He never would have believed that Sir John could drink this well. On the other hand, perhaps having a daughter like Anna made the alcohol go down easier.

Sir John smacked his wet and rosy lips. He admired his empty glass. "This is proper good," he said absent-mindedly. "Ah, yes ... Anna." He cocked his head at Jacob. "You said she told you she was tired?"

"Yes, sir."

"But not ill?"

Jacob shook his head. "I don't think so. She just kept repeating that she needed to sleep."

Sir John sighed. He put his glass down on top of the bureau and began to meander around the room. Jacob was relieved. He wouldn't have been able to keep up with Sir John if the man wished to continue drinking. Ordinarily, Jacob could hold his own ... but not before lunch.

"Damnit, I knew this would happen," Sir John said under his breath, and Jacob wasn't sure if it was intended for him. He remained silent.

"That boy has always caused trouble wherever he goes," Sir John eventually continued. Jacob had no doubt who "that boy" was. Phillip was the kind of man who would always be a boy, always putting his wants and needs in front of others.

Jacob studied Sir John as he moved around the furniture, picking up knickknacks and bric-a-brac and placing them down again. "I could tell Phillip to leave," Jacob offered. "I never wanted him here in the first place."

Sir John stopped perusing long enough to offer him a pitying smile. "Anna would never want that. It would embarrass and alert David that something is wrong."

"You mean to tell me that David doesn't know about their ... their ..." Jacob didn't know what to call it, because he didn't even know all the details of Anna and Phillip's affair. But Sir John did. From the pain in his expression, the father knew all too well.

Sir John shook his head. "David doesn't know all of it. Anna didn't want him to know. She didn't want to ruin their friendship. You see, David and Phillip have been the best of friends since they were children. Just as I was with Phillip's father. I've known that boy since he was in the nursery. Loved him as if he were my own. I knew what he was—*who* he was—but I never imagined that he would treat my family this way."

Every muscle in Jacob's body seized. He wanted to yell at the man, ask him what Phillip had done, but it wasn't his place. He would have to wait until Anna trusted him. It was her story to tell.

Sir John began to meander again, and Jacob understood what he was doing. It was something they had in common. Jacob liked to move his body when he was lost in thought as well. It helped his mind work more smoothly. "She's tired," Sir John said, craning his neck to stare at the embossed roses on the ceiling. "She was tired before when this happened ... after he left ... after she was ill. It lasted too long."

After he left? Something tugged at the reaches of Jacob's mind. "Sir John, did Anna become ill because Phillip left her? Was he the reason for the fever?" Jacob had never put the two occurrences together before. He'd merely assumed that Anna had suffered from a fever like so many others.

Maybe it was the alcohol or maybe Sir John was too lost in his thoughts to consider diplomacy, but the expression he threw at Jacob told him all that he needed to know.

After a pause, Sir John said, "My daughter is strong. But if she needs to sleep, then the best thing we can do is let her sleep. We will tell the servants not to say anything about her whereabouts, and we will inform everyone that she is under the weather. That is all."

Decision made, he moved to leave the room. There was no more to be said.

And yet Jacob couldn't stay quiet.

"So, you trust me," he blurted, just as Sir John was about to open the door. Anna's father turned back and looked at him quizzically. Jacob went on, "You trust me to have her in my cottage. You believe me when I said that my intentions are honorable?"

Never in Jacob's life had he ever asked a man if he thought his intentions were honorable. Jacob knew his heart, and he'd never cared to know what others thought. However, with Sir John, this was important—vitally so.

Sir John stared at him for an interminable length of time. Again, his mouth twisted, and Jacob could only wonder at what he wanted to say versus what he would allow himself. The irony wasn't lost on him. The man that he hadn't trusted—the man that he'd belittled and questioned ever since he'd invited him to his home—was now going to cast judgment on his intentions.

It would have been hilarious if it wasn't so sad.

Finally, Sir John put Jacob out of his misery. "Of course I trust you," he said. "I wouldn't leave my daughter in your care if I didn't."

And then he left. The answer had been thrown out so easily, so naturally.

Jacob only had one thing left to think.

Sir John wasn't bland. He was many things, but he wasn't that.

❊

ANNA FELT HER father's eyes on her as she shuffled about the cottage. After Jacob had left her that morning, she'd found a broom in the corner and swept the floor then tidied the bed. Now she was boiling water for tea.

She needed to stay busy. If she stopped, her rambling thoughts would take over. Worse yet, she would be forced to meet her father's gaze. And she *really* didn't want to do that.

"You do know this is ... awkward ... don't you, dearest?" Sir John asked as she handed him his tea. He sat on the only chair behind the desk, while Anna took a seat on the bed. The way his eyebrows bunched when she situated herself told her that he would have preferred her to sit anywhere else. Sir John trusted his daughter—she had no doubt of that—but the bed was awfully small. She could see the wheels turning in his head—he was wondering where Jacob slept last night, hoping that it was not with her.

Sir John placed his teacup on the table. He was polite, but he hadn't come to the cottage for pleasantries. "How long do you think you'll stay?"

"I'm not sure," Anna said truthfully. There was no reason to lie to her father. "I don't ... I don't want to see him."

"I know you don't, dear girl. I know." Sir John's voice was pathetically forlorn—defeated. It hurt Anna even more knowing that he would have given anything to take away her pain, but he couldn't. There was nothing anyone could do. "I told you to be careful."

"I was careful. I thought ... I didn't expect anything ... I didn't even want anything ... but when he said he needed to talk to me, I thought ..." Anna shook her head. "Well, I don't know what I thought."

Sir John nodded. "People are always different in our memories ... better, most times."

"Yes."

"I'm sorry that I didn't tell you about the letter."

Anna stared down in her lap. "You should have."

"I know."

"But I understand why you didn't."

Sir John placed his elbows on the desk, holding his head in his hands. "I wanted to give Phillip a chance to redeem himself, show me the man he could be."

Anna couldn't fault her father. Hadn't she just done the same thing? Phillip had failed them both.

She got up from the bed and went to her father, wrapping her arms around his neck. Sir John fell into her embrace, holding her forearms with trembling fingers. "I love you, Father."

"I love you too, my girl. So much. I love all of my children so much." He twisted out of her hold so he could look at her. His eyes were wide with fear. "This isn't like before, is it?" he asked. "Please tell me this isn't like before."

Anna's heart clenched. "No, Father, I promise. I'm not ill. I'm just tired, that's all."

"That's how it started before."

No, it hadn't.

Anna had fallen pregnant without knowing it and developed a fever after she'd miscarried. The malaise and despair took root in her body after the fever had lifted. The depression had been infinitely more difficult to recover from.

Anna brushed Sir John's bushy hair off his face. Suddenly, she felt like she was the parent, reassuring the child that she would always be there for it. "I'll be fine," she said. "I promise. I just need a break from it all."

Her father nodded, feathering a hand over his misty, worried eyes. "I understand. Mrs. Wright will as well; however ..." His voice trailed off as he glanced around the cottage. "You could have taken the break inside your room. It's spacious enough. Did you have to choose this place ... choose *him?*"

Anna's spine stiffened. She tried to pull away, but her father wouldn't release her waist. "You don't like him?"

Her father laughed. "I didn't at first. To be honest, the stubborn boy never gave me a chance to. Now, I might be changing my tune."

Anna was surprised by how happy that made her. "I haven't chosen anyone," she said in a defensive tone. "Jacob is my friend."

Sir John's gaze narrowed. "I don't know if he sees it that way."

"There's no other way to see it," she replied. Her voice dropped. "You know what I have to offer."

Sir John pulled her into a ribcage-busting hug once more, a sob bubbling from him before he could hide his face. "Oh, my dear girl. You have everything to offer. If only you would believe it."

Chapter Eighteen

JACOB'S BOOTS SLAPPED down the cold, stone steps. When he reached the entrance to the kitchen, he halted as if he'd run into a wall. All chopping stopped, all conversation stalled, all eyes blinked at him.

He swallowed the lump in his throat. "I need dough," he announced, finding his aunts and Anna's sister on the far side of the room.

Aunt Iris nodded, a contained smile on her face while Beatrice clapped ecstatically. "It's about time, my boy," she answered. "It's about time."

A half-hour later, Jacob was no closer to creating something that resembled a dinner roll, although he did feel better ... which *had* been the whole point.

As Aunt Violet drank a cup of tea, engrossed in her newspaper, Beatrice and Aunt Iris bookended Jacob, taking turns advising and ordering, instructing and downright scolding him.

"No, no, no," Beatrice said, dropping her own perfectly shaped bun on the flour-dusted counter. "That's too much pressure. We told you, you must be gentle. When you write, you don't hold your pen like you're strangling it, do you? Gentle. Soft."

Jacob exchanged a look with Violet, but she merely shrugged, obviously taking the girl's side over his. Though he did appreciate her analogy. His hands immediately relaxed as he rolled the dough against the wooden top. After a few painstaking minutes, something that someone might actually mistake for food emerged.

"Ha!" he cried, holding it up for his tutors to witness. His chest swelled at their approving smiles. Whoever thought he would be so proud of a piece of dough?

"That's wonderful, Jacob. Good for you!" Iris said. Then, with the grin still fresh on Jacob's face, the confounded woman snatched the roll out of his triumphant hand and tossed it on the table.

Jacob's expression lagged along with the pitiful dough. "Why did you do that?"

"Because playtime is over, Jacob," his aunt replied sternly. She crossed her arms. "What are you going to do about Anna?"

He looked over her shoulder to see Beatrice in the exact position as his aunt, with an equally menacing frown. Those formidable women were spending too much time with one another.

"She's resting," he answered. "She says she's tired."

The worry in Beatrice's voice was palpable. "Just like before—"

"No," Jacob snapped. "Your father said it's not like before. She just needs time."

"Time for what?" Iris asked.

"I don't know."

"How much time?" Beatrice said.

"She didn't tell me. I'm not sure she even knows." Jacob spun to face Beatrice. "How long was she *tired* before?"

"After the illness?"

Jacob nodded.

Beatrice's youthful face wrinkled in thought. She picked at the dried dough on her hands. "I'm not sure. I was only thirteen. No one told me anything, I had to listen behind closed doors. It was such a confusing time. Everything was changing—David left for India. I remember Anna became ill, and then, even when the doctors said she had healed, she still remained in bed. She lay there for days and days, maybe months. Father had to beg her to eat. He asked me to read to her to keep her from sleeping the days away. We all knew something was wrong but couldn't say exactly what it was."

Jacob recognized the confusion and despair of someone who wanted to help, who wanted to dress a wound even though there was none to be found. He'd had experience with that as a child when his father would descend into one of his dark moods and take out his frustrations and underlying anger on Jacob's mother. Sometimes, even after the bruises had faded and the cuts had mended, Jacob would still find his mother in bed, staring at the wall, as if she were waiting for it to swallow her.

To the young Jacob, that behavior had been unusual, but not alarming. In those early years, his imagination was still wild and impressionable. If his mother could take comfort in a blank wall, then who was he to say any different? Hadn't he found solace in his writing? His pen and paper provided a world of possibility far removed from his somber home.

In the end, only his aunts could bring his mother out of her melancholic spells. Their effervescence and strength pulled her back to the light—and him—every time. That was one of the many reasons Jacob would journey to hell and back for those women. He would deny them nothing; he would take care of them until his dying breath.

He felt Aunt Iris's hand on his shoulder and knew that they were thinking about the same things. He squeezed her hand before focusing again on Beatrice. "What was it that brought her back?" he asked. "What made her eventually get out of bed?"

Beatrice's eyes became shiny. "I'm … I'm not sure," she stammered. "I don't remember. One day she just joined Father and me at breakfast. and we were so happy that we didn't think to ask why. We just wanted to forget the past and move on … be the family we always had been."

"And Anna seemed the same?"

"Yes," Beatrice said slowly, considering. "Other than her hair, obviously. But she was the same Anna. I suppose she started playing cricket like a madwoman. That's when she heard about the club and got involved with those odd ladies. Father and I thought she was insane for a while with how much she practiced—and made me practice with her—but she was enjoying herself, so we left her to it."

"Cricket?" Jacob repeated, an idea dawning.

Beatrice shrugged. "Cricket."

"Cricket?" Iris repeated.

Jacob glanced over his shoulder, meeting his aunt's gaze. "Cricket."

She smiled at him. "It could work."

"It could work," he agreed, comforted that, once again, they were thinking the same thing.

⫸⫷

THREE DAYS LATER, Jacob had reached the end of his rope.

So had Anna.

"I don't want to go," she whined, flopping down on the bed. Her knuckles turned white as she clawed her hands into the bedsheets. Jacob watched her antics, aghast. Did she truly believe he was going to drag her out of his cottage kicking and screaming like some barbarian?

Though the idea did have merit …

"It's a beautiful day," he said, standing sentry by the door. "There won't be many more days like this. You should go out and enjoy the fresh air."

"I will go out," Anna said. "Later."

Jacob arched a brow. "Later." He snorted. "You mean at night, after everyone has gone to bed."

"I told you that I wanted to be alone."

"I understand that," he said, viscerally reacting to the hurt in her voice. He hated making her feel this way, hating pushing her, but today was the day his plan came to fruition. It was all he had, and he couldn't let her sidestep it before it had a chance to work its magic. "What if I promise you that you won't run into anyone that you don't want to?"

"You can't promise that."

"I can."

Anna yawned, making sure to catch his eye. She was laying it on thick. "I'm so tired. I think I need a nap before I consider a walk today. You know … you could take one with me."

Jacob had prepared for this. Over the last few days, it was the tactic she'd used the most. Whenever he mentioned leaving the cottage, Anna would circumvent his good intentions by suggesting they nap. And he'd be damned if he hadn't given in each time. The temptation had been too great. Holding her, watching her sleep, providing the succor and support she needed to feel safe, was like a drug to him. But, *unfortunately*, too much of anything was no good.

He moved in front of her. Anna batted her eyes innocently, opening them wide. "No more sleeping," he said firmly. He reached for her arms, pulling her up to his level. "Fresh air, blue skies, and a little exercise are what you need."

She twisted her arms from his grasp. "You don't understand, Jacob. It's not that easy to just … feel better. Feel like myself again. It's like everything inside of me is rebelling. I try to laugh and I try to smile, but it's as if my body is physically incapable."

Anna lowered her head, her cheeks going red. Jacob couldn't let her hide from him. He tipped her chin up. Her black lashes were wet. Her honesty had embarrassed her.

"You're right. I don't understand. But I do know what it's like to hide, and I don't want that for you. And I do know it isn't easy, even for someone so strong."

"I'm not strong—"

"Yes, you are," Jacob said, holding her gaze. "But now I need you to trust me. If you want to come back to the cottage after you've seen what I want to show you, then fine. But I'm begging you to try … for me. Can you do that?"

Anna stared at the buttons of his linen shirt for a long pause before eventually sighing. "Fine. Only for a few minutes."

"Good." He unhooked Anna's cloak and placed it over her shoulders while he opened the door, never taking his hand off her for fear that she might run back to the bed. "Everything will be fine. I promise," Jacob said, kissing the side of her head. Anna leaned into his kiss, and when he backed away, she fell against his chest.

"You can't promise that," she said as he nudged her past the threshold.

The sky was overcast. Clouds clung together, blocking out most of the sun. Anna shivered under her cloak, though Jacob wondered if it had anything to do with the temperature. From the corner of his eye, he watched her look around. He caressed the top of her hand with his thumb, hoping to reassure her. Didn't she know him by now? Didn't she know that he would never put her in harm's way?

Jacob had to calm his ego. Phillip had hurt her. Anna couldn't be blamed for her vigilance. It would be his job to continue to show her compassion and perseverance. He looked forward to it.

As the couple made their way out of the Asian garden, Anna's footsteps faltered. She turned to him, panic setting in. "I thought we were staying close?"

Only a little farther. "Just a little bit more."

"Jacob …" Anna's voice warbled. "What is going on?"

"Nothing is going on," he replied, before quickly adding, "Well, nothing you would mind."

Anna tugged her hand out of his, her eyes as sharp as knives. "I knew this was a trick! I told you that I didn't want—"

Crack!

She blinked. "What was—"

A whoop of delight cut her off. The noise was close by, coming from the other side of the tall hedges.

Anna frowned while Jacob sent up a silent prayer. *Just in time.*

Her feet began to move again. No longer needing to be dragged, she marched forward, rounding the hedges to identify the source of the commotion.

Jacob gathered that she had found his surprise when he heard her shriek. He hurried to catch up.

As he came to her side, Jacob saw three women stretched out on the lawn. Wickets were set up for a game of cricket, though nothing was happening at the moment. The women had stopped play and were staring at Anna as she remained stunned on the sidelines.

She opened her mouth a few times before anything came out. Her focus was on the brown-haired woman in the middle of the lawn, no doubt the leader of the trio. "How are you ..." Anna shook her head. "What are you doing here?"

The ostensible leader planted her hands on her hips. Her expression was hard, though not unfriendly. She nodded toward the other two women in the field. "We heard you needed to practice," she said matter-of-factly. "We also heard you were indisposed and couldn't come to the field, so we decided to come to you."

The leader's attention switched to Jacob, and he almost flinched. The woman was uncommonly direct. It was rather jarring. "Hello, cousin," she said, finally flashing a smile. "It's always nice to visit family."

Chapter Nineteen

"**I** GOT IT!" Anna called, focusing on the ball lofting above her. Her cricket club teammate, Miss Jennifer Hallett—now Lady Bramble—had been at bat and popped the ball up. It was an uncharacteristically shallow hit for Jennifer, who usually put the ball on the ground, giving her a chance for a few runs.

Anna positioned herself under the ball, catching it in her hands for an easy dismissal. It wasn't a hard hit, but the leather ball still stung her skin as she captured it.

"Nice job," Miss Myfanwy Wright yelled from the center of the field where she'd bowled the ball. She wiped wisps of her brown hair off her face. "Come in. Let's take a break."

Anna sighed. Her throat was parched, and despite the lack of decent sunlight, her back was drenched in sweat; however, she didn't want to stop. The moment she found the women on the lawn, she'd been overjoyed with the prospect of playing again. It had been months since their match against the Matrons. That win had marked the end of their season, just as it had in years past. However, Anna hadn't been ready for it all to be over. Waiting through another interminable winter seemed like torture. With everything that had been going on—with her father and Mrs. Wright, with Phillip, with Jacob—she'd needed this. She'd needed her friends. She'd needed to move her body and get lost in a game, if only for a little while.

Jacob was the only one who'd noticed that. He'd understood it even more than her.

The four ladies gathered around a table and chairs that the servants had set out. Scones, jams, and fruits were placed on trays along with a fresh pot of tea. Anna smiled from ear to ear as she claimed her seat. Cricket and tea ... *heaven.*

"Now," Myfanwy began after she'd poured tea for all the ladies, "are you ready to tell us what is going on?"

Anna flushed, feeling the heat of the tea—and the scrutiny of the other women—on her face. "I ... I ..." She hadn't the faintest idea how to start. Myfanwy and Heather stared at her expectantly. Anna had played with them for the past three years; there was a familiarity between them that broke through propriety. Only Ruthie Waitrose remained transfixed on her scone. Anna didn't know the young lady as well as the others. This had been her first year with the club, and she wasn't one for easy conversation. Anna had done her best to pull Ruthie from her shell, but it had been difficult. The woman was shy to a fault and preferred to get lost in the team rather than stand out. She was tall for a woman, gangly and rail thin, and always wore absurdly wide bonnets that dwarfed her frame and served to hide the patch of freckles splashed across her nose.

Not for the first time, Anna wondered how the trio had come to her today. Had Jacob written all three, or had he just contacted Myfanwy, asking her to round up the players that she could?

"Well?" Myfanwy prodded, dragging Anna back to the question at hand.

"I haven't been feeling at my best," she answered blandly. It wasn't a lie. It just wasn't the whole truth, either.

Nevertheless, it seemed to be enough for Myfanwy. She took a sip of her tea and nodded. "That's what my dear cousin told me," she said, one side of her mouth tipped up in a sardonic smile.

The others laughed. It was always odd remembering that

Myfanwy and Jacob were related.

Jennifer contained herself before the others and cocked her head at Anna. It was difficult to meet the woman's gaze. Anna had always thought Jennifer uncommonly beautiful with her clear blue eyes and wheat-colored hair, and she wasn't alone. The daughter of a soap merchant, Jennifer had made a brilliant match months ago and was now married to a baron. The story of the wedding day was still a little confusing—Anna didn't know all the sordid details—but both families had covered it up well enough so as to not invite *too* much speculation.

"But how are you *really?*" Jennifer asked in her soft, amiable way. "When Lord Newton wrote to Myfanwy, it all sounded rather urgent."

Heat rose on Anna's neck. She hated being talked about like this, like she was some wounded child or jilted wallflower. "I'm fine, truly. He shouldn't have alarmed you."

"Well … men are emotional," Myfanwy stated firmly. "It cannot be helped. He was worried."

"There's nothing to worry about," Anna replied stiffly.

Myfanwy's eyes narrowed.

"It's all right if she doesn't want to talk about it," Ruthie said, beating Myfanwy to the punch.

Anna gave the young lady an appreciative smile. "Thank you."

Myfanwy tossed her hands up. "Well, we can't help you if you don't tell us."

Anna laughed. Myfanwy was a true captain, upset when she couldn't fix a problem as soon as possible. "You are helping me just by being here and playing with me. I've …" Her throat closed up. "I've missed this … so much. I honestly don't know how I'm going to get through the winter without it."

The ladies nodded empathetically. Clearly, Anna wasn't alone in that sentiment.

"It will go quickly," Jennifer said, always the optimist. "We learned your brother is recently home from India. That's very exciting! And your father is thinking about remarrying." She sat straighter in her seat, her words gaining momentum. "And you have your younger sister. I'm sure she is a great comfort to you. Does she have an interest in cricket?"

"No," Anna replied. "She's actually very good, but she has no great love for the game. Besides, her thoughts are elsewhere of late."

Jennifer smiled kindly. "Boys?"

"Baking," Anna returned.

"Ugh," Myfanwy groaned. "I'm not sure which is worse."

"Ladies, really," Anna said, fiddling with the napkin in her lap, "I was just going through a rough patch. Things will come around. They always do. I thank you for your concern, but it's unnecessary. I will find a way to keep busy. Perhaps I will throw myself into charity work."

She hadn't thought about charity before, but now that she'd mentioned it, it made perfect sense. Yes. Charity work. It was just the thing to keep her from sleeping her days away or lamenting misfortunes. One must always look outward. The light inside her flickered at the idea, though it still felt abnormally weak.

Myfanwy took a hurried sip of tea, returning her cup to its saucer with a *clank*. "Oh, that reminds me. I forgot to tell you. Mr. Harry Holmes has donated money to the club."

Jennifer frowned at her best friend. "Donated? Why?"

"Because he's a despicable man who needs to atone for his sins," Myfanwy answered, adding with a shrug, "And I made him."

"Mr. Holmes … the gambler?" Ruthie said quietly.

Myfanwy nodded. "The very one. He says his gambling days are over, but I tend not to believe anything that comes out of his mouth. Once a degenerate, always a degenerate."

"Then why take his money?" Anna asked.

Myfanwy rolled her eyes as if the answer was obvious. "Because money is money, and the club needs it. If the man wants to try to buy his way into heaven, then I won't stop him. I just don't have to like him either."

"Is he that rich?" Ruthie asked. She nibbled on her scone, contemplating. "Does he truly have enough money to believe he can buy his way into heaven?"

"Good Lord, yes," Myfanwy replied. "The man is filthy rich. Some men are just made that way. They have a head for it. They can accumulate money like that," she said, snapping her fingers. "I've been thinking of ways the club could spend it, but I haven't come up with any ideas. Uniforms would be nice? Maybe planting hedges around the playing field? We don't need equipment. We're all set in that department."

The others murmured in collective thought. Thanks to Samuel Everett's sporting goods company, the club was never lacking in bats, balls, and wickets. But Myfanwy's comment sparked Anna's memory.

"What if we host a clinic?" she asked, the idea forming quickly. She had to speak fast to keep up with it. "We could send out an open invitation to all the young girls in the city. They could come for an afternoon and learn how to play cricket. We could use some of the money to provide *them* with new balls and bats."

Ruthie clapped her hands together, but Jennifer was slower in her approval. "Do you believe there are that many girls who want to learn how to play? You see the people who come to watch our games. It's mostly men, mostly voyeurs. Little girls don't grow up thinking about cricket."

"I did," Myfanwy said.

Jennifer grinned. "Yes, but I think we can all agree that you are different."

"I like different," Anna said.

"Me too," Ruthie agreed.

Anna's confidence picked up steam. She perched on the edge of her seat. "Most girls don't grow up playing cricket because they don't have anything or anyone to play with. They play with dolls because that's all they're given. What would happen if we gave them their own bat and ball? How might that change their belief in themselves? I gravitated to cricket because I was tired of feeling weak and lonely, and it provided a new way to express myself. I can only imagine how my life would have been different—how *I* might have been different—if I'd played sooner."

Ruthie regarded her curiously. "Do you want to be different?"

"Not now," Anna said. "But years ago ... maybe. I think many of us are afraid to be different when we are younger. Women are held to such exacting standards, don't you think? I didn't have the confidence."

"And you think cricket can help little girls gain that confidence?" Ruthie asked.

Anna pulled back her shoulders. "I do. I really do."

"I think it's a brilliant idea," Myfanwy announced. Jennifer nodded with an excited grin. "Pick a date and write a letter to the others letting them know what they can do. I'll tell Mr. Holmes and Samuel to get in touch with you as well so you can tell them what you will need."

Anna's stomach flipped. "No, wait. You don't mean for me to spearhead this event, do you?"

"Whyever not?" Jennifer chuckled. "It's your idea."

"Yes, but ..." Anna fought for a compelling argument. "I'm not the captain. I don't have experience—"

Myfanwy cut her off. "Then it's time for you to gain the experience." Her expression softened. "You're one of the players that has been with the club since the beginning, Anna. It's time for you to take on more responsibility."

"But you're the captain, and Jennifer—"

"I might be sitting the next season out," Jennifer interrupted swiftly. She didn't seem at all upset about the statement. On the contrary, her pale skin sparkled as if diamonds were under the surface. Furtively, she placed her hand over her abdomen before taking another drink of tea.

Oh. Now Anna understood.

Myfanwy wasn't half so discreet. "I'm expecting as well," she blurted merrily. A little too merrily, Anna considered, since the woman had only become engaged to Samuel last month. However, they were all friends, and Anna was proud that Myfanwy had shared the news. Her captain knew that her club would never gossip or judge her.

Myfanwy leaned back in her seat with a sigh, almost like she was relieved the information was out. "Samuel is beside himself with the news, but as I said before … men are emotional. He would only let me come today if I promised him that I wouldn't break a sweat. I kept my promise, but running a clinic might be too much."

Anna grinned. Myfanwy was intense about cricket during the best of times. Surrounded by a crowd of young girls, the captain might be too tempted to demonstrate every swing and delivery, giving every inch of herself in the pursuit of ushering in the love of the game to a new generation of female players.

Myfanwy zeroed in on Anna. "So that leaves you. Don't let the team down."

THE DAY ENDED too quickly. After tea, Anna gave her friends a tour of the grounds so they could experience the pagoda that she'd told them about. Prudently, she'd left the hermit's cottage out of the conversation, and they hadn't noticed it as they ambled by.

With the sun sinking below the horizon, she said goodbye to them, standing to the side of the carriage as the women took turns hugging her.

Jennifer squeezed her arms tightly, hesitant to let her go. Anna recognized an unrelenting concern in the woman's features and wondered what else Jacob had written in his letter. "I can't wait for the clinic," Jennifer said. "I know you will do an amazing job."

"I will do my best," Anna replied meekly. Her confidence had waned since she first announced her idea, and the planning that had to be done was making her regret opening her mouth. It would be a challenge, and only two days ago she hadn't the strength to get out of bed. But she would be ready for it. She had to be. The thought of letting her friends down was unthinkable.

Myfanwy inspected Anna as if she were debating which position to start her in a match. Anna raised her chin to the examination.

"You'll be fine," Myfanwy said. It sounded like she was trying to convince herself as much as Anna.

Anna put on a brave face. "It's just a bunch of girls. It won't be that bad."

Myfanwy didn't laugh at the attempt at a joke. "I wasn't talking about the clinic." She nodded toward the house. "I was talking about whatever is going on in there."

"Oh …" Anna's head fell. "It's nothing."

"It's not nothing," Myfanwy said. "How could it be when every time I look up at the window, I see him staring down at us?"

Anna's lips quirked. She twisted her neck to the house, and sure enough, she caught Jacob watching them from his office window. He jumped out of sight the instant he realized they'd spotted him.

"He's been doing that all day." Myfanwy chuckled.

"I know."

"Checking on you."

"Yes," Anna said. She didn't know what else to say about it. She couldn't explain his behavior, nor the silly way it made her feel. Like she was warm all over, huddled in his arms in bed. Safe. Cared for. It made her want to throw all caution aside, run to Jacob, and jump into his embrace, kiss him until he forgot his name.

But that notion was absurd—even more absurd than the idea that he was hers to do with as she wanted. If they had no future together, then what would be the point? Why start something that she couldn't finish?

"You know," Myfanwy began gently, "I never planned on getting married. I was adamantly against it."

Anna's attention snapped back to her captain. "You were?"

Myfanwy nodded. "I saw no point. I was fortunate enough to have an income I could live on. I had my club. I didn't think I needed anyone."

This didn't make any sense to Anna. When she saw Myfanwy and Samuel together, it was as if the stars had aligned. There couldn't be one without the other, they complemented each other so well.

"Then how did you … Why …?" Anna wasn't sure what she was asking, but she knew it was too personal.

Luckily, Myfanwy didn't see it that way. "I wanted a lover," she said matter-of-factly. Anna was certain that if she'd been drinking her tea at that moment, she would have spit it out. Myfanwy could be blunt at times, but this was *blunt*. "I thought I had a right to experience everything in life regardless of my marital status. And I wanted Samuel."

It was ridiculous for a woman as experienced as Anna to be blushing, but her cheeks felt like they were on fire. "So that's when your mind changed? After you …"

Good Lord, she couldn't even say the words.

"After we became *lovers*?" Myfanwy snorted. "Heavens no. I'm marrying the man because I love him. And he's made it very inconvenient to live without him. Love changes things. It makes them better in all ways."

Anna scowled. "That's not my experience," she muttered. "I've been in love, and I'm positive that it ruined my life." She hadn't meant to say all that. What good was dredging up her history with Phillip? The past could never be changed.

Myfanwy placed her hand on Anna's shoulder. "Did you ever stop to think that that wasn't true love?" she asked gently. When Anna didn't answer, Myfanwy continued, "Love is something that two people experience together. You give as much as you take. It's like cricket, really. One can't play it alone."

"Perhaps," Anna mumbled.

"You're too young to give up. I don't know what happened to you before, and I'm not going to demand you tell me. But you have your whole life in front of you. Don't give some bastard from your past the satisfaction of ruining your future."

"I'm not giving up," Anna returned.

"You're not living, either."

"You don't understand—"

"Then help me understand."

Anna spun around, tears coming hot and fresh to her eyes. She didn't want Myfanwy to see her that way. The captain never cried.

"Tell me, Anna," Myfanwy said. "Tell me why you can't move on. I've only been here a few hours and I can see how much Jacob loves you. What is stopping you from going to him?"

Loves me?

Anna's voice came out strangled. "Jacob doesn't even know me. If he did, he'd ..."

"What?" Myfanwy asked. "He might love you more?"

"He doesn't love me."

"You're not giving him a chance to."

"It's for his own good." Anna turned back to face Myfanwy. She and Jennifer would never comprehend it. They had their happily ever after. They had their husbands and fiancés and soon-to-be-families. They couldn't possibly realize how lucky they were. They had done everything right and been rewarded. They had waited for the right man, and now everything was perfect.

Anna had been impulsive, impetuous. She'd fallen for the first smooth-talking devil she came across and would never be able to live it down. Her father had forgiven her, but Anna knew now that she would never be able to forgive herself.

Myfanwy waited for her to speak. Anna didn't have any fight left in her, so she said the truth. It was the only way to make her captain see her for who she really was. "I am not an innocent."

Myfanwy glanced at her belly with a little smile. "Neither am I."

It would have been funny if it wasn't so sad. "Yes, but I cannot have children … *anymore*."

The last word came out in a rush of air, barely above a whisper. It was wrapped in grief, gifted in heartache.

Anymore. It landed like stone between them. *Anymore.*

Anna stared at the ground. "I can't give a husband a child."

Myfanwy came forward quietly. Without saying a word, she wrapped Anna in her arms, holding her tight. Like liquid into a cup, Anna poured herself into her friend. "I have nothing to give," she said into the crook of Myfanwy's neck.

"Shh," Myfanwy said. "You have so much to give." She pulled away so she could look in Anna's eyes. "Especially since all Jacob seems to want is you."

"But I'm not enough."

Myfanwy's lips hardened into a line. "The only person who believes that is you."

Chapter Twenty

JACOB SENSED ANNA was standing in the doorway before she knocked. Her scent infiltrated the room, an intoxicating blend of roses and lavender, but that wasn't all of it. Jacob could also smell himself on her. Sleeping together had created a unique mixture that clung to her, spicy and sweet, that would forever alter his consciousness. He'd been reduced to a bloodhound. He could locate Anna anywhere.

"Are you going to come in?" he asked, pretending to study the papers on his desk. It was all a ruse. He couldn't concentrate when she was so close. Hell, he'd barely been able to write a complete sentence since she had set foot in his house.

Anna lowered her hand, which had been poised to knock, and stepped lightly into the office. She made a point of wandering around the space, lifting random tomes from the shelves. Jacob watched her fingers trip along the various articles, gliding over book spines and smooth wood. He wanted those fingers to skate over his body; he wanted her to explore him with equal curiosity.

She lifted a stack of papers from his desk with a playful grunt. "I didn't expect this. It's much more cluttered than your cottage." *Your.* The word stung him. He'd begun to call it "theirs" in his mind.

Jacob took the stack out of her grasp and placed it neatly back where she found it. "I inherited it this way," he said gruffly. Straightening his shoulders, he shoved his hands in his pockets. "I don't care what it looks like, not enough to go to the trouble of changing it."

Anna nodded, though her brow pinched in between her eyes. She crossed her arms, scrutinizing his space. Jacob followed her lead, regarding the room that he spent most of his waking hours in. He'd never taken the time to judge it before. The yellow and red wallpaper and dark brown molding seemed fitting enough. He didn't particularly enjoy the color scheme, nor the fact that the old viscount had an obvious affinity for jungle animal figurines, but who was he to complain? If it was good enough for the old man, then it was good enough for him.

She lifted an onyx jaguar statue from a side table, scrunching her nose as she inspected it. "This doesn't seem like you."

Jacob scowled. Should be offended? Shouldn't all men want a woman to compare them with a sinewy beast, a king of any forest? He tried to pull forth indignation, but it proved too difficult. Jacob hated that ridiculous piece. Small red gems were inserted in the eye pockets, giving it a satanic appearance. It was why he always positioned it to look away from him. How could anyone expect him to think with that monstrosity directed at him?

"As I said," he replied, "it came with the house."

Anna returned it to its place. "And the house is now yours."

"And?"

"And you should make it feel like yours." She came toward him, and the more space she ate up between them, the more vulnerable Jacob felt. Was it what she said or her mere presence that did this to him?

Both. It was both.

Anna walked around his desk, stopping in front of him. "Maybe if you made this home feel more like yours then you wouldn't have to hide in the cottage so much."

"I thought you liked our little cottage," he teased. It was the only way he could put her on the defensive. Jacob didn't want to speak about his lack of decorating skills. He didn't want to discuss why he assumed the old viscount's dismal taste was probably better than anything he could dream up. With Anna so close, smiling so mysteriously, all he wanted to do was throw her down on his desk and ravish her. He only cared about the function of his furniture. Would it hold their weight? He didn't give one fuck about the form of it all.

Finally, Anna's little smile faltered, and he noticed her growing skittish.

Jacob took pity on her. "Did you have something you wanted to ask me?"

She lowered her head, seeming to need a moment to gain her confidence. Now he was truly intrigued. The past few days had created a fellowship between them, a bonding of mind and body. What could she be contemplating that would make her so nervous?

Jacob could no longer restrain himself. He reached out and wrapped his hands around her forearms, but when he tried to bring her closer, Anna resisted.

"No, wait," she said, placing her palms on his chest. Jacob stretched his neck from side to side. He loved it when she touched him there, usually because she would unbutton his shirt slowly, unmercifully next. However, her fingers didn't budge this time. They stayed exactly where they were.

"I need to thank you for inviting the ladies over," she began after a fortifying breath. "They were just what I needed."

"Of course," Jacob returned gruffly. It was difficult to accept thanks when visions of her naked body were dancing in his head. He felt like a degenerate wastrel.

Anna went on, "But I need to ask for more of your generosity."

"Yes?"

"The club has asked me to spearhead a cricket clinic for the young girls in town. I want it to be a success, and the only way I will be able to do that is if we get the word out."

Did she know her fingers were moving? Because Jacob surely did. They were playing with his button. How could her fiddling with such a small, inanimate object make his cock stiffen to attention so quickly?

He shifted his weight on his feet, flattened her palm on his chest, and lowered his forehead. "If you want me to actually listen to what you're saying then you should stop doing that."

"Oh! Yes … sorry."

"Go on."

Anna frowned. "Right. Yes …"

Jacob lifted his brow. "You want the clinic to be a success …"

She slapped her hand against him. "Yes! A success. So, we need as many families to know as possible, which means an article in the newspaper. So would you do it?"

"Do what?"

"Write an article about the clinic?"

Jacob was stumped. She was asking him to write about the club? His natural response was to say no. He had already told her that that life was behind him. Viscounts didn't have professions. But the way she was staring up at him, her green eyes hopeful and wide as she bit into the side of her cheek, Jacob felt like he was seven feet tall. He felt like a knight of the Round Table. He felt like he belonged … to her.

So he wasn't as bewildered as he should have been when he heard himself reply, "Of course." It was just one little article. Surely he could do that much without causing a stir.

Jacob knew he'd made the right decision when her grin, so wide and beautiful, struck him straight in the heart like Cupid had shot an arrow with all his might.

Anna wrapped her arms around his neck. "Oh, thank you, thank you," she cried. "I didn't want to ask because of what we'd talked about before, but I was desperate and I really want this to go well. I have to show the others that I can be a leader, and you're the only person I know who works for the papers, and I can't believe I'm going to do this ... I really don't have that much time. I better get started ... maybe I should ask Beatrice to help, although I'm not sure if that's a good idea, since her mind is stuck in the kitchens. What do you think? Oh, don't answer that. You're busy. Here I am taking up all your time. I should let you get back to whatever it is you were doing."

Jacob laughed through the whirlwind of words. He didn't even try to make sense of all that she said. He was just happy that she was happy—and doing something. Who would have thought that having a purpose meant so much to women? Perhaps more men should register this important fact.

"All right. All right," he said, unwrapping her arms from his neck. "Don't you know I'm a viscount? I'm a very important man with very important things to do."

Anna smirked. "Oh, yes, how could I forget?" She rose to her tiptoes and brushed a kiss on Jacob's cheek. He jerked back as if he'd been scalded. Didn't she know what she did to him? How could she expect to do that and then just leave as if it were nothing? *Was* it nothing to her?

She edged around the desk toward the door, her hips swinging merrily along the way. Jacob was just about to fall into his chair when she turned around suddenly.

"Oh, I should mention that I've moved out of the cottage," she announced.

The ease with which she said the words were like a knife in Jacob's gut. Was it all over? And so quickly? She didn't need him anymore ... and that was that.

He struggled to keep his cool, to stay nonchalant with the unexpected report. "Right," he replied placidly. "Yes ... that makes sense. Now that you're feeling better."

Anna's expression fell, but he couldn't read it. To be fair, Jacob was having a difficult time looking at her. He was afraid that if he gave her the chance to peer into his eyes, she would see how upset he was.

"I can't thank you enough for what you did," Anna said. Even those simple words made him burn with shame. They were laced with sympathy ... for him.

"It was nothing," Jacob said, his face like stone. He picked up the papers on his desk once more and shuffled them straight. God, he felt like an idiot, but he needed to do something while the woman ripped his heart out of his chest and threw it on the ground. "Good day, Anna."

"Oh, oh, yes ... good day," she replied slowly. After a pause, she turned once more to the door, as if she still had more on her mind. Why wouldn't the woman leave? What more could she possibly have to say to him?

Jacob sat down in his chair, hoping that would be enough to encourage her out of the room for good. Yes ... for good. He didn't need her ever coming back in. It would hurt too damned much.

Anna's skirts fanned as she twirled back to face him.

Jacob couldn't hide his grimace. In frustration, he dropped his head, just narrowly missing hitting his forehead on the wood.

"What now?" he asked pathetically. A man could only take so much distraction!

"I would like to come to you tonight ... in your room," she said quickly. She folded her hands primly in front of her. "I would like to ... be intimate ... have relations ... If that is agreeable to you?" She didn't wait for a response. "So, you should expect me after dinner, after everyone has gone to bed. Good? Good. Have a pleasant afternoon, Jacob."

Anna finally fled the room.

She wasn't there to see Jacob's forehead hit the desktop.

"WHAT'S WRONG WITH you tonight? You've already broken one glass, and if you aren't careful, you're going to break another!"

Jacob blinked, staring down the table at his mother, who had just chided him in front of the entire party. A few snickers were heard as he muttered an apology. He released the stem of his wine glass and carefully slid his hand away from the precious crystal. Drinking wasn't as good an idea as he'd thought it would be. He'd hoped it would settle his nerves, but it was making him feel like a discombobulated child.

"Is anything wrong?" Anna asked. She sat two places away on his right, but Jacob could still spot the suggestive half-smile she wore as she tucked into her sole. The little minx. She knew what she was doing. And she was enjoying every bit of his discomfort!

"I'm fine," he returned, showing her his teeth. Anna looked away. *Yes. Very smart. Be careful, little one. This wolf likes to play but he can also bite.*

Mrs. Wright spared them each a shrewd glance; clearly, his mother knew something was going on between them, but she hadn't figured out what it was yet. Thank the Lord for small mercies.

"We're so happy to see that you are feeling better, Anna," she said. She smiled at Sir John, who couldn't contain the glee he felt in having his daughter back with the group.

"Yes," David added generously, elbowing his sister playfully in the side. "It wasn't the same without you."

Anna brushed away the attention with a little laugh. "I was just tired. A little peace and quiet was all that I needed. The last few weeks have been rather stimulating."

"I think we can all agree with that," Aunt Iris said. "But we did miss you."

"I missed you too," Anna replied shyly.

Phillip shifted self-importantly in his seat. Jacob noted how he adored being the center of attention. The man had a knack for bringing every conversation back to him. "You know, I learned something in India that might be of use to you," he said, waiting for all eyes to float his way. "It's something the mystics teach. Apparently, you sit quietly alone and empty your mind. A meditation of sorts. It's supposed to be rather helpful for settling the nerves." He sniffed. "Or so they say."

"What do you mean, 'empty your mind'?" Beatrice asked.

Phillip leaned toward her conspiratorially, his lips contorting into a smile. Jacob darted a glance at Sir John, who didn't appear to appreciate Phillip's closeness to his young daughter. Why was the blasted man still here? For Anna's sake, Jacob refused to ask him to leave, but his presence was such a nuisance. Didn't the man have his own home to return to? What more could he need from Sir John's family?

"Well, I have to confess that this is where it gets confusing," Phillip explained. "One must sit for long periods of time and try not to think of anything." He pretended to pluck something from Beatrice's hair and toss it up in the air. "Cull your thoughts the moment they come to you."

"And then what?" Beatrice asked.

Phillip shrugged, returning to his plate. "And then something happens."

"But don't you have to think about something to happen for it to happen?"

Aunt Iris picked up her wine glass. "This is getting much too philosophical for me."

Phillip chuckled. "Forgive me. This isn't a proper conversation for ladies. I should have known that you would have a difficult time understanding the concept. It's ridiculous anyway. The people who do this meditation also believe in reincarnation. It's complete nonsense."

Anna's eyes narrowed into slits. "How lucky we are to have you always looking out for our best interests," she said, her tone chilly.

Phillip raised his glass to her with a tight smile, but she didn't repeat the gesture.

"Oh, do go on, Mr. Williams," Violet implored, leaning her elbows on the table. "What is supposed to happen if you clear your mind?"

Phillip stared at the offending elbows before continuing. "I must admit, I'm not an expert on the topic."

Anna snorted.

"I think I can answer," David said. "From what I've been told, one must clear one's mind in order to reach Nirvana."

"Nirwanna?" Sir John asked.

"Nirvana, Father," David explained patiently. "It's a term for spiritual enlightenment. Many religions in the east believe it."

"Well, I daresay enlightenment most certainly could be useful," Sir John said cautiously. "Even the spiritual kind." Mrs. Wright patted his arm in agreement.

David smiled. "It's supposed to be incredibly difficult to achieve. I've tried meditating, but I need lots more practice if I ever hope to master it."

"You practice this?" Beatrice asked. "Clearing your mind?"

David nodded. "It's actually incredibly calming. It can be beneficial especially if one has scattered, errant thoughts."

Jacob chuckled to himself. He doubted that all the meditation in the world could help his disjointed thoughts at the moment. He couldn't get Anna out of his mind. Would she truly come to him tonight? Why now? Did the answer have to matter so much?

"What does it feel like to reach Nirvana?" Beatrice asked.

"I have no idea," David replied. "I've never experienced it. But I read that it means complete peace, a release from suffering, a departure from the physical world."

Beatrice studied her brother, growing more animated. "Like heaven?"

"I think so," David said slowly.

"Do we have to die if we reach it?"

"I don't think so." The poor man was completely out of his element.

Beatrice looked around the table. "Oh, well then, that's lovely to hear." She clapped her hands. "I want to do it. Let's find it tonight, shall we? This Nirvana!"

Aunt Violet raised her glass of wine. "Oh yes, I want to find Nirvana. I'm sure this meditating can't be that hard—no offense,

David. Let's do it in the drawing room!"

"Ooh!" Aunt Iris squealed. "I'll bring biscuits in case anyone gets hungry! Meditating will be so much more fun than another card game." She turned to her nephew. "What about you, Jacob? Any interest?"

"Christ, no," he stated firmly. "No offense, David."

"Not at all, but I really must warn you all—"

But it was too late. The horse had bolted. David had sold the activity too well.

He attempted to rein in the excited conversations. "Ladies, no, I ... I'm not sure that's how it works ..."

However, the determined chatter could not be broken. A goal had been set. Nothing would stand in the way of the party's feverish belief in its capabilities. Nirvana would be reached tonight, no matter what.

For his part, Jacob sat back and enjoyed the frenzied discourse. He would thank David later. With the house focused on achieving this new endeavor, he could slip out early and wait for Anna to come to his room in peace.

Though he wished them luck. He wouldn't need it.

Jacob had no doubt he would find his own source of enlightenment tonight ... in the crux of Anna's thighs.

Chapter Twenty-One

THERE WAS NO point in knocking. Anna had told him to expect him, and she was right on time.

Or relatively on time. She was actually half an hour late. But she couldn't decide on what to wear. What should one look like when skulking through the corridors after everyone had gone to bed? This was all new to her. Her tardiness should be excused.

Confidence, Anna. Confidence. She stared at the cream-colored wood. *Just open the door. Just open the—*

The door swung open. A disgruntled-looking Jacob scowled at her before quickly craning his neck past the threshold.

"Get inside," he said, grabbing her forearm and yanking her into his room. He slammed the door behind her. "Christ, you're in your nightgown."

Jacob stood in front of her, running his hand through his hair. He didn't let go of it. He tugged at the ends while he regarded her with a ferocious scowl.

Anna wrapped her arms around her waist, feeling incredibly vulnerable … and annoyed. This interlude was supposed to be exciting, heartwarming, life-affirming … and the incorrigible man was behaving as if she was a large bother.

She gathered her courage. "Fine. You don't want me here, then I'll just go—"

Anna spun to the door, but she didn't get far. She felt Jacob's arms encircle her hips, holding her in place.

"Now, I didn't say all that." His mouth grazed her ear, causing the hair on the back of her neck to tingle. "I'm just trying to understand what game you're playing, is all."

"There's no game," Anna said, twisting in his embrace. Jacob hadn't disrobed yet and was still dressed in his dinner jacket. She ran her hands under the heavy wool. His waistcoat was white and silky, and she liked how she could feel his body underneath her fingertips, feel the bumps and ridges of his ribcage. "I told you I would come, and now I'm here. You won't let me leave, so I assume you are in agreement with what will happen tonight."

Like a piece of leather left out in the sun, his resolve was softening. "And just what will happen tonight?" he asked with genuine curiosity.

Anna almost rolled her eyes. "I already told you." Even in his arms in his bedroom, she didn't want to have to say it again.

But that man wouldn't let up. "But why?"

"Because I want to."

"But why?"

Anna wanted to pinch him. If she could find an ounce of fat on his body, she might have. She lowered her head so that she was staring at his chest. "You know why."

"I don't. *Ow!* Don't pinch me! I just want to make sure we're doing this for the right reasons."

What *were* the right reasons? Anna had made love to Phillip and thought his need was the only reason. He'd wanted her, and that had been reason enough for her. It was only now that she realized giving a man you thought you loved something that they wanted wasn't the same as wanting it yourself. She'd wanted Phillip so much that she'd given him everything without stopping to consider how it would affect her.

Not anymore. Anna wanted this. She wanted Jacob. And she was tired of not getting what she wanted.

She dredged up all the confidence in her body and finally

looked him in the eye once more. Jacob's face was so open, so accepting. But he was also wary. He was protecting his heart, and Anna couldn't fault him for that.

"I want to make love to you, Jacob. You once told me that you knew what lust felt like. I've never experienced that, and I want to with you. That's all I'm offering here tonight. I've already told you, I have no dreams of marriage or love. But I will accept passion, if you'll share it with me."

Anna's body felt light, like everything had just been dragged out of her and put on display. Jacob studied her for a long pause, making her stomach even more jittery.

"I thought you said lust was weak," he murmured. "And you are not weak."

He played with the short ends of her hair. It was like feeling the breeze on a scorching day, so blissfully necessary. "It's only a weakness if you let it rule you." Anna let her fingers explore. Starting at his throat, she unwound his necktie, not stopping until the long piece of fabric was on the floor. She wasted no time with the buttons, unfastening them at his waistcoat and then the top half of his shirt. He tensed while she worked. Even his breath seemed suspended between them as his entire being centered on her.

When she dipped her hands into the opening of his shirt, Jacob's shoulders finally trembled like a tiny earthquake, here one moment, gone the next. Anna leaned forward, filling her lungs with his essence, filling her future memories with the masculine aroma that was Jacob, the spicy scent that made her knees tremble so badly she had to lock them into place. She didn't know what had come over her as she rubbed her face back and forth against him, coating herself in that smell. "Lust doesn't rule me. I am ruling lust."

The black hair on Jacob's chest scratched her as he laughed. His arms tightened around her waist. A connection was made. Their bodies formed a knot that would not be broken tonight. "Silly woman." His voice was deep and husky, and a chill ran through Anna. Oddly enough, it made her want to rip off their clothes, as if being skin to skin was the only way she could feel warm again. "There's no controlling passion."

"There isn't?"

She tilted her head to see Jacob's lopsided grin. He shook his head.

Anna returned a teasing frown. "Then should I give up now?"

Jacob's embrace squeezed the breath out of her. "Where would the fun be in that?"

Anna let out a yelp as he hoisted her up in his arms. She had enough time to sweep her arms around his neck as he lifted her legs around his middle and palmed her backside with his hands. There was nothing lopsided about his smile now. He grinned from ear to ear as he led her to his bed.

His carefree demeanor was enchanting, and instantly Anna knew that she'd made the right decision. He would never lie to her or take advantage of her. Her heart was safe.

Gently, Jacob placed her on the bed. Anna only had a second to admire the soft royal-blue brocade and matching bed curtains before he stole all her attention. He stood to the side stripping off his clothes. Anna dug her fingers into the mattress as if it were a life raft.

Her giggle surprised her. Jacob raised an eyebrow at the sound but didn't halt in his undressing. He wasn't trying to be funny; however, the slapdash way he tore the clothes from his body, messing up his hair in the process, was adorably impatient.

Anna had never actually seen a naked man before. In the few times she'd been with Phillip, he had never taken off all his clothing, and she had never taken all of hers off either. It had all been so hurried, so clandestine, so ... *perfunctory*. Love, apparently, had a time limit.

Well, lust and passion did not. Because even after Jacob was completely naked in front of her—without a hint of shame or embarrassment—he didn't jump on her. His chest rose and fell while he looked his fill of her. As if Anna was the one on display.

As if she was the only gift that had been opened in that room.

"You're a beautiful man," she blurted out. Had she gone insane? Why else would her lips suddenly feel so untethered to her mind?

Nevertheless, Anna wasn't lying. Jacob's body was beautiful to her. His lineage was written in his blood, chiseled in his bones. She could see the knights of his ancestors carved into the lines of muscles that flowed effortlessly over his figure. How could anyone mistake him for anything other than a viscount?

For a man of his height, Jacob wasn't wiry or lanky. His limbs were long and well formed, his shoulders broad, his hips narrow. Hair was sprinkled across his chest and tapered down to his waist, where it nestled along his manhood.

Anna's cheeks flamed as she admired him—all of him.

"I've never had anyone call me that before," Jacob said.

"Fools, all of them." The flush along his cheekbones made Anna bolder. "Are you done standing there?" she asked, raising her knee. "Are you done begging for my admiration?"

Jacob choked on a laugh. He ran a hand over his face, attempting to contain himself. "Believe me, I'm not begging for anything. I'm trying to figure out what to do with you."

Anna's nerve wavered. "I thought that would be obvious, no? Our goal is to let passion and lust guide us."

Jacob's cheeks ballooned before he released a monumental sigh. Anna realized he was holding back. She just couldn't understand why.

"I don't know if that's a wise decision."

"Why?"

Mercifully, Jacob came toward her. He placed his hands on either side of her face, ducking his head until his lips were inches from hers. "Because once I taste you … once I taste what has been simmering between us, I'm afraid I won't be able to live without it."

Anna rubbed his shoulders, massaging the ball-like muscles. Her smile was thin. Her body was screaming for something to happen, and Jacob continued to take his sweet time. "That's what makes passion so special," she said, pulling him until he crawled on top of her. He held half of his weight on his arms, but the rest of him was enough. Jacob on top of her was like being covered in sand, warm and intense, claustrophobically safe.

She trailed her nose along his collarbone, licking at the thin skin covering it. "Passion fades. Lust fades. This is why we are taking advantage of each other now. This is the best it is ever going to be. There's no reason to hold on to something that is destined to end."

Jacob pushed her back to the bed. His scowl confused her. "And you're so certain our passion will fade?"

"All passion does. Cleopatra betrayed Mark Antony; Napoleon divorced Josephine; Peter Abelard was castrated by Heloise's father."

"Are we really talking about castration right now?"

"I'm just making a point," Anna said. "Happily ever afters are a thing of myth, so let's be happy now. Can you do that for me, Jacob? Can you make me happy now?"

He closed his eyes. It seemed like he was in the middle of some debate with himself. Why did he continue to resist her? What was the point? He was lying on top of her, naked—why torture himself with questions that needed no answers?

Anna reached up and kissed his neck, light, fleeting kisses that were meant to entice, to distract. "Please, Jacob," she whispered, undulating her hips. She heard a hiss between his teeth. "Share yourself with me. I promise, I won't bite."

Jacob's head hung like a flower with a broken stalk. She could feel his hot, quick breath through her robe. "What if I want you to bite?" he said finally.

Anna hooked her leg over his bottom, rubbing her feet down the back of his legs. Jacob lifted his head, and she could see his pupils grow big. "Then I will bite until you tell me to stop."

He dug his hand underneath her body. When he found the soft mound of her bottom, he palmed her flesh with an intensity that made her limbs feel boneless, her insides ache with raw need. She undulated into him again, and he returned the movement, rocking into her pelvis with a rhythm that made her wild.

All consideration was gone. In its place was a man with a woman he desired in his possession. Anna wanted him to use her, wanted him to slake that need with her until all that was left of them was sweat and exhaustion, and absolutely no regrets.

Jacob's hand continued to venture higher, taking Anna's robe and nightgown with it. Without finesse or any care for the poor garments, he slid them over her head and tossed them on the floor. She didn't have time for embarrassment. Jacob came back to her in an instant, clothing her with his body, his hands falling over her skin in naked abandon.

It was electric, this pairing. Their hands roved and their legs mingled. Anna worried that Jacob might try to kiss her. She hadn't reminded him that she wouldn't allow it, assuming that he would remember her dictates, but she didn't want to have to tell him here and now. She wanted no more breaks in intimacy. Anna only wanted to feel him inside her.

She reached between their slick bodies, pressing into his skin. Jacob's manhood was hard and swollen, and as he arched his hips back, Anna took him in her hand.

Jacob groaned, his elbows shaking as he almost buckled on top of her. "Yes, Anna," he raped, nipping her in the neck. He thrust into her hand, and the tip of his staff jutted into her lower belly. She ran her thumb over the sensitive tip, marveling at the delicate texture.

He laid his head in the valley of her breasts. Over his shoulder, Anna watched the delectable curve of his behind clench and release as he drove into her hand, the power behind the action, the way all the muscles clicked together in an elegant, animalistic design.

He licked her nipple, causing Anna to close her eyes, all appreciation diverted to what he was doing with his tongue. He flicked at it quickly, breaking away to blow cold air on the bud, driving her insane with the maelstrom of sensations. He palmed her other breast, fondling and massaging the soft mound.

Anna was weightless, light as air, and Jacob's words floated to her on this cloud of passion. "Place me inside you," he said, pumping into her hand once more. She opened her eyes and gazed at the ceiling. Jacob's hands were incessant, and his mouth even more so. His body controlled her; his touches bewitched her. Any more than this and she would forget her name.

But that was what she'd wanted, wasn't it? Pure, unadulterated lust. Jacob had been right. There was nothing weak about it.

Anna opened her legs a little further and guided him to her entrance. She felt herself open for him as he slowly nudged inside her, an inch at a time. Anna tensed. It had been years, but she remembered not liking this part, knowing it would hurt.

Jacob slid his hands under her shoulders, cupping them as he pressed inside her passage. "It will be all right," he said. "Just relax for me, sweetheart."

Anna couldn't begin to understand how she was supposed to do that. She was thinking too much. Anxiety was running rampant inside her, dousing all the excitement. She flexed her inner thighs and clenched her teeth as she waited for him to invade her.

Jacob raised his head from her breasts, a sympathetic smile on his face. His skin had a healthy glow. Anna imagined herself as pale as a ghost.

"I don't know how to," she said, embarrassed by the pathetic sound in her voice. What was wrong with her? She wasn't a virgin. Why was she making this so difficult? She tried to pull him back to her. "Can you just … do it? I don't mind the pain; I will deal with it. I want you to feel pleasure."

A deep growl rumbled from Jacob's throat. "It's not going to hurt. I promise you. At least … not like that. Here. Wait."

Withdrawing from Anna, Jacob grabbed the two pillows next to her on the bed. He lifted her pelvis to place them underneath. Her lower half was now at an incline toward him. Jacob took her legs and wrapped them around his hips and came back to her, once more pushing inside her with tender insistence.

"Is that better?" he asked, watching her intently as he seated himself inside her.

Anna didn't want to harm his feelings. But she didn't want to tell him the truth either. It felt … It felt like …

Jacob placed his hands on her belly, stretching out his fingers until he covered her. Then he lifted them until nothing was touching her except the tips of his fingers. Like a wing fluttering over her body, he tickled her skin, slow and languid. Her body was a canvas and Jacob was a painter, sweeping a brush over her hips and breasts, highlighting the curves and valleys of her expanse. She relaxed under his ministrations, delighting in the soft, barely there sensations that made her feel so incredibly cherished.

And with those soothing strokes came something deep and full between her legs. Jacob waited until she was ready for him, and the moment her guard went down, he charged forward, filling her core, connecting their bodies in this holy alliance.

"Oh, sweetheart, you feel so good," Jacob murmured as he arched back slowly and drove into Anna again. "I've never … Fuck … I can't …"

His hands continued to do what his words couldn't. Because even as he worked inside Anna, they didn't stop their dance. They roved over her, continuing to offer solace and a sweet distraction to the pain that never came.

It was like lying naked while rain dropped from heaven, like being kissed in a thousand different places.

It was like being loved. Wholly and exquisitely loved.

And Anna could not have that.

Jacob's pace was leisurely and pensive … a puff of wind causing a field of wheat to ripple. His hips were hypnotic, his gaze watchful and magnetic. They watched each other in silence as their bodies worked in tandem. Each giving. Each taking. A balancing act when all they wanted was to free-fall. Jacob's face betrayed him. There was too much caring. Too much affection.

Undiluted devotion scored into her bones.

And it frightened her.

Because that was not what she'd asked for. Because she still didn't deserve it.

In a fit of fury, Anna held tight to Jacob's forearms and slammed her pelvis into him just as he was filling her. They cried out at the heady sensation. He was so deep inside her. Anna felt him stretch her walls, felt him reach to the ends of her. The pain hit her then. But it was a good pain, a pain she could live with—a pain that shielded her from everything else.

It was another distraction, but this time of her own making.

"Harder," she said.

Jacob planted his hands at her sides. As if he were testing her, he slammed into her, jerking her body on the bed. Anna smiled while she arched her back to the ceiling.

"Harder," she repeated.

"I don't want to hurt you," Jacob replied, but he betrayed his words by charging into her again. He licked his lip as he watched her breasts bounce from the action, and he didn't wait for her to say anything more.

And then he couldn't stop, wouldn't stop. Not with Anna urging him on with her mews and purrs, with her insistent movements, her hips, which gave as good as they got. In no time, their bodies were wet and slick, their chests straining for breath. Jacob's pace was punishing, every push and pull finding him deeper, massaging her walls with ruthless abandon.

Passion took over. They weren't driving the carriage; they were mere passengers as lust showed Anna just how powerful it could be. All thinking was gone. All worry ran out the door. Their bodies and souls embraced in a way that minds couldn't.

The climax hit her without notice. An avalanche of sensations buried her, spurring Jacob to find his own. He grabbed her hips and crashed into her, again and again. The tops of his thighs slapped into her, making a sound that almost made Anna come a second time. She loved the primal way they poured into one another, the dazed look Jacob had when he pumped his final time, crying out in release.

When Jacob fell on top of her, Anna didn't even have enough strength left to fold her arms around him. She kissed the top of his head, though.

And then she smiled. Because she'd managed to avert disaster. Just in time.

All that was left of them was sweat and exhaustion. Minds perfectly clear. No thoughts to be found.

It was a good little death.

Chapter Twenty-Two

J ACOB WASN'T *FOLLOWING* the damn woman. If Anna had stayed in bed like she was supposed to then he wouldn't be chasing after her at all. Needs would have been met in the morning. It would have all been very convenient, very civilized. Yes, he probably would have started to look for her sometime in the late afternoon, but that could hardly be helped. Needs were needs.

However, it was barely midday and Jacob couldn't think. Well … he could think, but those thoughts weren't helpful. They were rather tawdry and centered on a naked Anna back in his bed. This was why he was on the hunt. This was why his work had suffered all morning. This was why he was behaving like a love-struck fool.

After an hour of active, embarrassing searching, Jacob finally caught sight of his elusive woman in the library. Sitting at a desk, head down over her papers, writing furiously, Anna had no idea that he was watching from the doorway. She was fastidious as ever, wearing a perfunctory yellow gown with a tartan headband over the top of her head. It reminded Jacob of something Anne Boleyn would have worn while she was busy seducing the king, only Anna wasn't trying to use her wiles on Jacob now. Her tongue poked out the corner of her mouth as she scribbled away. Jacob's body reacted instantly to that tongue. How he wanted to suck on it; how he wanted to take it in his mouth and mingle it with his own.

But … love.

Anna was terrified of it, which meant there was still an embargo on kissing. And Jacob was terrified of losing anything that she might give him. So he would accept her conditions. Beggars could not be choosers, after all, and Jacob understood who was in control of their rendezvous—and it was most assuredly not him.

He'd always believed that being a viscount would give him unimaginable power, and yet he felt nothing of the sort while spying on her through the crack in the door. Jacob was back to being a child, overwhelmed with hunger and need, uncertainty and anger—not at Anna, but at himself, because he'd gone along with her supposition that their lust would fade in time.

But Jacob had known hunger—real hunger—and knew that sort of desire tattooed itself on the skin, never to be forgotten. Even when the desires were met, that ache remained, like a broken ankle that clicked after it had healed.

One needed to feed that hollowness.

Jacob had intended to do it then and there, throw Anna on the desk and slake his passion when the sun was high, scattering her papers on the floor to be lost forever.

But, once more, his power had been made useless. Damn guests. Sir John had wandered into the hallway and discovered him, asking for a moment of his precious time. It was horribly awkward, attempting to hide a cockstand while speaking to the father of the woman who was inciting the cockstand, but nevertheless, Jacob managed. Sir John kept him for an hour, addressing Jacob's mother's concerns about his work habits. It seemed his mother was distressed about his lack of advisors and managers, and worried that he might be spreading himself too thin. She'd asked Sir John to consult with him on the matter.

At first, Jacob was blindsided and furious at the older man's intervention in his affairs. His mother knew better than to invite others into their private lives; however, Sir John, as ever, was kind and circumspect about his advice, handing Jacob a list of names that he could vouch for, men he'd heard good things about and thought they could trust.

In the end, Jacob could only offer his thanks. Sir John might be a meddling bastard, but he was a helpful one. They left on good terms, especially as Sir John did not ask about Anna. Jacob had been waiting for it, knowing that sooner or later the baronet might be slightly inquisitive about the time that his daughter spent with Jacob in the cottage. There was a moment—a second, a crinkle around that eye—as they were saying their goodbyes that Jacob felt the topic would break to the surface. But Sir John let him retreat. Perhaps the old man was content now that his daughter was back in the house, her health seemingly restored. Clearly, Anna was right as rain. She'd talked merrily enough at dinner the previous night. Maybe that was enough for Sir John.

Once again, the aristocracy bewildered Jacob. Sir John had trusted him to do the right thing—trusted him to *know* what the right thing was. Because of his birth or because of his character? Did the peerage know the difference between the two?

Needless to say, when Sir John was finished with him, Jacob had plenty on his mind. *And* he had work to do. He could have spent the remainder of the afternoon sending out letters to the names on Sir John's list.

But he didn't. He couldn't. Jacob's imagination swam with visions of Anna. Fighting it was fruitless.

Which was why, soon after that meeting, he found himself hiding in some sort of linen closet off the servants' staircase toward the base of the kitchen. Jacob had meant to locate Beatrice and ask her for Anna's whereabouts. He'd had no idea that Anna would be in the middle of the kitchen's maelstrom.

Jumping into the closet was cowardly—as was eavesdropping from behind a crack in the door. Jacob was man enough to admit it. But the notion of grabbing Anna and throwing her over his shoulder while taking two steps at a time out of the hectic room was comical. He decided to wait. He could have waited in the comfort of his study, but that held little appeal for him. Hearing Anna's voice rise above the din of the barking orders and the clanks of pots and pans was too exciting to resist.

Especially when Jacob heard his name … and a long, exasperated sigh after it.

"I didn't want to even ask," he heard Anna say, "but I'm desperate." She giggled, and Jacob smiled. Anna didn't giggle enough. The soft, uninhibited sound made him think of the twinkling lights of glowworms that flashed at night while he walked around his pagoda, mysterious and warm. "Not desperate like that," she went on. "I mean, I'm desperate to make this event special, and nothing tastes better than your scones and biscuits."

Jacob heard a *humph*.

"Don't be upset, Beatrice. I'm asking you to help too. We'll need quite a bit for the girls."

"How many little ones are you expecting?" Aunt Iris asked. Her voice held a hint of disgruntlement, but she was obviously interested, maybe even a little excited by the challenge.

"I'm not sure yet," Anna replied. "Jacob is writing an article for the newspaper. I'm hoping that that will pique interest."

When Anna said his name, Jacob searched for some inkling of feeling, some hint of breathlessness or shyness. He found none.

Someone began to clap. Jacob's guess was Beatrice. The vivacious girl always seemed to be clapping for something or another. Another voice chimed in, but it was more muffled than the others. The kitchen was in full swing with maids coming and going, deliveries being made and stored, but this sound was different. It was almost as if someone was speaking in between chews.

"… what will you do about … You know how he feels."

"Yes, Violet, I am very aware of our nephew's opinions on the subject," Iris stated, rather testily.

Aunt Violet. Yes, she never was much of a baker, but she had a sweet tooth that rivaled Marie Antionette's. Jacob should have known he would catch her with the others.

"What if I speak to him?" Anna asked. "It's for charity. Surely he won't prohibit you from helping if it's what you really want?"

Iris didn't respond right away. Jacob was taken aback. It was an odd thing to listen to others speak about you. Their back-and-forths made him feel like a tyrant. Was Iris truly so worried about upsetting him with her baking? Did she love it that much? He knew that she enjoyed it from time to time, but he'd chalked it up to old habits dying hard.

He would never take something away from her if it was a source of such happiness. Didn't his aunts understand that prohibiting them from working wasn't about control? It was a gift. Seeing them toil and break their backs for other families their entire lives had been difficult for him as a young boy, and he'd dreamed to save them from such drudgery.

But now they were tiptoeing around him, afraid of stamping on his pride or hurting his feelings.

Just like everyone had with his father.

Was Jacob any better? Or had he replaced an autocrat just to become one himself?

Footsteps came toward the staircase. Jacob jolted away from the door. Lavender filtered through the thin opening, and he knew it was Anna taking her leave. He waited half a minute in case the others were close behind. When he saw no one else, he exited the closet and followed her up the staircase.

Jacob caught sight of her yellow skirts rounding a corner as he emerged onto the main floor. She was heading to the main staircase. Her hand was reaching for the banister when Jacob finally struck. Like a viper, he caught her just in time. He muffled her squeak with his palm over her mouth and twirled her into the nearest room, rejoicing when he realized it was the library. Who said that lascivious dreams didn't come true?

He kicked the door closed behind him, releasing Anna in the process. She continued to spin into the room, her eyes wide, her hair ruffled as she found her footing.

"What are you doing?" she said, hand on her heart. "You gave me such a scare!"

Maybe Jacob apologized. He couldn't be sure. With Anna's hand so well placed next to her heaving bosom, all he could think about was sliding that clothing from her body.

Anna's hand fell to her side. "Why are you looking at me like that?"

Jacob stalked forward. "Like what?"

She back-pedaled, her gaze growing wary. "Like … like th-that," she stammered. "Determined."

Jacob's heart was pounding in his chest. Could she see that as well? His legs didn't falter. "Yes, I am very determined."

Anna bumped into the desk that she'd been scribbling on earlier. She reached back, holding on to the edge of the top with both hands. "Did … did you write the article for the newspaper today?"

Ha! The woman actually thought that she could throw off his intention with casual conversation. Not on her life.

Jacob answered with a slow nod as he stopped in front of Anna. He rested his hands on the desk on either side of her, caging her in. For a moment, Anna's green eyes brightened with something close to panic—like an animal ready to fight to free itself. Jacob continued to lean over her, and Anna bent back until her elbows hit the table.

He lowered his head to her chest, rubbing his nose and mouth over the curve of her breasts, imprinting his desire onto her. Anna's breath hitched at his audacity, a low purr emerging from her throat.

Spurred on by the fever Jacob could feel building inside of her, he ran his fingers over her shoulders, down the goosebumps on her arms to the top of her dress. He slowly pulled it down, exposing the lace undergarments hiding beneath.

"Jacob," she whispered. "You mustn't. Not here."

His mouth quirked into a mirthless grin. His blood was too hot for his smile to be anything other than predatory. Dipping his head again, he skated his tongue across the satiny expanse of her skin, savoring the salt and sweat and excitement as if it were priceless wine. "But you want passion. And I want you now. I want you here," he stated casually. He nudged her body flat on the desk, and her legs dangled over the edge.

"Here?" Her voice shook.

"I've been dreaming about it ever since I woke up this morning … alone."

She covered her face with her hand, and her voice came out muffled. "I had to go back to my room before my maid came."

"So now you're worried about propriety? When we've shared the cottage and one tiny bed?"

Anna picked her head off the table. An adorable frown was his reward. "So, this is my punishment? Ravishment in the library?"

With his other hand, Jacob worked on the buttons of his trousers. Anna's eyes darted to his movement, and he worried that he was going too fast. The woman wanted passion; she asked for lust. Nothing said that more than taking her on the table in the library.

"It's all about perception," Jacob replied, yanking his linen shirt from his waistband. "Most would see a ravishment as a reward, not a punishment."

She arched a brow. "It depends on who is doing the ravishing."

"Me, sweetheart," Jacob said, tossing up her skirts. "It will only ever be me."

Anna giggled, and once more, that sound made his heart pound all the way to his ears. It conjured images of moonlit nights, naked swims, and dew-drenched skin. And he wasn't alone. Jacob imagined Anna right there beside him.

The picture caused his stomach to flop over itself, his legs to wobble. It hit him like a ton of bricks. The scene was perfect in his mind. So incredibly idyllic. Jacob wanted it with a visceral need he'd never experienced before. He wanted her. With him. Forever.

He fell to his knees, pushing Anna's legs apart with clumsy force. He was losing control; his passion, his expectations, were getting the best of him. Taking a long breath, he forced himself to calm down, but her sex filling his lungs did the complete opposite.

Anna kept up her protests, but they were growing weaker. She tried to throw her skirts back down, obstructing his view. "Let's go back to your room," she said, her tone sleepy, like she was falling into a dream. "Anyone could walk in … My father—"

"I locked the door. Besides, your father is off with my mother to town. Something about art … or maybe horses."

You let them go alone? Why?"

Jacob shrugged.

Christ, he couldn't be expected to remember, not when he was faced with the dark curls of Anna's heat. He ran his hands up her legs, savoring the way the silk stockings molded against her calves.

Her laughter was husky and incredibly arousing. "Isn't that against your better judgment? I thought my father was to be watched at all times."

He slid his palms up Anna's upper thighs, massaging, devouring. Then he kissed her on each side, making her shiver. "I've come to appreciate when our parents distract each other."

Jacob glanced up and saw Anna gnaw at her knuckle. His cock was painful now as it bided its time. Everything about this woman was beautiful and made just for him.

There was that thought again.

Jacob frowned, returning to hide under Anna's skirts. Why did he keep ruining everything by thinking of a future? There wasn't one. Anna had already informed him of that fact. Fixating on it would only disappoint him and diminish the time she was giving him now.

He cleared his throat and came back to her center, leaning into the apex of her legs and licking the seam of her passage. A luxurious gasp came from the desk. And yet something still felt wrong. Jacob couldn't shake the nagging need to keep coming out from her shrine and watching her expressions. Not only did he want to give her pleasure, but he needed to watch her receive it as well. Never had he wanted that so much. He had to take control before he ruined everything, before he let lovesick words that he would ultimately regret slip from his mouth.

This was lust, pure and simple. There was no room for anything else.

Instantly, Jacob came to his feet and pulled Anna up to stand. Before she could question him, he twirled her around and bent her over the desk, hiking her skirts up to her waist once more.

Anna closed her eyes as she laid her cheek on the cold wood.

"I don't want to talk anymore." Jacob palmed her bottom with both hands, admiring the pale pink orbs with gluttonous hunger.

"We weren't talking."

She was right. But Jacob was thinking, so damned much, having a one-sided conversation with himself. He didn't want to think. He didn't want to worry about what he did or did not have. Like last night, he wanted to lose himself in her so fully and completely that all he could do was act. Let his body shatter and let his soul pick up the pieces later.

Anna shifted her weight back, softly pushing against his pelvis. Jacob hissed through his teeth; his cock was too sensitive. When she did it again, Jacob's control deserted him. With ridiculous speed, he lifted his shaft from his trousers and positioned himself at her entrance. Anna was wet and ready, her core primed for him. This time he didn't drive himself insane with subtle little movements. He thrust into her with one deep push, sheathing his cock between her walls, jerking their bodies forward on the table.

Anna pulsed and squeezed, and Jacob had to tense every muscle to stop from spilling inside her so soon. Like a lock to a key, a glove to a hand, her body was made for him. And Anna knew it all too well. She straightened her arms, bringing her torso off the table. Arching her back, she withdrew from him until they had almost broken contact, and then she slammed back onto his cock, impaling herself with a throaty groan.

And then it couldn't be helped. The act ... the *need* took over. Digging his hands into her hips, he charged inside her, meeting Anna with matching energy. This was no dance; there were no sweet nothings whispered in between light caresses. Their need was too much. The strokes were high and rapid, their breaths lost and then found. The pace was brutal and elemental, primal in its savagery.

Because they were both searching for something in the other. Only as Jacob's hips slapped into the back of Anna's thighs did he understand that he was never going to find it. Not this way. It would never be enough. He wanted all of her, not just her body.

With that thought plaguing him, Jacob reached underneath her torso to hug her through his thrusts. Even with his shaft inside her, he still wasn't close enough. He found an erratic vein on her throat and licked it up her neck as his hips flexed back and forth. He worked his way up to her ear, sucking on her lobe while their lower halves continued to fight for ecstasy.

Jacob wanted to give it to her. He pumped in and out, harder and harder, shaking the table with his ardor. Anna's moans encouraged him, coming higher and faster as she fought for her end.

Twisting her body, she reached behind and cupped the back of his neck, bringing their foreheads together. For a moment, Jacob almost forgot himself and captured her lips, but her gaze stopped him. Anna's eyes opened to him, flowing into his body as surely as he was coming into hers. They said nothing, only exchanged breaths, lips so close he could lick her, as she bucked into him. One. Two. Three more times.

Her mouth opened in a sultry keen. Anna hurried to place her knuckle in her teeth to stanch her cry, but Jacob beat her to it. He held his finger to her lower lip, begging for her to accept it into her mouth.

Thankfully, Anna wrapped her lips around him and swirled his finger with her tongue as her sweet cunt clamped down on his cock, milking him with her release. The moment he felt her teeth graze across his knuckle, he exploded, unleashing his passion into her in a great wave.

Jacob screamed out in surrender, his voice hoarse and unrestrained. Anna continued to hold his face, watching him acutely, as if his outburst magnified her own intense experience.

Somehow, Jacob found the energy to remove himself from her. He tucked himself back in his trousers and lay shoulder to shoulder next to Anna on the desk, where they both stared up at the ceiling. It took a few minutes, but their breathing eventually mellowed, their chests stopped heaving, and all that was left was the glow of the aftermath reflecting off their dewy skin.

Anna hid her laughter behind her hands as she covered her face. "My God, what were we thinking?"

Jacob snorted. He took her hand and kissed her palm. "We weren't." He rubbed it across his cheek. "It was beautiful, wasn't it?"

He couldn't see it, but Anna's smile was tangible, like the sun's rays breaking through the clouds.

"Nirvana," she said softly.

Jacob squeezed her hand. "Nirvana."

Chapter Twenty-Three

THE ROSE WASN'T a distraction. However, it was distracting.

On the morning of the cricket clinic, Anna woke to find the plump crimson flower sitting on her side table. No letter. No card. No vase. Just the rose waiting for her to notice it.

It lay on top of the newspaper that had arrived the day before, which had run yet another article from the Viscount Newton about the club's clinic, encouraging the girls of London to come out. Jacob hadn't stopped with one write-up; he'd surprised Anna with two.

In the week of planning, he hadn't mentioned anything about the second article. He'd come to Anna's room every night, but his lips had been too busy for words. Lust and passion left very little time for conversation, Anna realized. And yet she felt like she was beginning to understand—and covet—Jacob more with each passing hour.

That was the distraction.

Anna dressed carefully, wanting to provide just the right message to girls, eventually choosing a plain white gown with little lace and fuss and short, capped sleeves. She wanted to convey movement and agility. It was important for the girls to learn that women's garments could be for more than catching a man. Women needed to be able to catch balls in the air as well.

Anna planned to meet her teammates at the field early in order to set up and make sure they had everything they needed. She didn't have time to dawdle. She bounded down the stairs, hoping to have a quick meeting with Beatrice and the aunts before she left, making sure the food was set to be delivered.

But just as she was taking her last step, David and Phillip entered the foyer, with matching expressions that said she would not be doing anything until she dealt with them first.

Anna paused and caught herself before flying face-first onto the hardwood. She hurried to straighten and calm the ire simmering inside her. Phillip had been like a ghost ever since she moved back into the house—not because he'd been hiding, but because Anna looked right through him. Since their conversation in the library, she'd had no interest in speaking or hearing whatever mundane story he had to tell. Now when she thought of the library, she only thought of one thing … Nirvana.

Nevertheless, Anna couldn't ignore her brother. She'd barely muttered a few words to him since her return. Because he spent most of his time with Phillip, he'd been caught in the crossfire, and their relationship had suffered.

"Oh, good," David said, cautiously. "I was afraid that we missed you. I—we—wanted to ask if we could join you today. I'd love to see how it all turns out. Besides, maybe I—we—could help. You know how much we love cricket, and our knowledge is expansive."

"Yes," Phillip added, placing a friendly hand on her shoulder. Anna backed out of his grasp instantly, though he didn't bat an eye. "And it might be good to have family there, you know, in case you don't get the turnout you're hoping for. I'm not saying you won't, only …" He let his words trail off, tapping his white teeth together. "Girls and cricket … It's a bit of a hard sell, despite your charitable intentions. Besides, Beatrice is going to be there, no?"

Anna's smile was brittle. "But you're not family, Phillip. Anyway, my teammates will be there."

Phillip grimaced as if she'd slapped him. Catching on to the awkward encounter, David forced a laugh. "Oh, come now, Anna. Play fair. He's like family. More than your teammates."

Anna didn't want to argue with her brother, not when she had places to be, and he was oblivious of her history with his oldest mate. But Phillip was not family, no matter how long he'd known her. In her experience, family didn't cut and run. Her teammates had shown her more grace and patience than he ever had. The members of her cricket club had only ever looked out for her best interests. Phillip would never be able to say the same. They loved her. Maybe they didn't shower her with bouquets of flowers or write her terrible poetry, but their presence was enough. Their love and protection were felt in the smaller gestures. The older she became, the more Anna realized that love was all the little things.

And she would not forsake them now. Bringing Phillip and David would overshadow the club. Her brother wouldn't mean to, but he would take center stage, maybe even take over the whole thing, because that was what men like him were born to do. Standing on the sidelines listening to the women dictate the clinic would never work for them.

"I'm sorry, David, but everything has already been decided," Anna said genuinely. She turned a dead stare to Phillip, who still appeared confused by her behavior. "I appreciate your concern, but I can take care of myself."

He put his hands on his hips. "Now, I don't think you realize how difficult—"

"Oh, Anna! I've been looking everywhere for you." Beatrice rushed into the room. Wearing a royal-blue cloak and wide straw bonnet, she assumed the air of a general ready for battle. "Why aren't you ready? We're waiting for you."

Caught off guard by her sister's entrance, Anna didn't notice the butler on her heels. "The carriages are packed, miss. Lord Newton organized it all this morning," he said. "Everything has been taken care of."

Anna shook her head. *Jacob?* Was what he up to? "What do you mean, *carriages*? I only need one. What has been taken care of?"

"Everything," he replied.

"Everything," Beatrice repeated with a firm nod. "Iris and I couldn't decide on what to bake, so we just did everything. I even made a cake! It's delicious. Lemon poppyseed. I can't wait to see what everyone thinks!" She clapped her hands and then went into great detail with her list, ticking them off on her fingers. "Let's see, there's the blueberry scones, and rosemary biscuits—oh, and the date bars. Then the butter biscuits and sugar biscuits and—"

Anna threw up her hands. "Wait, wait. All that? I'm thankful, you know I am. but I don't think we're going to need all that—"

"Of course we will," Beatrice cut in with a confused laugh. "Jacob said so."

"How would Jacob know?"

Beatrice answered with an exasperated shrug and grabbed hold of Anna's arm. "I have no idea, and it doesn't matter. We need to go now so we can set up. Iris and Violet are already in the carriage. We have to hurry. A package of flowers came this morning, and we want to decorate the refreshment tables with them. We brought so many vases! It will be gorgeous!"

"Roses?" Anna squeaked.

"Yes. Roses! Did you see them?"

Anna shook her head as Beatrice continued to tug her away from the men and to the door. Words were too difficult to get past the lump in her throat.

Love was all the little things.

SAMUEL EVERETT STARED in acute bewilderment at the refreshment table—nay, tables. After Beatrice, Iris, and Violet were done primping and prodding, there were four in total. "What the holy hell?" he rasped, sliding the back of his hand along the stubble of his chin in a dazed fashion. "Is this a cricket clinic or damned summer picnic?"

Anna cocked her head at the extravagant display. The man had a point. The ladies had gone a bit overboard, though she wouldn't tell them that. Their generosity was incredibly lovely. Workers from Samuel's tavern had carried out the tables, and Beatrice and Iris had spent two painstaking hours decorating them to perfection. Roses were expertly placed throughout in various styles of vases, while the desserts were displayed on trays over crisp white linen that the queen would have admired. It was a work of art. Tasted like it, too, according to Aunt Violet, who made sure to sample each treat to make sure they had "held up" for the day.

"Well, this is a social event," Anna said, casting a nervous eye to the field. "And we wanted to make sure everyone had enough to eat."

"*Humph,*" Samuel returned, following her gaze. "Maybe you could have used another table."

Indeed.

Butterflies had bombarded Anna's stomach the moment she climbed into the carriage to leave the house, but they went positively berserk as the minutes before the event crept by. When one little girl eventually walked onto the field holding her father's hand, Anna almost wept with joy—and relief. But then another came. And another. And soon the field was so full of children that Anna had a difficult time finding her teammates in the confusion.

Now, she was so far past relieved, she was afraid she might be sick. How in the world was she going to wrangle all of those children into anything resembling order?

Samuel glanced down at his pocket watch. "I'd say it's about time to start," he said. Was Anna dreaming, or did she hear a distinct note of amusement in his voice?

Panic swelled. "What should we do?"

"We?"

"Yes, we! You're going to help me, aren't you? Look at all of this!" Anna flung her arms helplessly toward the throng. "I can't do it by myself."

Samuel turned to her, his one milky eye grabbing her attention. There was a time when she'd been terrified of Samuel Everett. His coaching style was intimidating at best. But the man was more bark than bite, and she would forever owe him for believing in the club … believing in her.

"There's no *we* here," he said. "I've got my hands full. Where do you think all these fathers are going to go once they drop their daughters off? To my tavern, that's where. So I'm going to be busy pulling pints behind the bar while also attempting to keep my fiancée safe by my side, where she belongs instead of running after you all. You're on your own, kid."

He offered Anna a pat on the shoulder before turning away. Just past him, she could see Myfanwy waiting for him near the tavern entrance. Her arms were crossed, and even from this distance, it was obvious that she was annoyed she couldn't take part in the afternoon. But Anna knew Myfanwy. She had a feeling her captain would sneak out to make an appearance at some point. Cricket was Myfanwy's life, after all. Marrying Samuel and bearing his children wouldn't change that.

Anna was about to call out to Samuel, beg him to stay one more time, when Ruthie ran up to her side. "Are you ready? I think everyone's getting a little restless."

Anna hesitated. Nothing in her body seemed to want to work. Fear had rendered her lifeless.

"What's going on? Why are we all just standing here?" The sharp question made Anna jump. Lady Everly stood in front of her, eyes narrowed. The widow was the oldest member of the club and even more outspoken than Myfanwy. Anna didn't know her well. Though Lady Everly was open with her opinions, she rarely spoke about herself and wasn't one for polite chitchat. But as a person who had suffered through tragedy, Anna recognized the sadness in Lady Everly and had given her space to open up when she was ready.

"I … I … I'm not sure," Anna stammered. Noticing she was wringing her fingers, she hid them behind her back.

"But you have a plan?" Lady Everly asked pointedly. "You discussed it in the letters you sent. Let's line them up and begin."

Anna's heart was pounding out of her chest. "Yes … a plan. I have a plan … and we should line them up. Yes."

Had she morphed into an exotic bird and resorted to parroting others? What was the matter with her? Maybe this day was too big for her after all. What if she wasn't strong enough to be a captain and a leader? It wouldn't be the end of the world. Some people were leaders; some people were followers. Teams needed both. Everyone had a role to play for the game to work.

She wasn't a complete failure. After all, she had orchestrated this entire event. When it was all said and done, Anna could take pride in that.

Feelings of hopelessness began to fall on her shoulders, weighing her down further. "Lady Everly, maybe you should take charge—"

Anna's words cut off. She had been ready to tell Lady Everly that *she* should be the one to command the clinic when a carriage stopped along the street, catching her eye.

A very tall, very muscular, very splendidly dressed woman exited the carriage, soon followed by a young girl. Even though she was fully clothed, Anna would have recognized her anywhere. The strongwoman—Helga Bitterman—walked toward the field, her daughter, Inez, close to her side.

Anna wasn't the only one who noticed their arrival. "Who in the world is that?" Ruthie asked, her jaw slack. "She has to be the tallest woman that I've ever seen. Taller than me."

Even Lady Everly was awed. "She's beautiful," she added in a hush.

"You think so?" Ruthie asked.

Lady Everly nodded, not taking her gaze from Helga. "Look at the way she walks … Confidence is the most beautiful thing in the world. Real confidence."

The crowd split as if Moses had entered the field. Helga smiled kindly, nodding at the gesture, taking all the gawks and stares as gracefully as one could. Her dress was demure but formfitting, with large flounces covering most of her arms. But there was no hiding the pure power simmering underneath the pearls and silk.

"Miss Anna," Helga said, stopping in front of her. "It is wonderful to see you again." Her accent continued to mystify, but Anna had no difficulty hearing her as the crowd died down to an eavesdropping silence.

"I'm so glad you came today, Mrs. Bitterman," she replied. "I had no idea."

Helga smiled indulgently at the daughter who clung to her like a limpet. "When we were told about your event, Inez wouldn't hear of skipping it. It's all she's talked about all week. We were so nervous we would be late, but you haven't started yet, yes? You are still leading the clinic, are you not? You've seen me work, and now I would love to watch you do the same."

Lady Everly stepped forward. "Actually, there's been a change of plan. I'm going to—"

"No there hasn't," Anna said quickly. "It's me. I'm ready. And yes, you're right on time."

Chapter Twenty-Four

RUTHIE WIPED THE sweat from her brow, upsetting her bonnet so it hung off the back of her head. In the full light of the sun, her face was red, and her freckles shone bold and bright like a ladybug's carapace. "Good Lord these girls can eat," she said, watching the lines form around the refreshment tables in rapt fascination.

Anna grinned at Beatrice and the aunts, who were in their element, directing the young players to and fro, advising them on what little morsels they should pile on their plates. "It's been a long day," she replied. "They're hungry."

Ruthie made an unladylike sound and crossed her arms over her thin waist. "When I'm hungry, my mother tells me to drink more tea," she grumbled.

Anna laughed, though when she regarded her friend, she realized it wasn't meant as a joke. She threw an arm around Ruthie's shoulder and nudged her toward the line. "Get in there. You deserve the biscuits just as much as they do. Treat yourself!"

After a moment's hesitation, Ruthie trudged forward, joining the horde, a pensive expression on her face. Anna had always thought that Ruthie was so skinny because she was so tall. Now she wondered if it was more than that.

She reminded herself to buy the aunts and Beatrice a thank-you gift later this week. Their efforts had paid off. Clearly, they had seen what Anna could not: girls enjoyed eating. Just like men, they worked up an appetite, and when you put them in a situation where they wouldn't be hounded or remonstrated for filling their bellies, they would do so gladly without shame.

It was a good day.

Once Anna overcame her nerves and self-doubt, she and her teammates had put their girls in their paces. It was daunting at first—similar to herding cats—but the children had come because they'd expressed interest in the sport. They only needed a little direction and then their excitement took over.

Coming in at two hours long, the clinic had lasted longer than originally planned, but it couldn't be helped. Anna and the others wanted to make sure that every little girl received one-on-one attention as well as a chance to bat and bowl with her fellow players. In the end, Ruthie informed her that over one hundred had shown up that day.

One hundred little girls who had been given the confidence to try something new and dream about being a part of a different kind of club, maybe even see themselves in a different kind of light.

As Anna continued to study the girls eating and laughing, cheeks rosy from exertion, wisps of hair fallen free from braids, she could barely contain herself. The need to hug and kiss every one of them flowed through her, along with the desire to tell them that this club would welcome them all.

The Single Ladies Cricket Club was a place where they could be different and still be appreciated.

Anna's ears twitched as footsteps sounded behind her. "I feel terrible accepting the bat and ball," the voice said, tearing her from her reflections. "We should let you give it to someone else, since we already have some."

Anna spun to find Helga behind her. "No, you keep it," she replied. "Inez will realize that one can't ever have enough."

Helga's smile was wistful, bordering on melancholy, while

they regarded the scene. "I envy these girls, don't you? When I was young, I was so alone. My husband was a comfort to me, of course, but those early years were difficult. People ... men"—her face dropped in disgust—"they used to call me such heinous names. Make me feel like I was less than a woman, all because I valued brawn and vitality. I wanted to push myself to see how strong I could be, not just listen to everyone else tell me what I could be. And now look." She raised her massive arms as if she was an ancient Greek statue on a plinth. "I am the strongest woman in the world."

Anna laughed, in the mood to tease. "You know ... there are others who are saying the same thing."

A shadow fell over Helga's face, and Anna's laughter died a swift death. "They are wrong. And they know it."

Anna cleared her throat, anxious to change the subject. "By the by, earlier you said that you heard about this event. You didn't read about it in the newspaper?" When Helga shook her head, Anna continued, "How did you find out?"

Helga returned a curious look. "Didn't your husband tell you?"

"My husband?"

"Lord Newton wrote to me urging me to come. I know many of the people here—peers love to come to my shows—and most of them said they also received a letter." Seeing Anna's confusion, Helga added, "I'm sure many read the newspaper as well."

Anna blinked. "No ... no, of course."

"Did I say something wrong?"

She let out a chirp of laughter, shaking her head. "Not at all. I was just thinking."

"About?"

"The little things." Anna rubbed at her temples. Suddenly, she felt hot, exposed, and exhausted. More than anything, now that her job was over, she wanted to rush home. To Jacob. But she still had to make sure the girls went home safely. And something else dogged at her—something only her companion could help her with.

"Tell me, Mrs. Bitterman. Do you ever cry?"

Helga snorted. "Cry? What kind of a question is that?"

Anna chuckled ruefully. "An honest one. Because you seem like the perfect woman to ask. You see, I can't figure out which me is the real one. Some days I believe in myself, and then other days I will freeze in fear. One moment I have confidence, and the next I am a frightened rabbit. At times I think I can live without love, and other times"—she blew out a long breath—"I believe the hole I've created inside myself might swallow me until there is nothing left."

Helga paused in thought, staring down at Anna. "Why would you want to live without love?"

Anna deflated. Perhaps because she'd given her everything today and was fatigued beyond measure, she couldn't do anything but lay herself bare. "I don't know if I'm strong enough to deal with it when it's over."

"Why would it be over?"

Anna bobbed her shoulders. "Because everything ends."

"Everyone dies as well," Helga replied philosophically. "Does that mean we shouldn't live?"

"I suppose not."

"Has anyone ever told you that you think too much?"

"I may have heard that before."

"Yes." Helga nodded. "Thinking too much can be a problem. It can get in the way of moving forward. If I thought too much about what others said about me then I never would have had the courage to be who I am. You understand?"

"I think so," Anna replied.

"Of course I cry," Helga went on. "Everyone does, even men when they think no one is watching. It is the only sensible thing to do. My body is perfect in every way. I work at it day and night. I know these things better than most. Holding in all those emotions … It creates a poison in your body, killing you from the inside. You see, there's nothing weak about crying or having doubt or being afraid. The weakness comes when you hide those emotions, from everyone and even yourself."

"So, the answer is to let it all out."

"The answer is to give yourself permission to live," Helga replied.

"And that will solve all my problems?" Anna asked.

"Of course not." Helga snorted. "It will only create more. But they'll be worth it because you'll be hardy enough to deal with them. The heart is a muscle too, you know. When you use it, it only gets stronger."

⇒⇒⇒✶⇐⇐⇐

JACOB HAD WAITED for her.

This was Anna's day. As much as he'd wanted to surprise her by showing up on the field, he hadn't wanted to distract her. The clinic was important to her, and it wasn't Jacob's place to insert himself.

Nor was it his place to force himself into her life—although he wanted to do that too. Jacob didn't bother throwing that thought away anymore. What was the point? It would just come back again. And again.

So, he waited. Hoping that she would come to him. Hoping that he would be the one she wanted to share her day with the most.

He wasn't hiding, Jacob told himself. Anna would know where to find him ... if she wanted to. The moon was round and full. The night held a wintry feel. The air tempted with possibility. Lavender infiltrated the garden, mingling with honeysuckle.

Then Jacob heard the soft rustling of leaves crunching under slippers. He closed his eyes, tempering the exhilaration speeding through his veins.

"Have you ever been inside the pagoda?" he heard her ask.

Jacob stood his ground, allowing Anna to position herself

beside him. Shoulder to shoulder they gazed across the pond, where the lonely pagoda sat stoically, highlighting by the vivid moonlight. The pond was still, covered with glossy green lily pads and a hazy magical quality that seemed to float above it like mist.

"Yes," Jacob answered calmly, ignoring the way his stomach jumped when her cloak swished against his arm. "Would you ..." He swallowed the lump in his throat. "Would you like to see it?"

Without waiting for an answer, he clasped Anna's hand and lead her to the bridge. Its planks were too thin, so they traveled across single file, Jacob first and Anna right after him, her hand never leaving his.

The door wasn't locked, but it required a swift push from Jacob to open. The pagoda's inside was blanketed in darkness. Thin swaths of light sliced through the small windows near the tops of the four walls. It was a small space, meant for decoration more than anything, but four people could stand here comfortably. Though if Jacob stretched out his arms, he might be able to touch each wall.

Still, Anna was entranced by the little structure. She meandered around the tight area, trailing her fingertips along the wood. "It's like being inside a dollhouse," she said, a note of whimsy in her voice.

It tugged at Jacob. If only he was the knight he'd dreamed himself to be when he was younger and this was a fairytale.

"How did the day go?" he asked.

Anna didn't need to say a thing. The way her eyes brightened and her smile crowded her face told him everything. She launched into her day, telling him about the horde of girls, Samuel's lack of help; how many biscuits a girl named Ruthie ate. She went into great detail about some of the girls and all the questions they had about the club.

Jacob leaned against the wall wearing a contented grin. He liked hearing the excitement in her voice, the way Anna's stories took over her body. It was love and confidence in action.

After a moment of hesitation, she said, "Helga Bitterman

came. She brought her daughter."

"Oh?" Jacob replied.

A sliver of moonlight rained in from the window above him, cutting her across her alabaster skin. "She said you wrote her a letter. She said you wrote many letters."

Jacob crossed his arms. "I realized that viscounts have many contacts. I decided to use them."

"Why didn't you tell me?"

Jacob didn't answer. He didn't know how to answer.

Anna did. She moved toward him. "You wanted to make sure the clinic had children. You wanted to make sure that it would be a success."

The closer she came, the more his muscles tightened. He held himself there. Waiting for her. "You were in charge of it," he said softly. "It was always going to be a success."

The corners of her sweet mouth inched up. "Maybe," she said. "Maybe not. Thank you."

Anna placed her hand on his chest, right above his heart. Like a puzzle piece had been locked into place, his satisfaction was intense. "I … It was nothing. A small gesture," Jacob said gruffly.

Anna's smile magnified. The room felt like it had been infused with light. He could see her so surely now. Her green eyes dancing with mirth. Her soft brown locks curling around her ears like ferns. How could anyone ever think she looked like a boy? Anna was all woman. The epitome of femininity.

"Many small gestures can turn into a large one. Roses … and newspaper articles … cold hands and warm pockets." Illustrating her point, Anna moved her other hand into the pocket of his coat, snugly keeping it inside.

"And …" Jacob's mouth stumbled. He was having a difficult time gathering his thoughts. He licked his lips. Anna leaned onto him on her tiptoes. He could see the striations of her eyes, the golden flecks that peeked through all the green. She pressed her chest into his, almost in a pleading way, begging him to hold it. Jacob needed no further invitation; he wound his arms around her waist and squeezed.

They exchanged breaths. "And what do you think that large gesture was?" he asked.

Anna's gaze flickered back and forth between his eyes. Her mouth was still curled in a knowing way, as if she knew all the secrets of the world and was bursting to tell him. But then her focus changed. To his mouth.

The hand on his chest slid up his throat, pausing near his lips. When her fingers grazed him, the feeling was fleeting and light. Jacob let himself lick the pads of her fingers, and her mouth opened with a slight intake of breath, showing her white teeth.

When her hand dropped away, Jacob thought that her exploration was finished. He girded his disappointment swiftly.

And then she came to him.

Anna's mouth landed on his with barely there pressure. Like testing the waters before one jumped in, she was measured and contained, her lips shut as she lifted her chin.

Jacob allowed her to feel him, to seek him out. He allowed her time to come to terms with her decision. And it was a decision. He understood that. It was a choice. And Anna had chosen him.

When her lips parted, Jacob accepted the invitation.

He hooked his hand behind her nape and crushed their lips together. No longer would they deny each other. A purr came from her throat, a heightened catch of noise that was both exhilarated and shocked, spurring Jacob further.

Nothing could have prepared him for her taste. A heady blend of mint and urgency, it addicted Jacob from the start. Thoughts evaporated as quickly as they landed. All he could do was stand in place and experience this onslaught of greedy need and wild abandon.

Their hands grew restless. Anna clawed at everything between them, pushing his overcoat from his shoulders, untying his necktie and tossing it to the ground. Jacob was equally as ravenous, ridding her of her cloak and working on the buttons on the back of her gown.

Their actions were clumsy, their lips wet and unskilled, and yet this time was beyond precious. As Jacob swept his tongue inside her mouth, Anna rewarded him with a groan that went straight to his shaft. Their tongues collided, playing with one another, licking and tasting, savoring and clinging. Explorations were made, turns were taken as they devoured one another, forsaking all sense of propriety and culture. Here in the little house on the stilts, in their pagoda floating above a sea of wonder and enchantment, they were free to release the leashes of their second guessing. Here they could love without words.

And it was love. Pure as snow and strong as a current, it could be nothing else.

Jacob pulled back, releasing her swollen mouth. Anna's focus was dazed, her lips plump and so very used. "Are you sure?" he asked, tipping his forehead to hers.

"I have to stop hiding."

Jacob clutched her face, kissing the top of Anna's head. "There is no more hiding between us," he said, his breaths shallow and frantic. If he wasn't inside her soon, all hell would break loose. "I swear to you now, my love will never fade. If you have to worry about something in life, let it not be that."

Anna jerked away from his hold, her eyes as large as saucers. She looked stricken, conflicted, as if she might run for the bridge and never look back. Jacob resisted the urge to sweep her into his arms again, knowing that she had to make the final decision. She'd come this far. He was only asking her to take one more step.

Jacob's voice shook as if his throat was coated in shards of glass. "Come back to me—"

Anna's movement stopped him. Slowly, she raised her hands to her shoulders and swept her gown to the gown. Underneath, she only wore a chemise, thin and translucent, and that soon followed the gown.

She stood before him completely naked, statuesque and regal, head high. A shiver swept through Jacob from the enthralling vision, but Anna did not waver. Her rose-colored nipples strained and puckered, her chest pumped, her thick eyelashes dusted her cheeks, but she did not waver against the cold or his dark gaze.

"I need you to do something for me, Jacob."

"What?"

Her voice was firm, and direct, hitting him to his core. "I want you to make me come so hard that I cry."

Fuck.

That should have been enough. But Jacob asked, "And then?"

Anna ran her gaze over his body, from top to bottom. Her smile was carnal. "And then I want you to dry my tears and do it all over again."

Chapter Twenty-Five

ANNA HAD NO idea how or when they'd ended up in the hermit's cottage.

She rubbed the sleep from her eyes, recognizing the shrill chirps outside, signaling morning. Jacob slept peacefully behind her, his arms draped over her middle as if even in his dreams he worried that she might leave.

Her mind told her to get up and run back to the house, but her body had a distinctly different opinion. A few more minutes couldn't hurt, not when she felt so blissfully alive, so acutely happy. It was a new feeling, unknown territory, because it came with no regret or shame. Her needs and wants were in perfect alignment. With Jacob.

Anna's skin still sizzled and hummed from the night. With kissing newly added to their bedtime repertoire, their lovemaking had taken on a whole new adventure *and* a new meaning. No patch of skin had been left unmarked, but it was her lips that Jacob had luxuriated in. He came back to them again and again with a raw fervor that left nothing to the imagination. He'd branded her with his possession.

Anna was his. And Jacob was hers. Nothing else mattered.

Nevertheless, the longer Anna remained in that bed, the faster her mind ran. Even in the warmth of Jacob's hold, with the heat of his breath on the back of her neck, Anna worried. Because she had done what she'd said she would never do. She'd fallen in love. With a good man. A decent man. A man who was brave enough to take what he wanted. To *take care* of what he wanted.

The last thing she wanted to do was disappoint him.

Her thoughts must have been loud, because Jacob began to stir. He stretched languidly, caressing her hips with his palm, rising along with the sun, in more ways than one.

He was the alchemist whose touch continued to transmute her. How easily Jacob made her body feel like it flowed with molten gold.

He repositioned her backside so it was snugly cushioned against his engorged manhood. He laid a lazy kiss underneath her ear. "Good morning," he said, his voice deep and sonorous. Hungry.

His forearm rested under her breasts, and he raised his palm to cup one in his hand. It was a casual motion, an action of ownership and worship. Anna sighed against the onslaught of delicious feelings climbing up from her toes, like water traveling from a root up the stalk of a plant. Her body was slowly filling with desire.

"We should go," she said.

Jacob rocked his hips into her in a restless, lackadaisical manner, like the two of them had all the time in the world, like there was nothing to fear, no worries to be had.

If only Anna could allow herself that reprieve. The only time her brain ever shut off was when they were making love.

"We have time," he said, kissing her neck again. Jacob didn't back away this time, keeping his lips on her skin, allowing them to wander in an idle and distracting fashion.

Anna's laugh was breathy. She lifted her arm and reached back to cup his head. "We really should go."

"We will," he said, nuzzling her. She should have known the hand on her breast wouldn't stay still for long. He kneaded her flesh, plucking at her turgid nipple between his fingers. "And when we do," he continued, nipping at her earlobe, tracing the shell with the tip of his tongue, "I will go straight to your father and explain everything."

He pinched her breast harder, and she let out a tiny squeak. "E-everything?"

Jacob's chuckle came from deep in his chest. "Well, almost everything."

Anna wanted to laugh too. She wanted to spin in Jacob's embrace and lock her lips to his in celebration of this moment.

But her fears were too great. *Everything* ... Everything was moving too fast. She still had so much to tell him. And it was so very difficult to locate the words, to pinpoint the perfect explanation with his shaft nudging insistently between her thighs.

"Open up, sweetheart," Jacob said, applying pressure to her hips, bending her torso away from him.

It was a war on two fronts. Jacob's attack was artful and merciless. She never had a chance. Anna bent her body and her will to him.

"That's right," he whispered. "Just like that, let me come in one more time, love." The passiveness in his voice was gone. Anna detected an edge of franticness now, an unraveling of control. His breath came quicker against her neck, and his hands shook while they roved across her front.

Anna loved Jacob like this, loved it when his veneer of respectability gave way to the rabid passions he hid so well inside. She relinquished her anxiety and control. She let the fears over the future rise off her, carried by the heat of their bodies.

She reached for his hand and held it on her hip, twining their fingers together, then twisted her neck to meet him, capturing Jacob's mouth in a long and lingering kiss that invaded her senses. They lost themselves in the kiss, clinging to one another, circling their tongues in play that felt both thrilling and dangerous.

When Jacob finally surged inside of her, she screamed into his mouth. His fingers came to her lips, soothing her fever before he captured her once more.

After that, their lips never parted again. As Jacob rolled his hips into Anna's, their mouths created their own dance, one that mimicked the rhythm of their bodies but was led by different music. The kisses were thorough and sweet, never-ending and ravenous. They spoke of love and trust, devotion and future. They were the stuff of daydreams, while their bodies evoked the wicked night.

Anna's pulse quickened. A frisson of energy was building. Jacob pushed inside her, his thrusts more erratic, needier. He pressed his fingers into her hip, while his other hand held on to her breast, stabilizing his pumping. He became harder inside her, thickening and stretching her walls, his appetite growing. Anna was mindless. She clutched and clawed at him; her kisses turned savage, her hips demanding.

Until she split in half. Shards of light cut through her, shattering her consciousness, of everything she thought she knew about herself in this world. As Anna pulsated around Jacob's shaft, milking him for all that he could give, she fell into an abyss; long and far she fell, with only darkness around her. And she had no fear. Because the light inside her broke her up into such small pieces that she became one with the abyss. Anna was everywhere and everything.

And she couldn't fear herself.

Jacob's release came fast, and he locked his arms around her as he jerked and convulsed, laying himself bare and empty against her. Their sweat-slicked bodies molded together as one; their panting reverberated like a mantra.

Inside their tiny cottage, they had created a temple. A sanctuary.

Anna held Jacob's forearms tight as he continued to shudder. Then she twisted to take his face in her hands, offering him a soft kiss, settling the emotion that held him in its firm grip. His eyelids were heavy, his mouth upturned, though he was too exhausted for a true smile.

Words were on the tip of her tongue. Words that Anna desperately wanted to say. Jacob's stormy eyes regarded her, and she could have wept at their kindness. The love she saw echoed through her soul and gave no hint of stopping. It clogged her throat, making any sound difficult.

So Anna told him how she felt in the best way she could, in a language that she had forgotten and that Jacob had helped her remember. She lifted her chin and brushed her mouth over his. It was a fleeting kiss. Over before it had begun.

But its message was clear. *This is only the beginning.*

DAYS LATER, ANNA would wonder why she didn't sense the danger sooner.

On returning to the house that morning, she heard the shouts and commotion just as Jacob did. There was a faint whiff of anger and dissension in the air as they stepped past the threshold. And yet she didn't pull back. She didn't grab Jacob and return to the gardens, allowing their love a few more days of cover.

Jacob's arm was wrapped proprietarily around her waist. Naively, Anna had thought she was finally safe from her past. That her penance was finished.

But the second they turned the corner into the drawing room—and Anna witnessed the blistering shade of red on her father's face—she understood that those thoughts had been foolish. Hauntings never ended because ghosts never died.

Phillip's caustic laughter tore her attention away from her father. He clapped at her appearance, curling his lips away from his teeth in a vindictive smile. Anna expected him to come for her. She straightened her shoulders, waiting for a biting comment; however, Phillip turned his ire on her father.

"And you say *I'm* a menace?" he asked Sir John, his voice abnormally high, laced with vitriol. "I didn't ruin your daughter. Clearly she's wanton. Just look at her."

A vein throbbed in the middle of Sir John's forehead. He stepped toward Phillip so quickly that the younger man moved back, hitting the back of his legs against a chair. "Don't you dare speak about her!" he exploded, shaking.

Anna moved out of Jacob's arms. "Father?" she asked.

Sir John attempted to contain himself, but his eyes were shifting, his hands clenching. "Go back to your room. I'm speaking with Phillip. We're almost done."

Phillip lifted a brow. "Are we?" He grinned. "So, you accept my offer?"

"What offer?" Anna asked.

Sir John sent her a helpless look. "Please, Anna, go upstairs."

"What is going on?" Jacob asked, walking to the center of the room. Anna watched him closely. His fists were clenched and his gaze was fixed on Phillip's devious expression.

"I apologize, my lord," Sir John said. "I didn't mean to raise my voice in your home. I … I …" He shook his head. "I momentarily lost myself."

Phillip scoffed. "Why are you apologizing to *him?*" he said, sneering at Jacob. "He just spent the night with your daughter. He doesn't even have the good breeding to hide it."

"How dare you!" Jacob went for Phillip, but Anna had anticipated it. She wrapped her hands around his arm, holding him back. It was a fruitless action. She was strong, but Jacob was stronger. However, Sir John aided her, positioning himself in front of Jacob.

"Please, my lord, I will handle this," Sir John implored. The lines of his forehead were deep and heavy; his panic was unmistakable.

Jacob took a steadying breath, pointing a finger at Phillip. "I want you out of my house," he stated firmly. "I never wanted you here to begin with."

Phillip made a face. "I never wanted to be here either, my good man. I just came to settle some business, and we're almost done." He focused on Anna's father. "Aren't we?"

Sir John's head shook back and forth as if he had lost control of his movements. "You can't have her," he rasped. "I can't let you."

Phillip waved a hand in the air. "Oh, Sir John. You act like I'm a fiend, some villain from a fairy tale. You know me. I'm a good man. I'll treat her with the respect she deserves—you have my word."

Anna's stomach dropped. *Wife.* Phillip still wanted her. How? Why?

"You can't do this, Father," she said. "I don't want him. I don't even know why he's asking."

"I don't want *you.*"

The words stabbed at her like a dull knife. Anna blinked. "What?"

Phillip huffed at Jacob. "Especially not *now.*"

"Then what?" Anna's mind reeled. "Then who—" Her blood turned to ice as realization struck her. The words tripped from her mouth. "B-Beatrice. You want Beatrice."

Phillip clapped. "*Brava.* Of course I want Beatrice. She's not damaged goods."

A flash of color whipped past Anna, giving her no time to react. Jacob's fist came out of nowhere, hitting Phillip's nose square and true. Anna cringed at the gruesome crack and the splatter of blood that flew through the air, landing on the drapes along the window.

"Fuck!" Phillip screamed, holding his face in both hands. He bent over in pain, which only served to make the blood gush over his fingers to the floor like a macabre waterfall. "I think you broke my nose!"

With a grimace, Jacob inspected his hand, stretching and clenching it to ascertain if it, too, was broken. He didn't seem upset by the prospect. "Good," he replied. "Now get out of my house."

"Don't you think I *want* to?" Phillip screeched. "I'm *trying* to leave. I'm just waiting on Sir John!" He stalked to the chaise, where he deposited himself with a comical sigh, holding his nose up in the air while blood dripped down his chin. Anna was bemused by his behavior—it was as if this wasn't out of the ordinary for Phillip. As if getting punched in the nose during a conversation was just a trifling inconvenience between gentle-men. She wondered how she'd ever thought she knew him at all.

"Now, Sir John," Phillip went on, growing impatient. "As we were saying, I need a wife—one with a generous dowry. I initially came for Anna, but since that didn't work out, I'll take Beatrice. I have no time or inclination to court another woman. Our families know each other. I will soon be a baron. She could hardly do better."

Anna sniffed. "She could marry a chimney sweep and do better."

Phillip rolled his eyes. "Oh, don't be jealous now, Anna. You had your chance. It's not my fault you're defective."

Jacob marched to the chaise, fist raised once more. "What did you call her?"

Anna caught him right in time. Murder was in his eyes, and no one in that room knew what to do with a dead body. Besides, her curiosity was inflamed. She needed Phillip to keep talking.

Sir John stamped a foot. "I've already told you. You cannot have her."

Phillip's blue eyes pierced through the blood as he scrutinized the man. "Even after all I've told you?" he said. "I would ruin you."

"Father?" Anna asked.

Sir John ignored her, continuing to meet Phillip's chilling gaze. "Some parts of me, no doubt. But not all."

The two stared for a few beats longer, engaged in a silent conversation, a battle of wills.

Phillip broke first. With an expletive, he hauled himself up from the chaise, more blood dripping to the carpet as he bowed to Sir John. "I don't want to do it, you know. You leave me no choice."

"Every man has a choice," Sir John replied.

Phillip chuckled. "Well, then I am giving you a chance to rethink yours. I will wait a few weeks hoping you change your mind and decide not to ruin your entire family. If not … Well …" He shrugged.

Then he exited the room swiftly.

Anna had to give her father credit. He waited for the odious man to leave before he collapsed on the floor.

Chapter Twenty-Six

JACOB GLUED HIMSELF to the wall, allowing his mother the space to move. She hadn't stopped clucking and worrying ever since Jacob had carried Sir John to his bedroom, nor administering to him with encouraging words, wet towels, and cold water to his parched lips.

He'd hit the floor like a cannonball after Phillip left. At first, Jacob had thought the worst. He'd seen his father do something similar before his death. Thankfully, Anna had kept her head, rousing the older man quickly, and after the shock subsided, Sir John convinced Jacob that a doctor wasn't necessary. He just needed to rest, he'd said. And then *they* would leave.

Leave. Sir John and his children.

Anna.

Jacob hadn't the heart to argue with an ailing man who spoke with a quivering mouth and whose face had turned the color of ash; however, as he pressed himself to the wall, watching the comings and goings of servants, he had to repress his mounting anger—his fear. Anna wasn't going anywhere. She was his now. It had finally been determined. No one—not Phillip, not Sir John— was going to take her from him.

He yearned to whisk Anna away, but she was as hellbent on nursing Sir John as his mother. The aunts understood the futility of interfering. They lurked in the corridor, whispering while attempting to listen in on the paltry conversation. Beatrice, like Jacob, clung to the periphery, anxiously waiting for someone to ask her to help.

David … Jacob had no idea where he'd gone. After the young man had checked on his father, he left the room in a hurry, not giving an inkling as to his destination.

"Stop it, stop it, please," Sir John begged, gently pushing the glass of water Mrs. Wright held up for him. "I can't drink any more. I'm fine, truly," he said, softening his words with a wan smile. "Please, dearest. I need you to stop fussing and listen to me."

Jacob's mother placed the glass on the side table with a demonstrative *thud*. "If it has anything to do with your leaving this afternoon, I don't want to hear it," she stated firmly. "You're not fit to travel. It's preposterous."

Sir John reached for her hand. "I have to, my dear. You have no idea what's about to happen. I can't put your family in jeopardy."

"Father, please," Anna said. She sat down on the side of his bed. "Let's speak in private. Then we can decide what to do together."

"No, Anna. She deserves to know. I will tell her of my mistakes—"

"*My* mistakes."

"No," Sir John snapped. "These are my mistakes. You did nothing wrong."

Anna's head fell. She buried her face in her hands.

Jacob had seen enough. With two swift steps, he came behind her. Just as he was about to scoop her up and carry her from the room, Sir John turned to him with a deadly stare, one meant to stop a man in his tracks. Jacob wasn't an ordinary man, but he wasn't used to this behavior from Sir John; frankly, he hadn't known the baronet had it in him.

"You will wait and listen," Sir John said.

Jacob's arms stopped in midair. For a moment, he thought to challenge the gentleman, but decided against it, returning to his place along the wall. Anna had been through enough. She didn't need theatrics from him.

Sir John turned back to his daughter. He put his hand under Anna's chin, forcing her to meet his eyes. "Always so sad, my dead girl," he said gently, brushing her hair off her forehead. "These past years have been difficult for you—for all of us. I realize now that I relied too much on you after your mother died. You took over so willingly, so efficiently, looking after David … raising Beatrice—"

"Oh, Father—"

"No." Sir John put up a hand. "Let me get it out."

Anna nodded.

Sir John's Adam's apple bobbed in the sagging skin under his collar. "When Phillip came to stay with us that summer, you started to smile again. You were so happy, and I didn't have the heart to question it. I should have watched him more and kept you closer, but I was just so relieved to be done worrying. I thought I could trust him with you. I thought he could give you what you needed." Sir John's face darkened like thunder clouds. "But all he did was take. And now he wants more."

Jacob couldn't see Anna's face, but he could feel the tension radiating from her back, the rigidity that had taken her body captive. "What will he do now?"

Sir John sighed. He laid his head on the pillow, a man resigned to his fate. "He said if I do not give him Beatrice, he will tell everyone about your liaison. He will ruin you. Ruin the family. We will be ostracized, cut off, ignored by everyone we know."

Jacob's mother sat on Sir John's other side, a bookend to match Anna. With her hand on his cheek, she forced him to look her way. "But, my love, those are just rumors and lies. We can withstand them. People will think he is just a jilted man, angry and vindictive."

"Maybe so," Anna whispered. "But he isn't wrong. They aren't lies."

"And rumors are always enough in our world," Sir John finished.

"Even so," Mrs. Wright went on, not able to accept defeat, "this doesn't mean you have to leave us. Leave *me*. I want to be your wife. I will stand by you as we weather this together."

"I can't let you do that, Violet," Sir John said. "I'm sorry I've let you down yet again. But you don't know what's coming." He propped himself up on his forearms, searching for Jacob. When he found him across the room, he said, "You were right, young man. You said your family was too good for ours. I wanted to prove you right, but I'm afraid I can't."

Mrs. Wright reached across Sir John's body to touch Anna's shoulder. "You don't deserve this," she said kindly. "People make mistakes. They shouldn't have to pay for them for the rest of their lives."

Anna laughed mirthlessly. "Some people's mistakes are bigger than others."

Jacob's mother shook her head. "I don't understand—"

"Is that all?" Anna asked her father sharply. "Or is there more?"

Sir John nodded. His eyes became glassy, his skin once more turning gray. "He will tell everyone about the baby. You must brace yourself, my child. This is only the beginning."

⊹⟫⟫⟨⟨⊹

"ANNA, WAIT," JACOB called out, but her feet didn't falter. She kept going, her steps determined as she climbed the stairs. When she reached the top, she went straight toward her room, not acknowledging any of Jacob's calls.

"Goddammit, Anna," he growled when she opened her door then closed it before he could follow her inside. He grabbed the handle and shoved his shoulder against the wood. It flew open, and he nearly crashed to the floor as he sailed through. Apparently she *hadn't* thought to lock him out.

Hands on his hips, Jacob hesitated, utterly perplexed as Anna paced around her room, throwing her clothes and personal items into a pile on her bed. Her maid sidled past Jacob into the space and bobbed when Anna instructed her to bring up her luggage from downstairs.

The resourceful maid vanished before Jacob had a chance to tell her to ignore the command.

Words felt anemic, useless.

In desperation, Jacob closed in on Anna, clutching her shoulders in his hands, forcing her to stop. But he couldn't force her to look at him. And she wouldn't.

"Anna, please," he said, compelling her to meet his gaze. She wouldn't raise her eyes above the fifth button of his linen shirt. "Talk to me. Tell me what's going on? What did your father mean? What …" His voice caught. "What baby?"

Jacob watched her struggle. Emotions cycled over her face, ranging from despair and heartache to steely resolve. Anna attempted to struggle out of his grip, but he refused to let go. Somewhere inside him, he believed that if he released her now, he would never hold her again.

Finally, Anna's shoulders fell. All her life and vitality appeared to vanish. Now Jacob's hands were doing more than restraining her—they were keeping her on her feet.

She lifted her lids slowly. "I lost a baby. That was why I was sick. The doctors told me it was childbed fever." She shrugged hopelessly. "I didn't even know I was pregnant. It happened a month after David and Phillip left. I was walking on the lawn, and all of a sudden I felt this pain, almost like something was ripping me in half. And then I started to bleed … and it didn't stop."

Jacob resolved to keep his expression blank. He couldn't risk Anna stopping. As much as it killed him to hear about her trauma, he needed to know everything. How could he save her—

save them—if he didn't?

Anna went on. Her voice was flat and dull, as if she were no longer inhabiting her body. Instead, she was somewhere safe, protecting herself until the moment passed. "Father called for the doctor right away. He knew what was happening before we did. He cut my hair; he informed my father to send for the priest." Anna shuddered as she was brought back to that terrible day. "And he's the one who told us about all the damage that had occurred." She placed her hands on her abdomen. "The damage that would guarantee that I can never have a child."

Jacob's control snapped; his face crumpled in anguish. Anna's head fell as if her slender neck had lost all power. His heart bled for this woman—his woman. She'd had to face so much on her own. So much had been taken from her … her innocence … her girlhood … motherhood. It was no wonder she ran from love. Ran from him. No one had ever protected her heart above their own.

"My love …" Jacob began, a million words cascading into one another in his mind. But he needed the perfect word. The magic one that would solve everything. However, nothing came. Jacob couldn't understand his failure. As a writer, he believed that there was a perfect word for every situation. Only now, he came up dismally short.

Taking advantage of his paralysis, Anna shrugged out of his hold. She went back to the bed, staring down at her things, wiping the back of her arm over her eyes. "It's fine," she said stoically. "I'm fine. It's my fault, really. I thought … Well, I don't know what I thought. I came here and everything became muddled, but I've been brought back to my reality. My father was right. The best decision is to leave. If Phillip is intent on revenge, then we can't put your family in the middle."

"I don't give a fuck about Phillip!"

Anna closed her eyes. "But I do!" she said, voice breaking. "You've taken such pains to be the viscount you want to be. You're trying to do everything right for your family and its future.

I won't allow you to put that in jeopardy … not for me."

"And do I have a say in this?"

Anna opened her eyes. The green shade that had bewitched him and enticed him these last few weeks had become murky and faded. Hopeless.

"This isn't right, Anna," Jacob said. "What you are doing isn't right. You can fight for me, fight for us."

"I'm so tired, Jacob. I'm so tired of believing that if I can only climb to the top of the mountain that there will be a reward at the end. But there never is! There are just more mountains to climb! I need to go home."

"You are home," he growled. Jacob could feel the rope in his hands. It was slipping away, and he couldn't find his grip. It burned and ripped his palms the more he tried to hold on.

She picked up a gauzy chemise on the bed and let it drop from her fingers. "No. This is your home. To me, it was a dream. And now I have to wake up."

"For fuck's sake," Jacob muttered. He raked a hand through his hair, trying to come up with anything that would convince her to stay. None of his arguments had any effect. His passion was falling on deaf ears. Anna had an answer for everything, as if she'd practiced this conversation, knowing one day that it would come.

And then he realized he didn't need words.

Ignoring her yelps, he gathered her in his embrace once more. He walked her backward to the door and draped himself over her, caging her from all but him. Jacob captured her mouth, plundering her sweet depths with relentless intention. He allowed her to pound his chest, kick at his thighs, but it didn't matter. Kissing Anna was the only answer. Loving her was his only hope.

When he felt the tension in her drain, Jacob relaxed his onslaught. Tenderly, he swept inside her mouth, caressing her tongue, stroking the heart of her. Tears fell into their mouth. Her or his, Jacob didn't know. Nothing was held back; nothing was restrained. With parted lips, their kisses became more measured, more skillful, each knowing what the other liked and wanted. Jacob's hands stayed fixed on her hips. He didn't need to explore. All focus, all intention was on their mouths as he said the words over and over again to her with his kiss.

I love you.

I love you.

And Jacob knew she heard him. Because when their legs went out, they went out together. As one they crumpled to the floor, landing on their knees, pelvises pressed together in a holy communion.

Jacob refused to let up. He tasted and sipped from her mouth, taking only as much as Anna was willing to give. And, as ever, gifting her more in return. He poured his soul into that embrace, begging Anna to drink. And, like the Holy Grail, Jacob hoped that this exchange would heal their present, fulfill their future.

Anna stroked the length of his back, around his shoulder, over his neck. Her fingers were like satin as they skimmed over his skin, up his jaw to his lips. She broke away from him to stare at his mouth while her fingers explored it in a languid, meandering motion that he felt down to the soles of his feet.

Her features were inscrutable. And even though Jacob could feel the fire raging inside of her, he remained worried. He held her closer, melding their bodies even more, hoping that as they burned, they might fuse as one.

"I want to kiss you all night, Anna," he said. "And not just your lips, but your whole body. And then I want to do it tomorrow and then the day after that. Can you accept that?"

Anna's gaze stayed on his mouth. A mournful smile emerged, and it terrified him.

"I love you, Jacob," she said gently, the words bussing his lips in tandem with the pads of her fingers. "I will always love you. And I can't thank you enough for showing me what real love is. I will treasure it forever."

"I don't want to live without you," Jacob said.

Anna attempted to stand, but Jacob's hold wouldn't break.

Neither did her resolve. She took his face in her hands, staring into his eyes.

"If I'm strong enough to withstand it, so are you. Goodbye, my love."

Chapter Twenty-Seven

WEEKS WENT BY and Anna's family settled back into their old routines. They weren't necessarily hiding—though none of them liked to point out that no one had left the estate since they returned from Newton Place.

Encounters were short and light. Conversations were shorter and lighter. Voices were rarely heard above a whisper. It was the calm before the storm. The family was hunkering down, covering all that was exposed, taking shelter before the rain threatened to drown them and carry them out to sea.

As Phillip had not given a set time for his repulsive plan, every day was met with anxiety. Every letter that came to the house was stared at with trepidation before being opened in a resolved panic. But nothing gave an inkling that Anna's secret had come to light.

Days dragged on and tempers became frayed. Wits were close to their ends.

Anna begged her father to write to Phillip to implore him to rethink his decision, but Sir John wouldn't budge. Giving in wouldn't help matters, he said. He wouldn't allow Phillip the satisfaction of his groveling. Deep down, Anna knew her father was right. Men like Phillip didn't have the capability to see situations from other people's perspectives. Their vanity, their selfishness, was too great.

Needing to assert her control over even a sliver of this horrid ordeal, Anna's main concern became her siblings. Beatrice had been taciturn and moody the moment she returned home. It took copious amounts of dough and dozens of biscuits, but Anna finally got her sister to confide in her. Beatrice blamed herself for their father's broken engagement. She insisted that the family stop treating her like a child. She would marry Phillip if only to make everything right again.

The girl was too naïve to see the situation for what it was. Even if the family placated Phillip, he would always hold the scandal over them. He had all the power. It was best to force him to show his hand now. That way the family could move on and figure out how to maneuver in their new world. Take the pain all at once instead of in brutal increments.

As ever, David was much harder for Anna to track down during this uncertain period. In the end, he was the one who came looking for her on a lonely afternoon as she had just finished up a good cry.

She had made it a point to keep herself from falling apart, especially in front of Beatrice and her father. But Anna's strength wasn't infallible. She'd taken to walking the gardens farthest from the home every afternoon, permitting herself to break time and time again behind the tall hedges and Corsican pines. Nature, she found, helped separate her from her rambling thoughts. And even though this method of finding peace wasn't as enjoyable as the one she'd shared with Jacob, she still appreciated it.

"You're a hard one to pin down, aren't you?"

Anna turned to find her brother meandering toward her. His face still held firm to the tan he'd developed in India, but his warm, rascally smile reminded her of their childhood together, the way they would play hide and seek in these labyrinthine hedges before their nanny forced them to come in.

When he reached her, Anna curled her arm in his, and together they strolled down a path they hadn't traversed in years.

Before everything had become so complicated. "I was just trying to think … or trying not to think." She chuckled.

David nodded knowingly. "And how was that going for you?"

Anna squeezed his arm. "I've had better days."

"Yes," he said plaintively. "Yes, I imagine we've all had better days."

The dismal note in David's voice caused Anna to steal a glance at him from the corner of her eye. As carefree as he pretended to be, she could feel the strain in his muscles, the tight clenching of his jaw.

"Have you seen him?" she asked, not able to say the name.

David answered with a disgusted sigh. "No. And I don't plan to. Never again will I speak to the bastard."

As much as Anna wanted nothing but hardship and foul luck to nip at Phillip's heels for the rest of his life, she hated seeing her brother suffer. He'd lost a friend—a best friend. That, too, deserved a mourning period.

"I'm sorry," she said.

With a jolt, David stopped and turned to her. "You have nothing to be sorry about, Anna. It is I who am sorry for allowing this fiend to come into our lives."

"He wasn't always a fiend."

David's mouth tightened. "I should have seen it coming. I knew what he was like, how he could behave."

Anna coerced him into walking again, hoping the action might release his anger. Phillip's destruction knew no bounds. Everyone in her family had taken turns shouldering the blame, when he was the man who'd brought it all down on them.

But he hadn't acted alone.

"He never forced me, David. You should know that," Anna said. "I wanted him."

David scoffed. "You were too young to understand."

"Maybe so," she agreed. "But you have to allow me to take responsibility for my end of it."

"Even if that means you will be gossiped about, shunned

from Society, while Phillip will go free?" David asked. He rubbed his chin with the back of his hand. "I had no idea how unfair it all was for women. I'd never really thought of it before. It doesn't seem right."

"I daresay it isn't."

He reached for the hedge and yanked off a patch of prickly green pine needles. "Sometimes I really miss India. I know I shouldn't go back—especially now—but ..." He kicked a rock down the path. "Everything seemed so alive there, vibrant and fast paced. I don't know how to explain it."

"Yes, you do," Anna said. "Tell me."

David's cheeks reddened, and his lips tilted up bashfully. The child who still yearned for adventure lurked inside the man. "You wouldn't be able to imagine the spices, the colors," he said. "Everything here is so muted. The same families, the same people, the same clothes, the same weddings. I just wish it could be ..."

"Different."

"Yes," David replied. "Different. We're taught to avoid it at all costs. But why?" He shook his head. "I'll never understand it."

"You should go," Anna stated firmly, tugging on his arm. "Don't worry about us. Go out and explore the world. It's what you've always wanted."

"And leave you all to face Phillip? I could never. I won't hide from my duty to my family."

"It's not hiding if we're telling you to do it. Besides," she added, "you just said that this life is too bland for you. Why do you care, then, what these people think? Be different."

David chuckled, but Anna could tell her words were having an effect. She could see his mind spinning, the possibilities taking form. A dormant root remembering to grow.

"And what will you do while I'm gone?" he asked. "Beatrice already told me she wants to open a bakery. Father is so lost right now I think he might just let her."

"Of course he will," Anna said, finding a true smile. "He

would never hold her back. He will let her do it because he knows it's what she wants."

"And you? What will you do, Anna? What do you want?"

She dropped her head back so she could stare at the tops of the pines. So tall and mystical, they mimicked the lofty pillars in the grand cathedrals. Anna closed her eyes in this holy place. Her breath slowed, centering her, clearing her thoughts once more. Just as David had said, the act did become easier with practice.

"Maybe I'll be a little different too," she said finally.

THE MOMENT ANNA and David returned from their walk, their father called them into his study.

They found him standing in the middle of the room with Beatrice, both glaring at two crisp envelopes on his desk.

The silence was deafening. Impending doom seemed to close in on them from all directions. However, Anna was swarmed with relief at the sight. She was tired of waiting for the worst. Whatever was to come, she could not be more ready for it than now.

"Who are they from, Father?" she asked, already knowing the answer. But she needed to speak; she needed to rouse Sir John into action.

"Lord Newton."

Anna flinched. "Don't you mean Phillip?

"No," he replied. "Lord Newton."

"What? Why?"

Sir John answered by going to the table, his pace dismally slow, as if this was his death march. His hands shook as he ripped the first letter open without using an opener. The envelope dropped to the floor while he tore out the contents. He unfolded the note and held it up to the late afternoon light pouring in from the window.

The delay seemed interminable. Anna was just about to snatch the letter out of her father's hands when a disbelieving chuckle bubbled from his chest.

"Father—"

Sir John cut her off. "It seems I'm being sued ... for breach of promise."

"What on earth?" Anna replied.

"It's perfectly understandable," he announced, though he appeared not as disheartened as Anna would have thought. "Lord Newton—and Mrs. Wright—are threatening to ruin us by suing me for breaking the engagement. They say that if I do not go through with the marriage as promised, they will take me to court and sue me for 'an astronomical amount' because of the 'emotional distress, loss of reputation, and'"—Sir John cleared his throat—"'loss of virtue.'"

"Loss of virtue!" David exclaimed. "The woman is old ... *and* she has a grown child!"

"Quite," Sir John replied before giving his son an acerbic scowl. "And be respectful! She's not old. She's *mature*."

"Well, what does the other one say?" Beatrice marched to the desk, swiping the second letter from its envelope. Anna watched her eyes run back and forth on the page as an odd smile came to her little sister's lips.

"Beatrice! Tell us already!" David yelled. "I feel like I'm watching a badly acted play!"

Beatrice's smile morphed into a grin. "It seems we've been invited to a ball. The first ball ever given by the new Viscount Newton."

"So?" David replied.

"*So*," Beatrice said, "he's holding a ball in honor of the engagement of Sir John Smythe and Mrs. Violet Wright." She shoved the letter into Sir John's hands. "It looks like you have a decision to make, Father. Would you rather be ruined or married?"

Chapter Twenty-Eight

THE CARRIAGE CAREENED to a halt.

Anna held her hair, careful not to upset the elaborate coiffure her maid had created earlier that evening. She hadn't the slightest clue how the evening might unfold—her father had spent the better part of a week convincing her to even appear at the ball—but she knew she wanted to look splendid. She needed all the confidence she could muster, and a gorgeous dress and a lovely, ornate beaded headband always helped.

Beatrice and David wasted no time exiting the carriage. Their excitement was palpable. Being locked away at their estate for weeks had nearly made them crazy. Sir John was equally as restless and eager. He'd taken extraordinary care with his ensemble. He wore an impeccable navy-blue jacket and plaid waistcoat, both tailored so beautifully to his broad, fit figure that they made him look half his age.

His fingers visibly trembled as he reached for the door. Anna knew he was champing at the bit to see Mrs. Wright. Delaying him felt mean-spirited, but Anna couldn't conjure the others' enthusiasm.

"It's time, Anna," Sir John said gently. He patted her knee with a heavy, comforting hand, something he hadn't done to her since she was a child.

Worry ran rampant inside Anna, coalescing into an uncomfortable, cumbersome ball in the pit of her stomach. "I just don't understand," she muttered. "Why did he do this? He hates these kinds of events."

She had asked that very question countless times since the family received the invitation. As suspected, Sir John decided against being sued and wrote back to Mrs. Wright confirming their engagement. He'd traveled to Newton Place only once before the ball, coming back to his children remarkably chipper. Whatever he had encountered there made him more than willing to move forward with the marriage, despite his earlier reservations about the scandal and its effects.

When Anna pressed him about Jacob, Sir John had maintained a tight lip. All he'd said was that the two men had come to an understanding, which Anna thought was beyond ludicrous. In the past, Jacob had had very little *understanding* of anything regarding Sir John. What had changed? From the very beginning, Jacob had been searching for a reason to kick Sir John out of his mother's life. Anna's past had provided that reason on a silver platter.

And yet now she was sitting in a carriage, waiting to enter a ball in the older couple's honor.

It made no sense.

But then, love rarely did.

And Jacob loved his mother. There was no doubt there. Perhaps the woman's persuasiveness had won over her son in the end.

"Come now, Anna," Sir John said. "We mustn't keep him waiting."

He urged her to rise from her seat, but Anna remained where she was. "Jacob won't be here," she scoffed, her voice unnaturally high, her panic evident. "He doesn't want to mingle with people he barely knows. He's probably in his hermit's cottage right now, scribbling the night away."

Why did that little picture make her heart jump? And why,

assuming that he was not inside the large house, did Anna still resist leaving the sanctuary of the carriage?

"Perhaps he is done hiding," her father replied. "Perhaps he has grown confident enough to show the *ton* the viscount he wants to be."

"And what kind of a viscount is that?"

"Well," Sir John said with a huff, "one that has a profession."

She blinked. "What do you mean?"

"Honestly, daughter," he said, searching in his pockets. He retrieved a folded piece of paper and took his time smoothing out the wrinkles. "I thought you enjoyed reading the newspaper."

"I ... I do ... But I guess I've been distracted," Anna mumbled, accepting the page from him in a state of bewilderment. For long seconds she searched it for clues as to what her father was talking about. Then, in a tiny section in the bottom right corner of the page, a headline jumped out at her: *Dutiful Wife Travels Long and Far for Love.*

Anna ravenously attacked the ensuing article.

This author has heard of a love story that will, no doubt, go down as one of the greatest of the age. I've heard that Mr. Phillip Williams of Larkshire, son of the Right Honorable Lord Savot, has finally been reunited with his long-lost wife, Miss Indira Phule. The pair met and married last year while Mr. Williams was engaged as a clerk during a short and undistinguished time for the East India Company. They exchanged their blessed vows at St. John's Cathedral in Calcutta on 27 March, 1847 with only the bride's parents in attendance. How private and romantic!

But disaster was destined to strike the young lovers! On hearing the terrible news of his older brother's death, Mr. Williams secured passage for England at once. Due to his newly elevated position in the family, he was determined to leave India behind. Unfortunately for Mr. Williams, he also left behind his Indian bride.

One can imagine the misery and absolute terror that Mr.

Williams faced when he ostensibly lost his wife before the fateful voyage! This author was told that the future baron was beside himself with grief during his painstaking trek back to England and moved heaven and earth to reunite himself with his love.

Luckily for Mr. Williams, his intrepid and resourceful bride was moving heaven and earth a little quicker. With the help of her family, Mrs. Williams, née Phule, boarded a vessel in search of her husband soon after he'd misplaced her. Learning our mother tongue during the arduous six-month journey, the seventeen-year-old woman swiftly located her wayward husband's whereabouts, and I'm told the reunion was one of breathtaking fireworks.

Love truly knows no bounds to those strong enough to fight for it ...

Anna dropped the paper on her lap, blinking at her father. "Who wrote this?"

Sir John smiled. "Who do you think?"

"Is it true? Is Phillip already married?"

"It would appear so," her father replied, smoothing his auburn hair into place. "Though I think Jacob was having a bit of fun. No one misplaces their wife unless they want to."

"Phillip just left her in India? The poor girl."

Sir John *humphed.* "It seems his perfidy and horridness aren't contained to this continent."

Anna shook her head. "Why didn't you show me this before? You knew how worried I was."

He appeared to shrink from guilt. "I only saw it yesterday. I thought ... Well, I thought that I would leave it for Jacob to explain it all to you." He peered out the window. "At the ball. The one that he's holding not just for me but for you."

Anna's heart seized. She wanted to believe her father. Every ounce of her being wanted to throw caution to the wind and share his optimism.

"But this doesn't change anything," she said. "Phillip can still decide to ruin us, even if he is married."

He nodded thoughtfully. "Yes, he can."

"Aren't you worried?"

Sir John contemplated his daughter for a long moment. "I am tired of worrying about what other people think, Anna. I allowed my father's opinion to rule me when I was younger, and I gave up the woman I loved. I can't let it happen again. We only live once, my dear." His eyes twinkled as he laughed to himself. "That's one good thing about getting old, you know. You stop caring so much. It's an unexpected blessing."

Anna returned a winsome smile. "But I'm not old, Father."

"Yes, but you're smart—much smarter than I was at your age. Smart enough to learn from my mistakes."

Music drifted in from the house. It called to her like a siren's song. Jacob was a master of showing Anna his love with a whole lot of little things. However, it seemed that the man was capable of over-the-top gestures as well. With the amount of people crowding the front steps, it looked like he'd invited all of London into his home tonight. He'd put himself front and center. For her.

She glanced down at the ridiculous and colorful article. "Do you think the *ton* will ever accept him?"

Sir John sighed. "I don't think it matters to the boy anymore."

"Then what does?"

Sir John winked at his daughter and started out of the carriage. "Not what, my dear. Who."

⭆⭅

JACOB COULDN'T STAND it. His patience was at an end. He'd already greeted Beatrice and David, and they had been milling about with friends for the past fifteen minutes. Where was she?

Why wasn't Anna coming to him?

He pulled at his collar. The insufferable thing! He blamed the formalwear for his inability to breathe, but it was more than that.

These people—his guests—walked around his home making polite chitchat, casting strange looks at him while they thought he couldn't see. They didn't know what to make of him or the fact that he didn't appear to give one goddamn about getting into their good graces.

That hadn't stopped them from answering his invitation, though. Thanks to his mysteriousness, Jacob was certain that few would decline—however, he hadn't counted on every single invitee to crowd his ballroom. It was a crush if he'd ever seen one. And he was the exotic animal on display.

He supposed he would have to get used to it. This was his life now. Like a young woman at her first ball, Jacob was officially *out*. But the mountain wouldn't seem as unclimbable with Anna at his side. Yes, as a couple, they would be subject to their share of gossip. People might always deem them a little too peculiar to be considered good *ton*, but that was fine with Jacob. He wouldn't have time to go to all their balls and musicales and dreaded picnics anyway, so it wouldn't matter if a few invitations never made it to his door. Jacob had a profession; Anna had her cricket club. And more importantly, they would have each other. Their life would be full enough.

If only the damned woman would get in his ballroom so he could start living it!

Finally, Jacob caught sight of Sir John skulking along the perimeter of the packed room. With a keen gaze the baronet stretched to look over the heads of the throng, clearly searching for Mrs. Wright, but the instant he met Jacob's eyes, he turned sheepish.

Jacob steered to him at once. "Where is she?" he asked, casting all formality and politeness out the window. Sir John was soon to be his stepfather/father-in-law and simply had to get used to Jacob's unpolished ways.

"She was right behind me," Sir John said quickly. "I thought she would come in, but then I heard her say she needed some air, and she just started walking!"

"Walking?" Jacob scowled. "And you didn't try to stop her? What he bloody hell—" His words caught in his throat as his mind raced to catch up with his rampant emotions. He ran a hand through his hair, the answer hitting him at once. "I know where she is."

Jacob pushed his way out of the room, toward the back of the house. "Dear boy, give her time. You can't leave your own ball! Anna will be here soon," Sir John called after him. "She just needs time to think."

"That's the last thing she needs," Jacob muttered. "She needs *me*."

Chapter Twenty-Nine

THE PICTURE IN Jacob's head couldn't have prepared him for what he found in the Asian garden.

Anna stood with her back to him at the edge of the pond. Silhouetted by the moonlight, she stared out at their pagoda like a fairy queen waiting for the magic of the mist to carry her over the bridge.

"I thought you would be here," Jacob said softly. Anna's cloak trembled. Her shoulders squared at the sound of his voice, an attempt to ready herself for this moment. "I was waiting for you inside."

Finally, she turned to him. Her face was luminescent and peaceful, as still as the water that surrounded their tiny temple. "I thought you would be here."

"No more hiding," Jacob said.

Anna hinted at a smile. "No more hiding." She reached inside her reticule and pulled out a piece of paper. Jacob was reminded of an earlier time when she'd done that very thing. How he'd fallen in love with her then and there, only he'd been too myopic to see it. "I saw what you wrote about Phillip. How did you find out?"

Jacob slapped his hands together casually as he made his way toward her. "Oh, it's a funny story, actually. Last week, a stranger came to my door—a Miss Indira Phule. She had heard that her husband, Mr. Phillip Williams, had been staying here. When I told her that he was gone, I asked her to rest inside, and we soon shared a pleasant, lengthy, and rather informative conversation."

Anna's green eyes bored into him. "Did he really leave her behind?"

Jacob was close enough to sweep her into his arms, but he resisted the temptation. She needed to know everything. There would be no more secrets between them. "Well, it seems that Indira's father refused to allow his daughter to be an Englishman's mistress. He demanded Phillip marry her and gave her a rich dowry, which Philip quickly and predictably squandered on bad business ventures. After that, it seemed he had no further use for her—in England, anyway."

"And David didn't know?"

Jacob shrugged. "David thought what everyone else thought, that she was his mistress. I'm sure Phillip will try to convince everyone of that fact as well, but I have to give her credit. Indira is a smart woman. Before she left India, she ripped out the pages in the church register and brought them with her."

Anna laughed, making Jacob's heart jump. "She *is* a smart woman."

Jacob nodded. "And naturally, being the chivalrous viscount that I am, I escorted Indira to her new home to reunite her with her dear, long-lost husband. If you could have seen his face …"

Anna's smile faltered. "He could still tell everyone about me. You could still be brought into this scandal—"

Jacob shook his head, losing enough of his restraint to take Anna's hands in his. Even with her gloves, they were dismally cold. Pulling her forward, he tucked them into the pockets of his overcoat—where they belonged. "I don't think Phillip will have time to cause trouble," he replied. "As I said, my conversation with Indira was incredibly informative. It seems that Phillip's bad decisions in India included attempting to steal trading partners away from the EIC and their shipping captains. He made many enemies of many powerful people. If he hadn't left India when he did, he was sure to be run out of the country in disgrace. I informed him that that news could stay in India if he preferred, although, being a newspaper man, I could choose to share it with my readers if I saw fit."

"You're blackmailing him?"

Jacob cocked his head. "Blackmail is a bit of a harsh word. We came to a mutually advantageous agreement."

"Ha! And that involved writing an article about the wife he conveniently abandoned?"

Jacob's arms found their way around Anna's waist. His grin was sheepish. "Definitely not. But I had to have some fun; the bastard couldn't get away with everything he put you through." He ducked his head. "Did you like it? I thought it hit the right notes. Who knows? I might see a future for myself in the scandal sheets."

Anna giggled, her fingers twitching in Jacob's pockets. He could feel her press against the fabric, searching for more of him, needing to touch him as he touched her. With a long, breathy sigh, she laid her head on his chest, finding a sense of calm. Jacob cradled the back of her head.

"I think I prefer you writing about more important things, like cricket," she said.

Jacob grinned, resting his head on the top of Anna's. "Well then, I'll stick to cricket and more serious things."

"Wait!" she said. Her head popped up, hitting Jacob's chin in the process. She grimaced apologetically. "Sorry. But I don't understand. You said Indira came to Newton Place last week. You sent the invitation to the ball days before that."

"Yes?"

Anna frowned, clearly trying to put everything together in her head. *Always thinking too bloody much.* She'd once said that Jacob dug too deep into things, which was like the pot calling the kettle black. "So that means that you agreed to our parents' marriage before the situation with Phillip was settled?"

"I never gave a damn about Phillip," Jacob replied. "You did."

"But you let me go."

"I never let you go. I let you have time to think, to find your way back to me."

Anna's neck wilted. "I didn't want to drag you down."

Jacob tucked his finger under her chin, drawing her gaze back to his. "You've only ever pulled me up."

"I want you to have a future."

"I see no future without you."

"But what if …" Anne bit her bottom lip. The fact that those were now Jacob's lips made him feel like the luckiest man in the world. His to kiss. His to pay countless attention to. His to worship. "What if I can't have children?" she asked.

Jacob held her pale face in his palms and brushed his thumbs along her skin. "Then we will have to make do with each other," he said. "Would that be so difficult … spending your life with me and only me?" He stared over her shoulder, considering. "And probably the aunts."

A single tear trailed down her face. Anna placed a sweet kiss on the inside of his palm. When her eyes met his again, they shone with spirit and love. Jacob locked his knees, determined to stay on his feet.

"I want you more than anything," she replied. "I love you, Jacob, more than I've ever loved anyone in my life. I wasted so much time waiting for someone to forgive me. I was wrong. I only needed the courage to forgive myself. I want to experience life again, and I only want to do it with you."

Jacob swayed, holding himself up by the skin of his teeth. He was unmoored, unworthy, and desperately grateful to have found this different kind of woman.

Attempting to stabilize himself, he leapt for the one thing that always cleared his mind. He seized his woman's mouth like it was a life raft, the only thing that could keep him afloat in this unpredictable world. Anna reacted with equal fervor, meeting him halfway, capturing his lips and tongue as surely as she'd captured his heart.

Jacob hadn't thought it possible, but this kiss was so very different from others they'd shared. It was not a kiss of passion or lust or even inevitability. This was a kiss suffused with expectation. It held the calm reassurance that it would not be the last—not by a long shot. A fever spread between them, but it was tempered by languid pulls and lingering strokes. This was not the kiss of night or dreams; it was a kiss of the morning ahead. A morning with endless possibilities.

"Let's not worry about what may or may not happen," he said, trailing his finger along the line in the center of her lip. "Let's just focus on now. I love you. And you love me. That's all we can control. That's all we need."

Anna tried to wrap her arms around him, but she also refused to withdraw her hands from his pockets. "That's all we need," she repeated, bussing him with another honeyed peck.

"It's a different idea, to be sure," Jacob said, directing her toward their cottage. There would be more balls for Viscount Newton. He would make an appearance at the next one.

"Well, my love, we are different kinds of people," Anna said, her feet picking up speed.

My love. It sounded so much better than *my lord.*

Jacob shoved the vines and branches out of the way and put his hand on the knob.

Before he opened the door, he gave her a look of warning. "I want you to think long and hard about this, my dear," he said. "If you walk over this threshold, you are agreeing to a lifetime of a husband cherishing you. He will kiss you many, *many* times a day, not just on your lips but all over your body. He will always cheer when you play cricket and take you to the circus whenever it's in town. He will even suffer through picnics just to see you smile. But, most importantly, he will love you with every fiber of his being, because life with you is as close to Nirvana as he is ever going to get. Can you handle that, Anna? Can you let me love you? I need to know."

Anna placed her hand over his. She twisted the knob and opened the door, at once stepping inside. Looking over her shoulder, she stunned Jacob with a soft smile. "I'm strong enough to handle you, Jacob. Now come in here and let me show you."

Epilogue

Three months later

Under the shroud of darkness, Anna handed over the package and rested back in her carriage seat, careful to hide her curious expression.

Miss Ruthie Waitrose sat across from her. She hugged the package to her chest, her heavy sigh of relief the only noise breaking through this clandestine appointment.

"Thank you," she said softly, lifting her head. Dressed all in maudlin black and wearing a heavy, satin-covered bonnet that all but swallowed her face, the young woman looked like she was on her way to a funeral.

Not that one would take place in the middle of the night.

Anna would have laughed at the ridiculous drama if the moment wasn't so perplexingly odd. Yet again, she wondered why she'd agreed to any of this. Clearly, Ruthie Waitrose was up to no good—or at the very least, doing something she shouldn't be— and Anna was now an accomplice.

"Please don't look at me like that," Ruthie said, no doubt reading the alarm on Anna's face that couldn't be contained. "I won't tell anyone. And I'll be careful."

Anna laughed, though it tripped out nervously from her

throat. "Why should I be worried?" she asked, feigning nonchalance. "I'm sure there's a perfectly good reason you needed to come to my home under the cover of darkness in order to pick up a handful of my brother's old clothes."

Anna's sarcastic tone was completely lost on her friend. For all her reassurances, Ruthie was too on edge. Her gamine body betrayed a strict tension, like she could snap at any second. "He won't mind, will he?" Her long fingers made wayward circles over the rough cotton bag she clutched in her lap. "I'd hate to put him out or get you in any kind of trouble."

Well, it's a little late to be worrying about that. Anna waved a hand in the air. "David won't even notice. As I said in my letter, he's on a boat for India as we speak." Anna leaned across the aisle of the carriage. Her knees bumped Ruthie, causing the girl to almost jump out of her seat. Poor Ruthie. A successful life of crime was not in her future. "Is there anything you want to tell me? Maybe I can help."

"You are helping," Ruthie replied quickly, pulling her shoulders back. "I can't thank you enough for this. I thought to ask my cousin for his, but"—even through the darkness, Anna could see the girl's cheeks turn crimson—"he's not as tall as I am."

Anna frowned, biting back a *tsk* before it escaped her mouth. Her suspicions were confirmed. For some inexplicable reason, Miss Ruthie Waitrose intended to wear David's clothes. But in the back of Anna's mind, she'd already guessed that. It was the *where* and *why* that had her stumped.

However, those questions would have to wait. Gravel rustled outside the carriage. Feet were growing restless. Anna's new husband was making his anxiety known. He desired this furtive meeting to be over and done with. So did Anna, for that matter.

Husband. Just thinking the word sent warm shivers of pleasure up her spine.

She felt Ruthie watching her. A shy smile showed on the young lady's face. "You look different, Anna," she said, cocking her head. "Good different. Oh, I'm sorry," she added with a laugh. "I should probably call you Lady Newton now."

More warm shivers. Anna and Jacob had only been married for two months, and the newness had yet to wear off. *Lady Newton*. Who would have ever thought?

"Anna is just fine," she replied. "It's all new to me too. Sometimes I wake up in the morning and forget until ..." It was Anna's turn to burn red. She clamped her mouth shut, allowing her words to trail off. It probably wouldn't be proper to tell the unmarried woman about Jacob's lovely habit of waking her, something Anna now craved as much as her morning tea. "Never mind that," she rushed out, hearing more gravel being kicked up outside the carriage. Jacob was pacing.

She lowered her chin, leveling Ruthie with a stern look. "I am here for you—always," she said, hardening her tone. "If you ever need me, don't think twice about sending for help."

Ruthie squirmed in her seat. "Honestly, Anna, there's no need for this—"

"Just promise me," Anna cut in. "You are my friend, and I am choosing to respect your privacy. I won't ask what all this is about; I will wait until you are ready to tell me. Just ... don't make me regret it."

Ruthie held her gaze. After a long pause, she nodded. "Thank you."

Anna's expression softened. She hated sounding like such an older sister, but old habits died hard. Besides, Ruthie didn't have an older sister to provide advice and guidance. This was a service Anna could provide, along with the bewildering clothes. "I told you. There's nothing to thank me for. David won't miss any of it."

"No," Ruthie said. Her eyes were round and large and took up most of her skinny face. Their earnestness struck Anna straight in the heart—and her conscience. "Thank you for saying you're my friend." She shook her head ruefully. "I wasn't sure."

Anna snorted, lifting her hands in exasperation. "If this isn't friendship then I don't know what is."

"I'll be careful," Ruthie added, laughing. "Now, I've taken up enough of your time. I must be getting back before Mother notices I'm gone. Off to bed with you, Lady Newton."

Anna rolled her eyes, reluctantly reaching for the door handle. "You as well, Miss Waitrose. Will I see you at the next club meeting?"

"Of course."

Anna opened the door and was about to exit when a nagging thought stopped her. She twisted back to her friend. "You won't be wearing my brother's clothes to the meeting, will you?"

Laughter bubbled from Ruthie's chest. "Can you imagine Myfanwy's face?"

Anna took the time to contemplate the scene. "You know … I don't think she'd mind."

"You know … I don't either," Ruthie agreed.

Their laughter flitted away into the crisp night air, and Anna shared one more warning look with her friend, imploring her to make prudent *if not proper* decisions. After she was certain the message was received, she exited the conveyance. Jacob was on her in an instant, helping her down the carriage steps and closing the door firmly behind her.

He wrapped an arm around Anna's waist as they watched the groom drive Ruthie away, not uttering a word until the carriage was out of sight.

For a moment, snuggled into her husband's cozy side, Anna almost believed the whole encounter was a dream, until Jacob's deep, highly skeptical voice pulled her back to reality. "Do I want to know what that was about?" he asked, directing them toward the house.

Anna hesitated, glancing over her shoulder one more time. Ruthie was gone. There was nothing more to be done. Anna only hoped she wouldn't regret acting a part in this little play. "I don't think so."

She rested her head against Jacob's shoulder, loving the way she could feel his chuckle vibrate through her skin. "I could make you tell me," he declared, his determination evident.

Anna kissed his shoulder. "You could," she replied evenly. "But you won't."

Her husband's put-upon sigh made her smile. "You know me too well. Still," he added grumpily, increasing the proprietary pressure of his hand along her hip, "no more nighttime rendez-vous—with anyone other than me. It can't be good for you."

Anna placed her hand over his, intertwining their fingers. It continued to amaze her that she could never be close enough to him. "The doctor said that I'm perfectly fine. Fresh air is good for me."

"I doubt he meant it to be taken at midnight."

Anna giggled, though immediately sobered when she saw her husband's face. Jacob's expression was like thunder, serious and concerning and not a little bit frightening.

He was also wildly excited, and, of late, that emotion was exemplified by a fearsome, ever-present scowl.

Anna reached up and traced a light finger along his furrowed brow, coaxing the harsh lines from his forehead. He grabbed her hand, kissing the inside of her palm, breathing deeply, settling his worries.

"Did you tell her?" he asked quietly as if the secret—their secret—was so delicate and fragile that it could be challenged by a few little words.

Anna shook her head, feeling a deep flutter inside her. "No. It's still early … not the right time."

Jacob released her, but only so he could place both hands on her stomach, staring down in wonder at the miracle that was only just beginning to show on Anna's small, strong body. She knew he was waiting to feel the baby move inside her. That day couldn't come quickly enough.

She still couldn't believe that their love had created this life inside her. At the start of their marriage, she'd resolved herself to the fact that their family would always consist of them. But life had other plans. And this baby hadn't been shy about making its presence known. A month ago, the realization hit her like a wave. Anna's morning sickness lasted all day, and eating anything other than a few pieces of bread was out of the question. Her complexion reminded her of a dead fish, and her legs ached in the most random of places. And this was only the beginning. She still had so many months to go before she held a tiny, sweet baby in her arms. But Anna had never been happier.

Jacob's words were painfully shy when he finally spoke again. "Do you mind if it stays *not the right time* for a few months longer?"

Anna cocked her head curiously, enjoying her husband's bout of embarrassment. "Why?"

Jacob shrugged, spreading his fingers across her midsection. "I like having something that is just ours."

Anna's face split into a wide smile. "You don't think our child will be *just ours*?" she teased.

"Of course not," he huffed indignantly. "It will be the aunts' and my mother's and your father's. This child will be inundated with love and attention the moment he's born. Everyone will want him all the time."

Anna arched an eyebrow. "Him?"

"Or her," Jacob replied quickly. "Either will do."

"Well, that's good, since those are the only options," Anna remarked dryly. She led him into their home. With everyone in their bedrooms, it was one of those times when the house was quiet and peaceful. After their wedding, the family had proposed to leave the couple alone for a few weeks, give them their space to grow into a true married couple, but Jacob and Anna had declined the offer. Newton Place could handle everyone, and she loved the constant hustle and bustle. She'd been alone for so long. Every member of her new family felt like links on a chain, only serving to make the unit stronger. Besides, whenever the house became too crowded, Anna and Jacob could retreat to their little cottage. It worked.

"You know," she said, "there are worse problems for a child

to have—being hounded with love from his or her family."

"That's true," Jacob grumbled, though Anna could tell he needed more convincing. She lured him toward the stairs, towing him gently behind. "I just can't explain it. The child isn't even born and I have this incredible desire to be with it always, to teach it everything I know, to be the father that I never had, the father that I always wanted."

Anna's heart swelled. She turned to Jacob, cradling his face in her hands. It wasn't every day that he displayed his vulnerability so openly. She wanted to hold the burden for him, keep him safe from his self-doubt. "You will be, my love. You have nothing to fear."

"I just don't want to let you or this baby out of my sight—ever."

"Ever?"

"Ever," he repeated, nodding for good measure.

Anna climbed the staircase once more, a frown marring her tranquility. "And what about at night?"

Jacob's voice had regained its confidence. Clearly, he'd given this much thought. "The baby will sleep with us. Or next to the bed, if you prefer."

"And during the day?"

"I will carry him always, take him for walks, rides. I was thinking of fashioning a swath of fabric that would bind him to me to free up my hands. The ancient people used something similar. I've been doing much research on the subject."

Anna tripped on the step. *Much research?* They'd only known about the baby for four weeks!

"But what about being alone?"

"Alone?" Jacob said the word as if he'd never heard it before.

"Yes, alone." Anna would never admit to this, but she may have given her hips a little more sway as she ventured higher up the stairs. She may even have lowered her voice into a husky whisper that never failed to turn the tips of her husband's ears pink. It was lovely that he wanted to lavish their child with unbridled attention, but it was her that needed it now. "With me." Using the tip of one finger, she caressed the banister lightly, languidly as they climbed. "You will still want that, yes?" she purred seductively. "Still want *me*?"

Anna felt his hands at her waist, but she pulled just out of reach. "What kind of a question is that?" he growled. Anna grinned to herself. Plain as day she could hear it. She could hear the wanting in his question. The hunger. She could also hear the wheels turning in his head.

"An honest one," she answered coyly. "After all, just a few months ago you were a man living as a Spartan in a hermit's cottage. Now you want to strap a baby to your chest morning, noon, and night."

Jacob cleared his throat. "Perhaps ... Perhaps it wouldn't be such a bad idea to have family who want to watch over our child ... every *so often*."

"Oh?"

"Advantageous ... really," he went on. "It probably isn't beneficial for a child to be with his parents *every* second of the day."

"Maybe you could do more research on it," Anna suggested, feigning concern.

"No, no, no" Jacob replied quickly. He was no longer being towed. He ate up the stairs next to his wife, his expression thoughtful. "No research is necessary. It's just pure sense," he remarked. "It would be in our best interest to allow the family to watch our child *some of the time*."

"If you think it's best," Anna said, nodding. The couple reached the landing, and she finally allowed Jacob's wandering hands to catch her. His arms snaked around her middle and he nudged her down the corridor toward their bedroom door.

Too overcome with passion, Jacob didn't register the mischief on his wife's face. His words caressed her face seductively. "Now that I'm thinking about it, it would be *unfair* of us not to share our child with our family *as much as possible*," he said, ducking his head into Anna's neck, placing little, haunting kisses over her sensitive skin. "I understand that having one's first child can be overwhelming. It will be important for us to make a little time for ourselves … to be alone."

"Alone can be a good thing," Anna squeaked as Jacob settled on her ear, tickling a line over her lobe with his expert tongue.

He shifted, and Anna heard his hand twist the knob. He held her upright as he swung the door open, lobbing her inside with a playful shove. "A very good thing, wife," he murmured. "Now let me demonstrate how good."

About the Author

I'm a lifelong reader of romance novels. Some of my earliest memories are of sneaking into my mom's room at night and stealing any books I could find.

After moving around quite a bit, I've finally put down roots in New England with my two sons and husband. I've always been a writer, starting out in newspapers, but it wasn't until my sons began going to school full-time that I began working toward my dream of becoming a romance author.

I enjoy crocheting toys for my kids, hiking with my Saint Bernard, and watching Real Housewives on the couch with my very old and very fat pugs.